I NEED
YOU TO
READ THIS

ALSO BY JESSA MAXWELL

The Golden Spoon

I NEED YOU TO READ THIS

A NOVEL

JESSA MAXWELL

ATRIA BOOKS

New York London Toronto Sydney New Delhi

ATRIA
BOOKS

An Imprint of Simon & Schuster, LLC
1230 Avenue of the Americas
New York, NY 10020

First Atria Books hardcover edition August 2024

ATRIA BOOKS and colophon are trademarks of Simon & Schuster, LLC

Simon & Schuster: Celebrating 100 Years of Publishing in 2024

For information about special discounts for bulk purchases, please contact Simon & Schuster Special Sales at 1-866-506-1949 or business@simonandschuster.com.

The Simon & Schuster Speakers Bureau can bring authors to your live event. For more information or to book an event, contact the Simon & Schuster Speakers Bureau at 1-866-248-3049 or visit our website at www.simonspeakers.com.

Interior design by Joy O'Meara

Manufactured in the United States of America

1 3 5 7 9 10 8 6 4 2

Library of Congress Cataloging-in-Publication Data
Names: Maxwell, Jessa, author.
Title: I need you to read this : a novel / Jessa Maxwell.
Description: First Atria Books hardcover edition. | New York : Atria Books, 2024
Identifiers: LCCN 2024009646 | ISBN 9781668008034 (hardcover) | ISBN 9781668008041 (paperback) | ISBN 9781668008058 (ebook)
Subjects: BISAC: FICTION / Thrillers / Suspense | FICTION / Thrillers / General | LCGFT: Thrillers (Fiction) | Detective and mystery fiction. | Novels.
Classification: LCC PS3613.A8997 I3 2024 | DDC 813/.6—dc23/eng/20220629
LC record available at https://lccn.loc.gov/2024009646

ISBN 978-1-6680-0803-4
ISBN 978-1-6680-0805-8 (ebook)

To my mom, my first and best reader.

I NEED
YOU TO
READ THIS

Dear Constance,

He'll be back now at any moment. I know that he'll be angry. I should be leaving. I should be packing my bags and getting out of the apartment but instead I'm sitting here, paralyzed and replaying the whole thing in my mind. I should have known better than to think I could outsmart him. It's impossible. I can't think the way he does. He has his own logic.

And he knows me so well. He has all of my passageways memorized, places I don't even know myself, dark corners where he can hide and wait for me. You were wrong about him. It's not your fault, we both were. We thought if I just made myself stronger, I could escape it all. But it doesn't work that way, not with him. He's solved my brain like a maze. He will always find new angles to attack from, new places in me that are soft and weak. I don't know where this ends, but I expect it will be soon. I should be deciding what to bring with me to start my new life. But it feels pointless, an exercise in extreme futility.

I can hear his key in the lock. It's too late now. Too late to pack a bag. Too late to even send this to you. If I survive it, I will write and tell you. But maybe you won't even see it. Maybe no one will know what's become of me either way.

PROLOGUE

Francis has been avoiding the computer since she arrived this morning, keeping herself busy by puttering around the summer house, cleaning the counters, anything to distract herself from the message that popped into her inbox late last night. Driven by nervous energy, she'd found herself outside, pausing only momentarily to look out at the deep-blue ocean at the far side of the lawn before turning toward her fallow garden beds. There isn't much to work with now that it's fall. She surveys the beds. A few dry stalks left over from some late-blooming asters tremble in the wind. There's no urgent need to pull them but she kneels in the dirt anyway. Gardening has always helped her make complicated decisions about her writing. Maybe it can help her now too. She doesn't bother with gloves, pushing the sleeves of her thick Fair Isle sweater up her arms and plunging her fingers into the cold soil. She always thinks best when her body is occupied by something else.

But now that the sun has nearly set, she feels the tug of her little office room. In thirty-five years, Francis has never been late with a column. Returning to the house, she drops into her chair and moves her mouse so that her computer hums to life. The monitor brightens and she sees the letter there in her inbox, down at the bottom of the screen, and feels a sick twist in her stomach. She looks away quickly, moving her eyes to the top of her inbox, where the unread messages stack up in bold font.

Francis scrolls through the subject lines. Despite the *Herald*'s assurances that she reads each and every message sent to her, it is rare that she actually gives most more than a cursory look. There are topics too well trodden to revisit. By now her readers already know what she'd say about a noncommittal man (walk very quickly in the opposite direction), a sibling rivalry (therapy), or a go-nowhere job (probably stay put for now unless something better is available).

One email with the subject line reading simply *I'm lost* intrigues her. She clicks open the email and begins to read the story of a woman whose marriage of forty-three years has recently fallen apart, sadly coinciding with the deaths of both of her parents. Francis sits and considers her predicament for a moment, allowing herself to truly feel the woman's life as though it is her own. Her chest aches for the woman. And yet, being so lost, so incredibly rock bottom, comes with a kind of freedom if you are able to harness it. Isn't there something almost delicious about being able to start fresh? It's like that Janis Joplin song, *freedom's just another word for nothing left to lose*. Rarely in life do you have the opportunity to start completely from scratch. She shakes herself free from that train of thought. It isn't the right question, not for this week. Reluctantly she closes the message, guiltily shutting out the woman and her loss, and returns to the inbox.

In just the last few minutes several new letters have come in, pushing the email, the one she came all the way up to the beach house to try to avoid, to the very the bottom of the screen, nearly off the page. Sunday is her busiest day for new questions. It is a natural time for reflection after the rush of the early weekend but before work picks up again—the time of week when people seem to feel the most depressed and dissatisfied with their lives. Francis, on the other hand, loves Sundays, the pleasant rush of new letters coming in, the feeling of being needed and helpful. She doesn't let herself linger on the idea that other people's pain is her pleasure.

She is about to settle in and read another letter when she hears a faint scraping noise behind her, coming from the front of the house. Francis stands up, startled, and spins around. She looks for the most likely culprit but finds the cat asleep on its favorite chair. She cuts through the pantry into the kitchen and peers out the kitchen window at the empty driveway.

There's a flash of someone passing by the window. Something yellow like the hood of a jacket blurring through the near-dark. Francis's heart pounds as she walks back into the hall. The front door to her house hangs wide open. That's odd. She knows she didn't leave it like that. She looks around for signs of another person but hears and sees nothing.

She steps tentatively out onto the front porch in her slippers. The wind rushes up from the beach, smelling of the ocean just barely tinged with woodsmoke and the bite of approaching winter. She stands still, her body tense, her ears prickling. The Atlantic churns darkly at the edge of the lawn. She thinks she can see the bluish flicker of the television in Bertie Robertson's house, her neighbor down the road. She should go over there, she thinks. Have some company. She suddenly regrets coming up. Francis had thought she'd feel safer here, that she'd be able to gather her thoughts. But she hasn't come close to having any clarity. If anything, the solitude has only made her feel more agitated and uncertain.

"Hello?" she calls out. "Is someone there?" Her voice, unused for hours, catches. It comes out hoarse as a whisper. She makes her way down the front steps. The grass is cold on her ankles as she steps into the yard, walking to the edge of the house. *Be brave, Francis, for goodness' sake.* She steels herself as she leans out and peers around the side.

A dark shape on the ground below the window startles her, but quickly she recognizes the coil of her garden hose. The light from her study shines out onto the lawn. She notes how her office would be completely visible to any interested person looking in. She'd always meant to buy curtains, but the years had dulled her motivation. Besides, who cares enough to watch an old woman on her computer? A car passes on the road behind the house. She finds her breath slowing. Everything is fine. She shakes her head. *Honestly, Francis.*

She turns and heads back to the porch. Sometimes there are just sounds that cannot be explained, she tells herself. Still, when she goes inside, she makes sure to twist both locks on the door. She'll have trouble going to sleep tonight now. She often does these days, even without a scare. If that is even what it was? Just as likely, she thinks now, that it was just someone walking their dog, or a vacationer cutting through her yard to get to the beach the way the tourists always do in summer. It doesn't take much to scare her, it would seem. She pushes away a vision of the flash of yellow at the window. It could have been a trick of her mind, a bird or a leaf in the wind. After she gets some work done, she'll make some tea, possibly watch something on TV. She'll leave the letter and its disturbing contents for tomorrow and keep a light on in the hallway tonight.

Comforted by the plan, she makes her way through the house toward the still-bright computer screen in her study. Approaching the desk, she can see that the email has fallen off the home page now, and she breathes a deep sigh of relief. She feels better not seeing it, knowing it's buried. Why not do one better and get rid of it altogether? she thinks. Better to have it gone, to pretend she never saw it at all.

She begins to pull her chair out to sit but something catches her eye and she stops short. She sees herself reflected in the window. There is her chaotic hair, even wilder in the humidity, her fuzzy cardigan. Her eyes travel past herself farther back into the room, where she sees the reflection of something behind her. It takes a moment for her to place the outline of a figure in a coat, its hood pulled up. Her chest seizes up at the shimmer of something above her. A startled scream escapes her throat before everything goes silent.

ONE

Eight Months Later

Alex Marks sees her reflection in the door of the Bluebird Diner as she approaches. She steers clear of mirrors most days, but she can't avoid herself now, the wavy brown hair and small pointed jaw. The dark eyes, deeper set than she'd like and on the small side. The dire clothes—a pair of track pants and a V-neck T-shirt—are something she tries not to dwell on. She pushes through the door into the restaurant, breathing in the familiar smells of toast, bacon, and syrup.

"Well, look who it is," Raymond calls out, raising a piece of buttered toast in greeting as she makes her way down to the end of the L-shaped counter. "Alexis, I saved your seat."

"You know Alex doesn't go by that name," Janice scolds him as she brushes past, her wide arm loaded with plates of pancakes and omelets like some sort of breakfast-themed circus performer. Alex smiles at the Bluebird's head waitress as she slides onto the empty stool.

"No name for a young woman," Raymond grumbles. "I'll call her by her given name, no offense, Alexis."

Alexis is *not* her given name either, but she doesn't correct him. Despite his many shortcomings, Raymond will have been sitting there vigilantly saving her spot next to him since the diner opened at seven. And who else could she say did anything like that for her? Nobody.

"Usual?" Janice asks, not pausing for an answer. Though Alex has been coming to the same counter every day for nearly seven years, Janice has only recently accepted her. You have to put your time in at the Bluebird to be deemed worthy of having a usual. Alex is proud of the accomplishment.

"Yes, please," Alex says. The usual being a sesame bagel toasted with cream cheese and raspberry jam.

"Don't know how you eat those things," Raymond mutters. "It's truly a tragedy. Not how bagels are meant to be consumed." He's right. It's nearly blasphemous. And the Bluebird's are not even close to being the best bagels in the city or even the neighborhood, but the combination reminds her of her childhood. Of mornings getting ready for school and the smell of bread in the toaster, sticky knives left out on the counter. Of the way things were before she left everything she grew up with to come to a place where she knew not a soul.

Raymond is eating his early bird special of scrambled eggs and home fries at a glacially slow pace. He will now be on his third, possibly fourth cup of coffee. His hand trembles ever so slightly as he lifts it to his mouth. *Ol' Gray Hair,* Janice calls him with only a very small sprinkling of affection.

Janice's own wiry hair is dyed a deep, unnatural red and pulled into a bun the size of a gumdrop on the top of her head. She glides by Alex now, dropping off a thick porcelain mug of black coffee.

"I'll have some more toast, too, please, Janice." Raymond pushes his empty plate away and shakes open his copy of the *Daily Press.*

"I don't know how you read that tabloid garbage," Janice says, stationing herself in the crook of the counter as she pours him a fresh cup.

"The *Daily* is a New York institution," Raymond says, not lifting his eyes from the front-page photo of some politician drinking beer from a keg under the headline *What Does She Really STAND For?*

"At least the *Herald* is respectful," Janice argues, bringing up the *Daily*'s rival, the venerable *New York Herald.* "Back when we were young the news was unbiased. Walter Cronkite. Not whatever garbage this is!"

"You think the *Herald* is unbiased?" Raymond says, his voice rising. "You don't think that they are in the Democrats' pockets with all their politics? And don't get me started on how they covered those protests last year."

"Oh, right, because you were a cop they must all be good." Janice rolls her eyes.

"I was a *detective*, Janice, and I didn't say that."

"Bah!" Janice isn't having any of it.

Oh boy. Alex leans back with her coffee mug and ignores them. It's an argument they have at least weekly. She takes a bite of her bagel. The work she will have to do later is already weighing on her. Her copywriting job is so boring sometimes it makes her want to cry.

"You wouldn't understand nuance, Ray," Janice says. "Not if it came up to you and bit you on the ass." Her red-polished fingernail taps the counter for emphasis.

"So I want to be entertained, sue me!" Raymond says, exasperated. The two of them know exactly how to rile each other up. "More toast, please."

"More? You've just had four slices." Janice narrows her eyes.

"What, are you the toast police now? Last I heard this was a free country where a man could order as much toast as he can pay for!" Raymond pushes his plate forward. Alex watches warily as Janice's lips tighten. To her relief, the shriek of a fire truck outside interrupts them. By the time it passes, Janice has moved back toward the kitchen and Raymond seems to have calmed down. Alex picks up her mug, settling into the hum of the diner, appreciating the whir of the coffee makers and clatter of silverware.

It may not be perfect, but there are things you need to keep grounded when you live in a big city. Routines that you create for yourself, the small town you make of your daily movements. These mornings at the Bluebird had kept her from collapsing with loneliness when she first arrived in the city. Alex remembers herself then, shy and skittish. When she first moved into the apartment above the nail salon on Eighty-Sixth Street, she didn't venture far. The Bluebird was convenient, right across the street, a place from which she could retreat quickly if needed to the safety of her shoebox of an apartment.

All she wanted to do then was to be a part of it all, to be one among those millions in the swirl of Manhattan's streets. And she thinks, taking a sip of weak coffee, that she has probably succeeded. No one really knows her here. Except for Janice and Raymond, she is nearly invisible. It's part of the magic of New York, Alex often muses, that you can be completely anonymous while also feeling so interconnected to the people and places around you.

"Oh, look, Alexis, isn't this that advice columnist you loved?" Raymond says as he turns the page in his paper. "Frannie? The one who was murdered?"

"Francis?" Alex's heart jerks in her chest at the thought of her hero, Francis Keen.

"That's the one, yeah. Looks like they are trying to replace her."

"What? No!" Alex yanks the paper from his hands. "They wouldn't dare."

"Grabby, grabby," Raymond tuts, letting go of the pages. Alex smooths the paper out onto the counter in front of her, her heart pounding.

In the photo Francis Keen is standing behind her desk at the *Herald*. She wears a white shirt rolled up at the sleeves, her gray-blond hair loose around her shoulders. A chain of heavy gold links glitters below the V of her collar. She smiles at the camera so warmly that you'd think she knows the photographer. Through the window behind her, Midtown Manhattan gleams geometrically. It's the same photo they ran last year when Francis's body was found on the floor in her beach house.

The headline reads:

For the Herald's *Beloved Advice Column Dear Constance,*
Attempts at a New Beginning after Tragedy

"Well, it's not like she can write it herself anymore, can she?" Raymond says. "Why not give someone else a chance? People loved that column, didn't they?"

Alex shakes her head. "You don't understand, Ray. She was the best. There's no one who can give advice the way Francis Keen did."

Since she first picked up a copy of the *Herald*, Alex was a religious reader of Dear Constance. She doesn't know how anyone could not be drawn to Francis's column. That special way she had of perceiving things about people by reading between the lines, things that they probably didn't even know about themselves. Despite her ability to understand what a person should do in any given situation, her advice was never preachy, never condescending. Francis's words felt like those of a true friend, one who innately understood you, who would do whatever was in her power to make sure you succeeded. Nothing could make you feel like you weren't alone in the world like reading one of her columns.

After Francis's death Alex had looked for comfort in other advice columns, but the magic just was not there in any of them. The advice was staid and unimaginative and often just plain bad. It left her with a cold, sad feeling.

"I still can't believe they never caught the person who killed her," Alex says, shuddering. Francis Keen's murder was so unexpected, so terrible and violent and senseless, that Alex had felt off-kilter for weeks after.

"It was a bad detective on that case," Raymond grumbles, his fingers shaking as he tries to open a single-serving creamer cup. "That Delfonte twit. I knew him back in the day. Spoiled brat who never wanted to work for anyone." Raymond's tremor has gotten worse lately, Alex notes, watching out of the corner of her eye as he struggles to find a grip on the creamer's paper tab.

"Oh, and you would have solved her murder single-handed, I suppose?" Janice swoops by with the long-awaited toast, clearly skeptical.

"I would have," Raymond insists, still grappling with the plastic container. "There's a reason I was a good detective, Janice. There is a logical order to these things, you have to be methodical and patient." His fingers fumble again with the creamer and he smashes it onto the counter in frustration.

"That sounds like you, Ray," Janice says dryly.

Alex takes the creamer from him and peels the lid back. He gives her a silent nod of appreciation and tips it into his mug.

"I should go," Alex says, feeling suddenly agitated.

"Off to sell drugs?" Raymond snorts as she slides off her stool.

"Girl's gotta eat her bagels," Alex replies, dreading the copywriting she'll be doing today for the pharmaceutical company that employs her. But she is grateful for the work, or tells herself she should be.

"Can I take this?" Alex asks, already folding up Raymond's paper and putting it into her purse.

"Sure, sure. I was done with it anyway." Raymond waves her off. "Wouldn't want to rot my brain with all that celebrity news in the back."

"See?" Janice says. "Good start, Ray."

Alex walks toward the door, the murmur of their banter receding behind her. She doesn't hear it though; all she can think about is Francis Keen.

TWO

Alex spends the rest of the day writing promotional copy for a new medication that claims it's able to stop cyclical thinking. She does her best to make the little pink pill appealing, wondering how cyclical her thoughts would have to be to make up for the fact that one of the side effects listed is death.

In the late afternoon she turns in her copy to the boss she's never met and puts on her sweatpants. It is one in a series of rituals she has made for herself that keep her sane. *You can't work in your sweatpants* is rule number one. She pads into her kitchen and pours the first of her nightly glasses of wine and a bowl full of kettle corn from the bag, one of her main food groups. With her provisions she settles back on the couch and takes out the newspaper Raymond gave her, opening it up in front of her on the coffee table. The photo of Francis makes her chest tighten for a second time.

Alex remembers the shrine that went up in front of the *Herald*'s Manhattan office, the piles of bright flowers and handwritten thank-you notes lining the sidewalk, all while a killer walked free. The scene described in the articles was beyond disturbing. Francis on the floor of her summer home. No sign of a break-in. No DNA. No murder weapon. No credible suspects. No witnesses.

And now, apparently, the *Herald* has moved on. Alex has tried to put it behind her, but her Sundays feel empty without Francis's column to read. It feels like she's lost a wise older relative. Dear Constance gave Alex something to look forward to, something to cling to in those years when she was working up the nerve to make her move to New York and then later as she navigated life here, provided a bit of motherly wisdom as she came of age in a city that was often less than nurturing. Without Dear Constance, what would have happened to Alex? She shudders, thinking of the direction her life might have taken. It's quite possible she wouldn't be here at all.

Alex reels at the prospect of someone new taking her beloved Francis's place. The idea of a person doing the job poorly is somehow more terrifying than no one doing it at all. She rereads the final paragraph of the *Daily*'s article.

> *Ever wanted to be an advice columnist? The* Herald *will attempt to replace its longtime columnist Francis Keen, who was tragically lost just last year. To apply for the position, go to Theherald/careers. net and fill in the online application form. May the person with the best advice win. Our advice to the* Herald *is: good luck replacing the irreplaceable.*

It was a strange choice to make it an open call, Alex thinks. It feels almost vulgar to advertise the position like that. After all, it isn't just anyone who could match Francis Keen's sly humor or the depth of her compassion. She reaches for her laptop and types in the address for the job listing. A link takes her to the *Herald*'s career page, where the position for advice columnist is at the top. She just wants to see what the questions are, she tells herself as she fills out the first part of the application. She wants to see what metrics they are using to replace her beloved Dear Constance. First, they ask for a list of basic things like name, address, prior work experience. Alex types in her information, but next the electronic form directs her to a page that looks very much like a Dear Constance column, or a series of them. There are several letters formatted the way they appear in the *Sunday*

Herald, and below them blank spaces for answering, like the essay portion of a test.

Alex starts to read the first letter. It is from a man who feels his life has no meaning even though he has two young kids, a good relationship, a stable home. But still, he is dissatisfied. He writes that he often finds himself standing outside his house at night looking up into the sky and asking himself if this is it. Is this all he is good for? Or has this very normal existence trapped him, stopped him from becoming all he was meant to be? As painful as it might be, he thinks the answer might be in leaving his wife, in giving himself a fresh start, but he isn't sure.

So, I'm asking, begging really, for help knowing what to do. This can't be all there is, can it?

Reading along, Alex finds herself thinking with complete clarity that this person's problem isn't to be found in his wife, who by his own account is lovely and patient with him, nor is it anywhere else in his external circumstances. She grows slightly frustrated with the man. His real problem, Alex thinks with sudden conviction, is his complete lack of appreciation for his own life. The answer is obvious. He has to change the way he sees himself, to dismantle the image he has of himself as some sort of unappreciated genius. He needs to start living the life he actually has. If he fails to do so, he is destined for a lifetime of misery either with or without his wife and kids. Alex has a strong sense that she knows what to do and that if she could just tell this person, he'd be able to make things right for himself.

Before she even means to, Alex is pouring herself another glass of wine and is writing it all down. Time passes in a blur of focus. As she finishes, she moves to the next one; this question is from a woman who is afraid of growing up. The sentences fall into place with the satisfying snap of puzzle pieces.

She hadn't intended to get here, fill in all of the questions. Her finger hovers above the Submit button. She takes a last swig of wine, tilting the glass to get the dregs. The bottle is now completely empty. She can feel the regret of it already beginning behind her eyes. Before she lets herself think about it any further, she drops her finger onto Submit.

Her pulse buzzes with adrenaline. She watches with her heart in her throat as all of her writing disappears. There is a moment of nothing, and then the screen refreshes and is replaced with one blue sentence against the white background: *Congratulations, your application has been submitted.*

She sits back and looks up from her computer, blinking into her dark living room. The clock reads nearly 2 a.m. But she isn't tired. If anything, she feels a zippy buzz of energy. It is surprisingly satisfying solving other people's problems, she thinks. Much easier than fixing your own.

Dear Constance,

Ever since I was a little girl, I've wanted to leave the town I grew up in. I know that might sound silly, but it is true and I don't have anyone to tell it to.

My mom and dad never had much in common. The few times I remember seeing them together they were fighting, or worse, silent. Now Mom has Sid, her boyfriend. They are obsessed with each other in a way that leaves no room for anyone else to get involved. I move around the house where I grew up like a ghost; no one makes eye contact when they talk to me. I know Sid wants me out almost as bad as I want to leave. "When are you going to get your own place?" he asked me the other day, looking at me over the back of the couch when I came into the house.

"As soon as I can," I shot back at him. But honestly, I don't know when that will be. It takes a lot of money to get a place of your own, even somewhere as cheap and lackluster as Wickfield.

I guess if I'm going to ask you for life advice you should know a few things about me. I am twenty-two and live in the same town I grew up in, even in the same house I grew up in. But I want desperately to try something new, to grow up and move away, but I don't have the money. Maybe I'm just not brave enough.

Ever since Sid showed up when I was fourteen and Mom disappeared into him, I have been the one responsible for myself. I've watched my friends all go off to college while I stay here in Wickfield working at the hardware store. When I was a little kid, I remember it being kind of fun downtown, but now Sam's is one of the only businesses left. Sam, my boss, is in his early sixties. He wears a pair of coveralls every day and can fix just about anything from car engines to screen doors. He's owned Sam's Hardware on West Main Street since I was a little kid and probably even before that. I started working here four years ago when I was still in high school. I like it at Sam's. Unlike my house, it feels safe and predictable here. I like the rows of tiny bins filled with different-sized nails and mixing paint colors. I like that everything has a place and that Sam can answer nearly any question. Except he can't help me figure out the things I need to fix, like the fact I go home every day feeling miserable, that I hate it here in Wickfield, or why I am twenty-two years old and have never had a real boyfriend. I am all on my own with those.

All my life I have felt like I was at sea alone in a boat that was bound to sink unless I kept my hands on the oars. But the problem with paddling like crazy is that sometimes, just focusing on surviving makes it hard to know what direction you're heading or if you are going anywhere at all.

I am spinning in circles, Constance, and all I want is to find a way out. Can you tell me how?

Please help,
Lost Girl

THREE

Wednesday morning Alex switches on her bathroom light. Outside on her apartment's narrow window ledge two pigeons coo and shift, swiveling their little orange eyes toward her. "Hi, Mildred. Morning, Percy," she addresses the pair with the names she's given them as she reaches into her shower and turns the water on. They ruffle their feathers in response. Alex knows a lot of people think of pigeons as an unsanitary nuisance, but she can't help but feel impressed by their resilience. They're just trying to get by like the rest of us.

She puts on a podcast on her phone. She's chosen one called *Reaching*. It is hosted by an expensive-looking blond woman who interviews other women with aspirational jobs. It will be the perfect accompaniment to her shower. She has a wide variety downloaded to fill in the silence of living alone. Her only constraints are that nothing be too complicated or depressing. Too much quiet can be damaging, can lead to spiraling thoughts and unproductive days. Alex can't afford to dig herself out from that, so *Reaching* it is. She props her phone on the edge of the sink and steps out of her pajama shorts, leaving them on the tiled floor as she gets into the shower.

The soothing voice of the podcast host penetrates the steam. She is interviewing a woman who started a bespoke line of candles named after herself. It is the kind of vanity business that suggests the woman already had plenty of money.

"I gua sha first thing every morning," the woman is saying. "Lymphatic drainage is key to my well-being. Then lemon water, an oat milk latte, these are my nonnegotiables. They truly make me feel grounded and give me a sense of inner joy." Her voice sounds thin and fragile. Alex frowns. There is something between the lines that she is hiding. And it isn't just the obvious fact that no amount of lemon water can make a person truly happy.

Alex shampoos her hair, thinking ahead to her own day. On today's docket: Colesna, a stomach pill to offset the damage from one of the company's other medications. From there the day yawns and then contracts. An afternoon snack, rarely a full dinner. Some popcorn from a bag, kettle corn if the corner deli has it. Maybe a few cookies or a bowl of noodles. Always a glass of wine, maybe two, usually three. And then to sleep, though it often doesn't come easily. Her days are always the same. A patchwork of order she's created for herself out of the nothing she came to New York with seven years ago.

"And would you say you feel content now?" the host asks her guest. Alex closes her eyes and lets the water trickle down over her face, soaking her hair. *No.*

The woman on the podcast pauses before she replies. "It's taken me a long time to get to this place of peace and stillness in my life, but yes, through my daily practice I am happier now than I've ever been." There is a slight tremor in the woman's voice. "I just have to stay consistent. That's the key." It's fear, Alex realizes. The rich candlemaker is afraid of something. But what could she possibly have to be scared of?

Alex picks up her body wash. It's in a glass bottle with a gold top. *Enjoy the transportive scent of Ylang-Ylang*, the packaging says. She'd bought it on a whim while wandering around the Upper East Side. *Cheaper than therapy, and just as good*, she likes to lie to herself about her daily walks. In her seven years in the city, Alex has walked nearly every block of Manhattan, expanding her circle every week. There are places she's been only once and others so well-trod she can walk them without thinking. Walking might not be as good as psychotherapy, but it is the only way to feel like she is still moving forward in her life, even if she isn't.

She isn't sure what had possessed her to go into the store and buy the fancy body wash. Maybe it was the faint smells of rose and sandalwood wafting out onto the sidewalk. But more likely it was a group of women inside. They were laughing and chatty, making each other sniff various perfumes until the whole store was a cloud of essential oils and musks. It reminded Alex of who she thought she would be at thirty. A businesswoman with a gaggle of friends. Or perhaps she might have been one of the other women, the one pushing a bassinet up Madison Avenue and serenely gazing into shop windows with a Ralph's coffee in hand, her Celine sunglasses pushed back onto her head. The kind of woman who stopped in on a whim to do whatever she liked, who had a sort of lightness to her as if nothing terrible had touched or could touch her. Alex had felt almost like crying as she looked around the shop at these other women whose full and beautiful lives she might have had if only things hadn't gone so horribly and irrevocably wrong.

And so, she'd gone into the store and bought a fancy body wash. To be near them. Alex had imagined the scent of it making her calm and content. Instead, the bottle sits on the side of the old porcelain tub, and it just makes the rest of her shower look shabby. It serves to remind her of things she wanted for herself that never came to pass, of how far she still has to go. She swallows back images of her old self before they overwhelm her and pours some of the precious liquid into her hand, knowing she can never fully join them, the rich podcasters or the carefree women who shop on Madison Avenue.

When she gets out of the shower the pigeons are gone. She wraps herself up in a towel. The podcast is nearly over. The women's conversation has moved on to exercise routines and food. "I like to nourish my body with chia pudding," the woman says. Alex can practically hear the thinness in her voice. "Sometimes I'll put a touch of cinnamon in for sweetness." It is her admission to this sad indulgence that makes Alex suddenly understand that the woman's major fear is of losing control. Of failing. Before she has time to explore that thought further, the podcast is interrupted by her phone's chiming ringtone.

She steps across the bathroom in her towel to look down at an unfamiliar New York number lighting up her screen. She stares at the phone as it vibrates on the vanity. Alex does not answer unfamiliar numbers. It is one of the rules she has for herself, one of the long list of things she does every day to keep herself safe. But at the last second, something makes her snap the phone up and drag her finger across the answer button.

"Hello?" Alex says suspiciously.

"Hi, I'm looking for Alex Marks?" a man's voice replies. Alex's stomach twists at the sound of her name in a stranger's voice.

"Yes?" she says, her mouth dry.

"Hi, Alex. This is Jonathan Amin. I work as an assistant to Howard Demetri, editor in chief at the *New York Herald*." He sounds crisp, efficient, slightly irritated.

Her heart thumps. *The application.* She leaves the bathroom wrapped in her towel and crosses her small living room to the table where Raymond's copy of the *Daily* is still folded open to the article about Francis.

"Alex?" The voice is impatient. "Are you still there?"

"Yes, sorry. I'm here." Droplets of water from her hair spatter onto the photo of Francis Keen.

"Good. Howard was very impressed with your sample letters. He'd like to schedule an interview with you to discuss your application," Jonathan says. Alex's mouth opens and closes. She yanks the phone away from her face to reaffirm the phone number. She'll google it later to make sure no one is fucking with her. *Howard Demetri, editor in chief of the most respected newspaper in the country for over three decades, was impressed with her?*

"In person?" she says, quickly bringing the phone back to her ear.

"Yes, that is how Howard likes to do things." Of course, *the* Howard Demetri isn't going to have some sort of sad virtual meeting. There is no way he could ever appear as a talking head in a square on her desktop.

"Yes, of course. I'm sorry. When should I come in?"

"Thursday. He has nine a.m. available."

She scrambles to process this information. "Yeah, like this Thursday?

Tomorrow? I can do that." She writes the numeral 9 with a blue pen on the margin of the newspaper and circles it several times.

"Thursday would be tomorrow, you are correct," he says impatiently. "Bring your ID to the front entrance and the doorman will give you a pass. Just give him your name and say you are coming to see Howard Demetri. They'll send you up to the forty-ninth floor."

"Okay, I'll be there," Alex says.

"Great."

"This is very exciting," she adds, cringing at her unconcealed enthusiasm.

"I'm sure," Jonathan replies, clearly disgusted.

Alex hangs up the phone and continues to stare down at the newspaper, watching as the drops of water form dark crimps in the page around Francis's face. She remains rooted in place, her skin prickling under the thin towel despite the sun beating in through her apartment window.

Standing there, Alex feels something beginning to shift, gears and cranks turning that haven't been used in years. Answering the letters was the first unwitting step toward the change. Or maybe it started even before that, with the impulsive purchase of the ylang-ylang body wash. To even have put herself out there like that Alex knows she must have wanted it on some level, that part of her has been ready and waiting for the right moment to make her grand reentry into the world.

Before she can tamp it down, she feels a hum of excitement pumping from her heart into her extremities. It has been so long since she's experienced this sensation that she almost doesn't recognize it. She clutches the towel to her, a smile slowly spreading across her face. All she knows is that for the first time in many years she feels on the cusp of something momentous. She only hopes that this time she can keep herself safe.

FOUR

The *Herald*'s Manhattan office gleams a steely blue in the morning sunlight. From a distance it looks clean and sterile, like a fresh start. But as Alex gets closer, the older, less shiny part of the building becomes visible. The Herald Building is split into two parts—the bottom third is one of the city's original skyscrapers, dreamed up in the 1920s by a student of William Van Alen, designer of the more famous Chrysler Building just down the street. Constructed from gray marble, the original Herald Building is a fever dream of geometric patterns and brass accents. Its entryways are still decorated with minimalist reliefs—a woman in a long dress holding a single blade of wheat, a man with boxy muscles heaving an entire globe above his head. This original part was kept partly intact even through the extensive renovation that cleaved a modern glass skyscraper into it, Frankenstein-ing the building into a strange architectural hybrid. It is now part new and part old, as though the original base has been taken over and is playing host to the modern high-rise bursting like a shiny skewer up into the Manhattan sky.

Alex's stomach turns as she walks toward the revolving doors, watching her reflection grow larger, wavering in the mirrored glass. Her face, at once familiar and not, above the V of her shirt. The short, delicate frame and pointy chin, the light-brown wavy hair pulled back into a low bun. She takes a deep breath, tugging her cuffs down over the tops of her hands—a nervous habit.

She emerges into a soaring atrium made almost entirely of tempered glass that bends into a series of modernist arches far overhead. In front of her, a long security desk is dwarfed by a giant slab of marble, taken from the exterior of the old building and repurposed. An art deco relief etched into a piece of brass shows a stylized man whose angular muscles appear to strain under the weight of a closed book. She tilts her head back to take it all in. Imagine coming in here every day. Alex doesn't think a person could walk through this lobby every morning and not feel like they'd made it.

She has her photo taken by a man at the desk and is sent through a glass turnstile and into an elevator that whisks her up to the forty-ninth floor as quick as an artery pumping blood. The elevator door glides silently open to a U-shaped reception desk. The *New York Herald*'s trademark owl logo engraved on a gold plaque hangs on the wall behind it. Its talons shine coldly as she approaches the desk where a slim, stylish man wearing a turtleneck and sleek wire-rimmed glasses gives Alex an insincere smile.

"Can I help you?" His tone is flat and unwelcoming. And familiar.

"I'm Alex Marks. I'm here to see Howard Demetri?" She cringes at the way her voice rises, as though each sentence were actually a question. "You're Jonathan, right? We talked on the phone."

He purses his lips, not giving Alex the satisfaction of recalling this exchange. "Let me just call Howard and see if he's ready for you." Alex settles herself onto a polished concrete bench. As she looks past the desk at the purposeful strides of the people in the newsroom, this place already feels out of her league. Alex hadn't even had the right clothes to wear today. She'd made a quick and desperate trip to Century 21 after turning in her copywriting last night, yanking a random assortment of workwear off the racks and dragging it into a dressing room an hour before they closed, coming away with only two shirts, neither of which she loved. She'd walked away from the shopping expedition feeling worse. *Calm down, Alex,* she tells herself, clasping her hands in her lap. *They asked you to come here, remember? It's not about how you dress.* Though part of her doesn't quite believe it.

She already knew who Howard Demetri was before filling out the application. He is one of those old newspaper editors who now has the word *legend* attached to their names.

"Alex Marks here to see you," Jonathan says crisply into the phone. "Yes, that's the one." Before she has time to wonder what he could possibly mean by the last part, he has leapt to his feet and is tapping the toe of his extremely stylish tennis shoe on the floor.

"He's waiting for you," he says as though she has caused the delay. Alex stands up too quickly, feeling the blood rush from her head. Jonathan recoils slightly and gives her a critical once-over. Alex glances down at her black pants, which she can now see clearly in the unforgiving office light have developed the sort of sad, faded look that comes with too many washings and not the right soap. Her shirt is not as bad, a crisp white button-up that only looks okay because it is right off the hanger, the plastic tag bitten off a mere hour ago in her bedroom. Her fingers find the hems of her cuffs and tug them down over her knuckles.

"I'll take you back to see Howard now," he says as her stomach bubbles nervously. He leads her past the front desk into the belly of the newsroom. The center of the floor is open and spacious, with several long tables for collaborating and a maze of cubicles half-filled with people, their heads bowed over their computer monitors. As she passes, she can hear the faint clip of keyboards being typed on, that first wave of productivity in the morning, before coffee number one wears off.

"Follow me," Jonathan says, taking her around to the far side of the floor. The periphery of the newsroom is ringed with modern glass-fronted offices. They walk by several conference rooms, one where a small group of worried-looking people talk animatedly in front of a white board. The person giving the presentation pauses when she sees them, her eyes following Alex as she walks past. They come to an abrupt stop at the corner, where a plaque adhered to the front of a glass-enclosed office reads: HOWARD DEMETRI, EDITOR IN CHIEF.

She can see him through the open blinds, sitting behind his desk.

Behind his trademark tortoiseshell glasses, his eyes are intent on his computer screen. A legend in the flesh. Alex's chest seizes. *The* Howard Demetri. Howard is not just any editor in chief. He's part of the old guard, an editor's editor from the era when newspapers were still the gold standard for how people ingested their daily news. He'd helmed the paper, steering it through wars and scandals, and in the process winning it more Pulitzers than any other newspaper in the country. He'd also hired her hero, Francis Keen.

She could pinch herself. His eyes remain glued to his computer monitor. His mouth quivers slightly, as though he is reading something that's upsetting him.

Jonathan knocks on the glass, and he looks up, startled. In the split second before he registers her standing before him, Alex sees pure misery on his face. In an instant, he rearranges his features into a neutral expression. He gestures for them to come inside. She lets Jonathan push open the glass door and usher her into the office.

"Hello," she says. She awkwardly comes to stand in front of his desk, unsure how to address him. *Howard* seems far too informal. *Mr. Demetri?* She worries that will make her seem like an eager kid. She can feel Jonathan growing impatient in the doorway behind her.

"This is Alex Marks," Jonathan says, clearly exasperated. And now a welcoming smile transforms Howard's face. He is handsome, more so in person than in his photos, with a strong jawline and thick gray hair that has come undone from its side part.

"Alex. So good to have you here." He stands up and she watches, amazed, as his legs unfold like stilts. He is strikingly tall, broad-shouldered even at his age, which she's read is currently sixty-one. He is dignified, his face naturally serious, the kind of man she'd have chosen for the job if the part were being cast in a play. All he needs to complete the image is a hat with a press pass tucked into the brim.

He wears a tailored gray suit that sags a bit into his lean legs and arms, making him look even more like a giant. He holds back his tie as he leans over his desk and shakes her hand firmly. She glances down and notices that the desk is littered with half-empty coffee mugs and stacks of papers. An old-fashioned day planner lies open across everything. He glances down and flips it quickly shut, gesturing for her to sit.

"It's a pleasure to have you here, Alex. Thank you, Jonathan. I'll let you know if we need anything else." She is relieved to hear genuine warmth in his voice.

"I can't thank you enough for having me," Alex says delicately as the door closes behind Jonathan. She realizes that a big part of her is actually waiting for him to tell her that there's been a processing error in the applications, that he doesn't want her here at all. But there seems to be no mistake. His expression is serious as he gazes back at her. He leans back in his chair, tenting his fingers in front of him.

"As you might have guessed, we received a huge number of applications for the position. It seems that many people believe they have what it takes to helm the new era of Dear Constance. I think the tally came in at over five hundred, actually. Of course, some of these were not serious applicants. There are a lot of people who think that they can give good advice, but so few actually can."

Alex tries to keep up. Is he saying that she is not a real applicant? *Is* she? Alex doesn't even know herself. It's rare for her to be unable to read someone's intentions, but she is finding that with Howard it is nearly impossible. It feels nearly laughable that she'd be an actual contender for Francis Keen's old job.

"There were also quite a few applications from established writers. A Pulitzer-nominated journalist, a few famous novelists even." Alex feels her insides sink. This is where he tells her that she is not one of the serious ones, that this meeting is a courtesy.

She braces herself for the fall. But instead, he leans forward, his desk chair squeaking, and looks at her intently.

He picks up a piece of paper on his desk and begins to read: "This was in response to a woman who wrote in feeling distressed about growing older: *I wonder if you are not missing your youth at all—being young is never as easy as we remember it—but rather the feeling of being true to who you are, of letting time stretch out in front of you in such a way that you don't need to guard it or worry about its end. Or maybe you miss feeling hopeful."*

He puts the page down. "You wrote that, correct?"

"I did." Alex feels her face growing hot. Is he really saying he liked her answers? It is such a wild idea that her brain spins. She begins to feel flustered.

"Pretty insightful stuff."

"Oh?" she says, her voice thin and strangled. She can't let herself hope. Until this moment she didn't even know this job was something she wanted. But she finds to her own surprise that she does. She wants it more than she has ever wanted anything.

"What is your current position?"

"Well, um, I work in pharmaceutical copywriting currently. Not at an office, I work from home. It's not my dream job, but it's given me a chance to practice writing and practice delivering on a deadline. Though to be honest, the subject matter isn't exactly something I'm passionate about."

He nods and leans back, tenting his long fingers in front of him. She feels that she can see the gears in his head spinning. "Can I ask what made you apply for this position?"

"I just saw the application and thought why not, I guess. I have been a fan of Francis—Dear Constance, I mean—for years and years. Her columns have given me so much. Really more than I could even say."

She continues, cautiously, noticing the pained smile on his face.

"She got me through so many troubled times. In fact, every time I smell fresh newsprint it brings me immediately back to reading Dear Constance. The column was the thing that kept me sane, the one constant in my life that felt safe and secure." Alex's fingers find her sleeves and pull. "Francis is—was—a hero of mine." She pauses, unsure how exactly she should acknowledge the other giant in the room. The one who is dead. The air in the room shifts.

Howard's hooded eyes flick to Alex. His interview persona is suddenly gone. He leans in now, his arms resting on the desk confiding in her. "Listen, I worked with Francis for over thirty years. There was no one, and I mean *no one*, as perceptive as she was. We all know there will never be anyone like Francis Keen. She is irreplaceable. But Dear Constance is a pivotal part of the *Herald*. Readers love to have an escape from the news. They love to see problems being solved for a change." As he speaks, he spins his gold wedding band with his thumb. "It helps people to be able to focus on sometimes smaller but no less important problems."

"I can see that," Alex says. "The day-to-day is all we really have control over. You can't solve wars in other countries, or end poverty, not as an individual human being. But perhaps you can mend a rift with your in-laws or help someone in need of encouragement."

"Exactly!" He bangs a hand down on his desk.

She is enjoying Howard's intensity, his take on the world. She can see right away the qualities he has that would make him a great editor, legendary even.

"You understand. I had a good feeling about you, Alex Marks. Not everyone can do what you did with these letters." He jabs his finger down onto the paper in front of him. "Hell, almost no one can. That kind of wisdom. We were very impressed with your answers. There were none that we felt even compared, honestly. We are prepared to offer you the job on a probationary basis."

The words rush out, washing over her so quickly that as soon as he stops speaking Alex immediately wonders if she just heard them. "Really?"

"Yes, really." He allows a smile now. "Starting next week. If you are still interested, of course." Alex feels her mouth open and close uselessly as she tries to absorb what he is saying.

"It would be such an honor, I don't even know how to respond," she says.

Howard nods. "You have to know that this isn't just a job. It's a vocation. It can be a lot of work and very consuming reading people's struggles every day. Kind of like being a therapist, except your advice is out there for the public to read. And criticize." He raises his eyebrows. "It's a good thing usually, but it does make you more exposed."

Alex's chest tightens at the word *exposed*. The application, this meeting, they were all pretend up until now. But if she is really going to do this, it will require her to put herself out there, her name. *Oh God, her photo?* She can't. This just won't work.

"I don't mean to dissuade you," he says quickly. "This is the kind of job that is truly a once-in-a-lifetime opportunity. It will give you more than you could possibly imagine."

"Oh, I know, and I am so grateful. It's just . . ." What should she say? That she has been in hiding for years and barely leaves her apartment? His eyes flick to his computer screen. Alex realizes that he must have other, more urgent issues to address. She has to tell him. She'll thank him and say that he's made a mistake, that she can't take the job. *Go on, Alex, tell him now.* But the words remain lodged in her throat. How could she possibly say no to being edited by Howard Demetri? She doesn't want to turn it down.

She wants this job more than she has ever desired anything in her life. All these years she's tried to stay safe at the expense of so much. And now she is nodding yes like a big fool.

"That's great news, Alex. We are absolutely delighted. You're going to do great here." He looks relieved, doesn't he? "Jonathan will send you an offer letter this afternoon."

"When would you like me to start?"

"We were hoping to have you in and going on Monday. That will give you enough time to turn a column in by next Friday morning and I can edit it to run in Sunday's paper. There are mountains of letters piling up in that old email account. It's summer. This seems like as good a time as any for a relaunch. What's better for escapism than other people's problems?" He gives her a rueful grin and she sees the younger version of Howard Demetri, the one from the old Kodachrome-tinted photos she saw online. The charmer. So he is going to be the one editing her column. The thought of it gives her a shiver of excitement and fear.

"I'll do my best." She finds herself grinning back at him. Her new boss. Her heart swells with gratitude for the opportunity he's given her.

"If all that sounds amenable to you? I assume you'll have to put in some sort of notice at the pharmaceutical company." He says the last few words with more than a tinge of sarcasm.

"Yes, of course. All of that is fine. I might just be a bit in shock," Alex says breathlessly. She will do anything she can to make him glad he hired her.

His mouth tugs down at the corners as several consecutive dings come from his computer screen.

"Welcome to the dusty old world of newspapers, Alex Marks. You're going to do great. I haven't felt this confident about a hire since I met Francis," he says. He stands up, putting an end to their meeting. As he reaches over and shakes Alex's hand once more, he adds, "As you may know, she didn't have much experience either. And look how well she did."

"You're right," Alex says, though part of her can't help but think that she ended up dead.

FIVE

Alex pushes through the revolving doors of the Herald Building, blinking her way back into the bright morning on the sidewalk. Her legs feel rubbery as she walks aimlessly for several blocks, following the flow of Sixth Avenue foot traffic, a strange floating sensation overtaking her body. The whole interview feels like she must have imagined it. There is no way that she was just told she would be writing the country's best-known advice column. She replays it in her mind. The conversation. Howard reaching to shake her hand. The way he looked at her, so directly, like he already believed she could do it.

It is already getting warm outside, turning into one of those June days when people are still happy about the feeling of the sun on their skin, where the city feels full of promise. Before the heat makes everything and everyone unbearable and the smog and the smell of trash choke you as soon as you hit the streets. The sidewalks teem with people in light summer clothes. In just a few weeks that will all change when the rich leave en masse, escaping to the Hamptons or their country homes upstate, leaving the others behind to fend for themselves.

Alex crosses Fifty-Ninth Street and cuts up through Central Park, letting herself enjoy the wild and impossibly rare sensation of having just gotten what you want in life. The park is bustling. Tourists are everywhere. Families cluster on the pathways; couples lounge on blankets, kissing in the bright sunlight. Friends sit together under the trees on their work breaks drinking coffee and probably gossiping about their coworkers. All this connection makes Alex reach for her phone. Without thinking, she opens up her contacts list. It is minimal—Raymond from the Bluebird, a woman who is her singular contact at work, a couple of Middle Eastern takeout places down the street from her apartment. Before she knows it, she is at the end of the list. Her heart sinks. It is the biggest news of her life but there is no one for her to tell. A face flashes through the back of her mind and her heart constricts. The temptation to call some people never goes away, no matter what you've done to rid yourself of it.

Alex spots a trail leading out of the park and turns quickly toward it, dodging the men walking dogs and couples pushing strollers. She is feeling claustrophobic now. All these cute little scenes press in on her, making her wish for a life that she can't have. She rushes across a patch of lawn and cuts out of the park as fast as she can. Once she is far enough outside of the park and its scenes of domestic bliss, she slows down, panting in the bright sunlight.

A notification dings from her phone. Alex stops walking, tucking herself under the awning of an expensive-looking French restaurant so she can see. It's an email from Jonathan Amin. The subject line is *Offer*. She holds her breath as she opens it.

Dear Alex Marks,

We are writing to officially offer you the job of columnist for the New York Herald's *long-standing advice column Dear Constance. In this role you will answer one question a week from the letter of your choosing, due each Friday and printed weekly on Sundays. In addition, you will read all of the letters that come into the* Herald *addressed to Dear Constance.*

We are offering a starting salary of $125,000 paid biweekly as well as a 401k, medical insurance, and fourteen days of paid vacation.

Howard Demetri was impressed with your written skills and looks forward to you joining our staff. However, this is an exploding offer, which means that if you do not accept by end of day today, we will have to rescind our invitation for you to join the Herald. I'm sure you'll understand, as this is a very rare opportunity.

We look forward to your response.

Regards,
Jonathan Amin

Alex stares at the salary. It is more than double what she makes now. Alex is self-aware enough to know that money won't buy happiness, but it can sure help with comfort. She thinks about the women she saw in the shop where she bought her expensive soap. How they nearly glittered with possibility. She'd be a fool not to take it. *It will expose you*—wasn't that what Howard had said? Her stomach turns.

"Miss?" a voice says from somewhere. She looks up. She had been so focused on the email, she wasn't paying attention to where she was. The doors to the restaurant are propped open. Near the polished wood bar, a portly man in a starched white shirt gives her a welcoming smile. "We have a delicious lunch. A nice glass of cold Sancerre?"

Several women have already claimed a table up front. They sip crisp white wine, their sweaters draped over their shoulders, Chanel sunglasses perched on their perfect noses, chatting comfortably with one another. Alex looks longingly. She thinks of the number they'd quoted in the offer letter. Why shouldn't she have a fancy lunch? She smiles and goes inside the restaurant, claiming a stool at the end of the bar near the open doorway.

"Make yourself comfortable," the man says, going behind the bar now and pouring her a glass of ice water. He hands her a stiff red menu. He turns his back to her as he prepares another round of wine for the women.

Feeling decadent, she orders herself a goat cheese salad and hamachi crudo. At the last minute she calls out to the bartender: "And a martini, dry, please." She isn't normally a martini drinker, particularly not at twelve thirty in the afternoon, but she feels the need to mark the occasion. It's been so long since she celebrated anything, even a birthday. And it isn't every day that you get offered your dream job. She watches the dappled sunlight hit the bar, relishing the feel of the warm wood under her arms. All at once, everything feels right with the world. Of course she should take the job, she thinks with sudden clarity. It's incredible how much her life has changed in the span of a few days. Miraculous, even. Things like this do not happen more than once, certainly not for her. It's almost enough to make her feel hopeful about life. She opens her phone and replies.

Dear Jonathan,

I am happy to accept the offer. I can't wait to join the New York Herald's *staff as columnist for Dear Constance. I look forward to continuing Francis Keen's legacy.*

Sincerely,
Alex Marks

She presses Send with a flutter of nerves that dissipate as the bartender pushes the martini across the bar. Her fingers melt the frost as she lifts the glass to her lips. She can already taste the cold bite of it, the hint of olive brine. Right now, she is Alex Marks, newest employee of the *Herald*, and if she can't celebrate with someone she may as well do it alone.

"Hot day out there," a man's voice says. She looks up, startled. He is large and wide, dressed in a polo shirt and chinos. He takes up the entire end of the bar, throwing her seat into shadow. She hears the scrape of the stool next to her being pulled out and feels the weight of his body sitting down, unnecessary when there are plenty of places farther down the bar, she notes, her chest suddenly feeling heavy.

I NEED YOU TO READ THIS

"Yep," she says, careful not to give him any sign she wants to get into a conversation.

"This place is great though. A martini, huh? Looking to take the edge off?" He gives a loud laugh that ends as a cough.

She glances at his face, which is rectangular, a scattering of orange and white stubble across his chin. She gives him a tight smile and turns away from him, looking back down at her phone. She can feel his eyes lingering on her.

"Oh, come on. Really? No one comes and sits at the bar wanting to be left alone," he tells her as though it is common knowledge. They do, she thinks. *I do.* But she has a feeling he is the kind of man who won't do well being rejected. She fumbles for her purse, wanting to pay and leave.

"Let me get that for you." His thick hand reaches out onto the bar holding a wallet imprinted with the Gucci logo.

"No, thanks, I've got it," she says, recoiling slightly.

"You sure?" When he looks at her this time his eyes are hard, empty as marbles.

"Yep, I'm good." Alex cranes her neck, looking for the bartender, but he is out in the bright sunlight talking to the women at the front of the restaurant.

"I'm just trying to be friendly," he says, though it doesn't feel that way. His jaw sets angrily. She reaches again for her purse. She can't stay here, not now. But his hand is suddenly on her wrist, pinning it down against the bar.

"Hey, let go," she says, a hot wave of panic starting in her belly.

"What's going on with you? I was just trying to be nice and buy you a drink," he says through gritted teeth, a sheen of sweat forming on his face. Should she scream? Is there even a reason? Instead, she leaps down from the stool and jerks her arm away from him. But the man's beefy hand remains clamped around the sleeve of her shirt. It tears as she twists away from him.

He looks down at her exposed skin, his eyes going wide at the sight of her wrist. "Whoa, whoa, what is this? You cut yourself, lady?" She looks down in horror at her exposed wrist crisscrossed with white scars. Now this man has not only frightened her, but he has humiliated her. She is no longer afraid of him; she is furious.

"Let me go," Alex hisses with as much ferocity as she can. He does as she tells him, dropping her arm suddenly as if she is contagious, holding his hands up in surrender. His face goes slack. His mouth drops open.

"Listen, lady, I was just trying to be nice. I didn't know you had problems." He leans away from her now, waves his palms in the air as if she were the one attacking *him*. Shaking, she takes three twenty-dollar bills from inside her purse and drops them on the bar. She walks quickly away, leaving behind her cold martini and any chance for a meager celebration.

"Miss?" the bartender calls out as she runs to the front door. He is holding a plate in his hand, probably her perfect salad. But she doesn't stop. She can already feel the pressure building behind her eyes.

"Fuck, did you see that? That girl was crazy," she hears the man say to the bartender as she ducks out the open door. Out on the sidewalk the sun is hard and unforgiving. The shame of all of it burns a hole in her back as she flees the restaurant.

It was just a random asshole, she tells herself, trying to calm down. *No need to let it color everything.* But she feels shaky and vulnerable as she skitters her way uptown to her apartment. The whole thing feels like a bad omen. Maybe she is putting herself in danger by accepting the job. By the time she reaches her corner she wonders if she should write Jonathan and rescind her acceptance. Alex climbs the dingy staircase to her apartment, a knot of panic growing in her chest. She closes the door behind her as always, tapping on each of the locks with a finger to be sure that it's turned—*one, two, three.* Next she goes to the living room windows, moving the blackout curtains aside to check that they are locked as well. She pulls the curtains tight even though the sun is still blazing.

In the dim quiet of the bathroom window Mildred and Percy shuffle closer together. Alex breathes in and out. She splashes water on her face.

What if this is all a terrible mistake?

Dear Constance,

One day last week this guy Brian just appeared in Wickfield out of nowhere. He came into the store and I couldn't stop myself from staring. Unlike most of the guys here, he has a certain style about him that I noticed right away. He likes to wear crisp blue shirts with rolled-up sleeves and a heavy-looking silver watch. He is lean and fit with stubble on his chin and a thick leather wallet he takes out when he pays for things.

I try not to act like I'm super impressed by him, but I have to stop myself from staring when he comes into the shop. It's always for something small, caulking or tape or some envelopes and pens. We sell all sorts of things here. I started getting the feeling like he was looking at me when he checked out. Like he wanted to talk. So finally, today I said, "Hey, you're new here?" He looked startled and then a big grin came across his face.

"Is it that obvious?" he asked.

"Oh, just a little. I tend to recognize everyone who comes in," I said, and nodded to the side of the store where a few local guys were picking out paint colors.

"Brian. But you probably already know that."

"I am quite the detective," I said, handing him a paper bag with the tape inside and his credit card with his name, Brian Pulman.

"Well, if you know a lot about it here, maybe you can tell me where I can find a decent meal? I've been living off of those hot dogs from Benji's."

I cringed and laughed. "Oh no! Those are not fit for human consumption. Well, there's the Red Barn, which is like a diner. Good grits, eggs, sandwiches, nothing fancy. Then there's the Shoreline farther down Route 12. That's more your white-tablecloth sit-down-style meals, seafood and steaks, that sort of thing." He was watching me, smiling in a way where I got sort of self-conscious and trailed off.

*"That sounds good. You want to go tonight?" His eyes
sparkled at me, which is a thing I don't think I ever could have
said about anyone's eyes before in my life. But Brian's did. They
sparkled. I sort of choked and burst out laughing.*

*"Wait, me?" I looked around the store like someone was
pulling a prank, but it was empty except for the guys looking at
paint.*

He grinned. "Who else?"

*"Um. Yeah, sure, I'll go." I tried to be cool and shrugged like
this sort of thing happens to me all the time. Lies! Could he tell?*

*"Great! I'll swing by and pick you up. When are you done with
your shift?"*

"Six thirty."

"Done."

*For the rest of the day, I worried about what I was wearing: a
pair of black jeans and some boots and a red T-shirt. I wouldn't
be able to go home and change. I also worried that he wouldn't
show, but his pickup truck rolled up outside the hardware store
at exactly six thirty.*

*I got in, sliding over the plush seat. He smiled. "You tell me the
way."*

*I smelled something woodsy on him when he opened the door
to the restaurant. I walked in and tried not to look out of place.
Until tonight I've never gone inside the Shoreline. It's the kind
of place where people go for special occasions. People with more
money than my family. My mom and Sid always turn up their
noses at it, but I know it's only because they've never been. The
hostess is a girl from my high school. She looked startled to see
me with someone like Brian. I could feel her eyes on me as she sat
us down at a table overlooking the river.*

*During dinner I learned he is an architect, which is what
brought him to Wickfield. He's working on a project to renovate
an old, abandoned shoe factory on the edge of town into a series
of designer lofts with businesses below. He also told me that his*

parents are still married. "Thirty-two years now," he said proudly as he ate a Brussels sprout cooked in a mysterious way that made it actually taste good. I also found out that he has a much younger sister who he adores, and his family all live in Holly Acre, a college town about two hours away.

"What about you, what's your story?" he asked me between bites of food. He had really good manners, I noticed, like he never talked with his mouth full, and he put his fork down between bites and really listened to me. All that attention directed right at me made me feel shy. I drank more of the wine before I answered.

"I'm from here," I told him, a little embarrassed. I didn't know what else there was to say that he wouldn't already know. "I've been working at Sam's since high school, but eventually I'd like to do something else. Maybe interior design, or even something like social work," I rattled on nervously, and he smiled, not seeming to mind that I had so little to offer, such a small story. I felt him looking at me in a way I wasn't used to. His eyes are clear and deep blue. I wonder what he sees when he looks into mine. I felt a shiver go all the way through me.

When I got home my mom was watching TV. Without turning around, she asked me where I'd been. I considered lying, but at the last second, I said I went on a date.

This made her swivel around and look at me over the back of the couch. "With who?" I told her about Brian coming into the hardware store lately. I wanted her to be excited the way I felt, but instead her eyes narrowed at me.

"Why did he ask you out?" Mom asked me. "He must be weird."

"He's not weird," I said quickly, but everything in my body had already sunk into the floor. She could tell that she hurt my feelings. My mom isn't a monster, she's just preoccupied with her own stuff and doesn't always know what to say.

"I didn't mean it that way, he just sounds too old and too fancy for you. I just don't want my baby girl getting hurt," *she said, turning back to the TV. It made me mad the way she treated me as though I had no idea what I was doing, like I was ridiculous and young. What is wrong with him or what is wrong with you? I wanted to ask her, but then Sid came in the door, and I went back to the old me, the one who is invisible. But just to them. Because something has changed inside me now. After the date I feel like someone is looking at me like I'm an adult who can make choices for herself. Please help me, Constance, I don't want to mess this up. I think I may have found my only way out of this trap.*

    I think it might be Brian.

Please help,
Lost Girl

SIX

"There's something different about her," Janice says when Alex sits down at the Bluebird's counter in the morning.

"There is, isn't there?" Raymond agrees. They turn on her, suspicious.

"Are you okay? You look nervous or something. Your cheeks are all pink."

"Well . . ." Alex has been dying to share it with someone. "I got a new job."

"Congratulations, Alexis. I didn't know you'd been applying."

"Good job, honey. What is it?" Janice says, pouring her coffee.

"It's at the *Herald*," Alex says, unable to contain her excitement. "I'm going to be the new Dear Constance."

Raymond puts his paper down and turns fully to her. "Wait, you got that dead lady's job? The one we were reading about the other day?"

"Yes, Francis Keen. There were five hundred applicants," Alex says, her cheeks feeling warm.

"Your dream job, Alex! And me and Ray will be able to say we knew her back when she ate bagels with jam each and every morning!" Janice sighs, and Alex swats her playfully on the arm.

But Raymond looks concerned. "Alexis, how are they going to keep you safe? I mean, someone really didn't like the last Dear Constance."

"You mean disliked her with a knife a few times," Janice says un-helpfully.

"Thank you, Janice," Alex says, taking a sip from her coffee.

"I'm not sure, Alexis, I get a bad feeling," Raymond says.

"You always have bad feelings," Janice snips. "You're practically one big bad feeling."

"How do you think I became a detective? You've got to have instinct." He taps his chest proudly.

"I always assumed the murder was personal, that it had to do with her, not her job," Alex rationalizes. It is what she's been telling herself in an attempt to calm her nerves. It hasn't done much to help.

"Of course, honey. I just can't believe our girl is going to be the new Dear Constance. Giving advice to the masses," Janice says wistfully.

"Unless she gives the wrong person the wrong advice and then, boom, dead at her summer house."

"Well, luckily I don't have a summer house," Alex reminds him. Though she has begun to feel queasy. She puts down her bagel, unable to take another bite.

"Don't scare the girl! She's excited! And besides, you don't think anything is safe," Janice says, clearing plates off the counter.

"That's because the world is a dangerous, terrible place." Raymond's hand comes down on the counter, rattling everyone's plates. "You need to be vigilant."

"Yeah, yeah," Janice interjects, rolling her eyes.

"You don't know the things I've seen in this city, the messed-up, crazy things—"

"What, in the eighties? Things have changed a little since then, if you haven't noticed. New York has changed. And Alex is going to be up in that big building with the security guards. She'll be protected."

Raymond shakes his head. "No one is protected twenty-four hours a day. Nobody."

Janice rolls her eyes. "Ignore him, Alex, he reads too much of the *Daily*. It makes a person paranoid." But deep down Alex knows Raymond's right. She won't be protected. Her current life is a known quantity. She can control who she interacts with and when—but at the office she will be putting herself out there, unable to hide when she wants to. Or run.

"I've got to go," she says, sliding off her stool and grabbing her purse from its hook. As she makes her way to the front of the diner, Raymond calls after her: "They never found him, Alexis! Remember that!"

SEVEN

Later in her apartment, computer on her lap, a bowl of popcorn balanced next to her on the sofa, Alex googles Francis Keen. How sad that her death is the first thing that comes up, pages upon pages of tabloid and news articles detailing the nightmarish circumstances of her murder. Most of them are highlighted, indicating she's read them before. It is far from her first time googling the crime scene. She knows the contents. Francis goes alone to the house and after spending one day there is brutally executed with a knife.

She clicks on an article several pages in. It describes how an anonymous source close to Francis said that she had been stressed about work and had gone away to try to relax. In the middle of the article is an image of Francis Keen's idyllic cedar-shingled beach house with its stacked-stone fence and sprawling English gardens. It would look like the setting of a fairy tale were it not cordoned off with crime tape and surrounded by emergency vehicles.

She reads the caption. *The grisly scene where Francis Keen's body was found by longtime editor Howard Demetri.* She stops, startled. So Howard was the one who found Francis. She read it before, but now that she's met with Howard, Alex can imagine it. The way she must have looked. How awful it must have been for him. Alex tries to clear the horror of it from her mind.

Now she types her new boss's name into Google. Her search brings her to a series of photos of benefits and charity balls. Howard, tall and dignified with a swoop of salt-and-pepper hair and sophisticated glasses, a scattering of gray stubble across his square jaw. There he is on his way into the Met Gala, looking dapper. A woman stands beside him, her delicate hand clamped onto his arm. Alex remembers the wedding band Howard spun on his finger. She zooms in to read the caption. *Howard Demetri attends the Met Gala with his wife, Regina Whitaker.* She'd heard Howard's name before but never his wife's.

She is an impossibly glamorous woman, the kind who feels to Alex like she might be her own separate superior species, wearing a gown that looks to be made from row upon row of overlapping tabs of silver. They catch the light like beautiful fish scales. Her perfect lips are parted to reveal a set of flawless white teeth.

Alex broadens her search online to include Regina Whitaker and finds a tour of her and Howard's West Village brownstone in *Architectural Digest*. In the first photo, Regina lounges sideways on a wide white sofa in a room so luxurious, so rich with dark woods and veined marbles, that it looks like a movie set. She scrolls through the photos of their home, absorbing the expensive antiques alongside minimal, modern art. All of it in perfect refined taste. Alex allows herself to imagine living there, the plush feel of the throw pillows, the perfect warm lighting in each room. Isn't this what New York does to people? Make them long for things? She stops on a photo of Howard Demetri in his home office. He sits stiffly behind an expansive desk, an antique globe and a Pulitzer Prize medal side by side on a bookshelf behind him. Alex zooms in on the image. Howard's fingers are clenched unnaturally in front of him, a small tight smile on his face telling her that, despite all of the trappings, the awards, and material success, Howard Demetri is not a happy person.

There's a sharp yell from somewhere out on the street. Startled, Alex pushes her computer off her lap and stands. Her ears prick like a wild animal listening for danger. She hears it again. A man's voice, low and angry, shouting something unintelligible. She moves to the living room window, carefully pulling aside the blackout curtains. Across the street the Bluebird Diner is already dark, closed for the night. A man stands in front of it on the corner. His back is to her, but her chest tightens. There is something familiar about his stance—the slightly bowed legs, the broad shoulders. He paces, his face turned away from her. What is he doing out there? He's stopped yelling but continues to pace, a few yards up and down the block, saying something ferociously into the his cell phone.

He turns finally, the side of his face catching the streetlight. Alex realizes that she has never seen it before. She releases a breath as the man crosses the street, disappearing around the corner and into the night.

She goes back to her computer. Another result farther down the page catches her eye.

Meet the New Dear Constance

She clicks on the link. It takes her to a press release. A photo of her own face stares back at her.

EIGHT

On Monday Alex anxiously reports to the Herald Building for her first day of work. Her heels click against the marbled floor, the sound echoing up through the glass of the atrium. At the entry desk she collects her badge from a security guard. She looks down in wonder at the stiff plastic card attached to a lanyard. ALEX MARKS, THE HERALD. On the right side of the badge is a small photo, taken quickly by Jonathan on her way out of the office the last time she was here.

In it, Alex is looking into the camera, a stunned half smile crookedly plastered onto her face. Will everyone else see the absolute terror in her eyes? She flips the badge over and waves it in front of the electronic sensors, watching in awe as the plexiglass gate parts for her. She slips through the opening silently, nearly expecting the security guard to leap over the barrier and confront her, to tell her there's been a terrible mistake. But no one tries to stop her as she continues to the bank of modern silver elevators. One of them opens on cue, and when she steps inside, the number *49* appears on a screen without her pushing anything. She looks into the mirrored brass of the ceiling, looking down on herself in the reflection. She takes in the somewhat crooked part in her brown hair. She'd brushed it back into a tortoiseshell clip, but now she wonders if she looks ridiculous, like someone pretending to work at a newspaper.

She'd meant to shop for some new work clothes but she doesn't want to go back to Century 21. She wants to go somewhere beautiful, to buy clothes befitting this office, things that will make her look and feel like she belongs here. But in order to do that she will need to wait for her first paycheck. So for now she's cobbled together something from the pathetic assortment of clothes in her closet. Alex is wearing the same white shirt from her interview (its torn sleeve carefully mended), tucked into a slightly flared pin-striped skirt. She smooths her hand once more over her hair as a tonal *ding* announces her arrival at the forty-ninth floor.

The elevator doors open to Jonathan Amin, again sitting primly at his desk. The *Herald*'s gold owl insignia gleams coldly on the wall above him. His head is bowed as his finger silently and fervently scrolls through something on his phone. As she draws closer to the desk, Alex sees amusement flickering on his lips. If he registers her approach, he makes no sign of it. After a moment has passed without any acknowledgment of her presence, she clears her throat. His smile dissolves when he looks up to her standing there.

"Oh, look, it's Alex Marks," he says as though he wasn't expecting her to dare show her face again. "Ready to solve the country's problems, are we?"

"Yes. I'm actually a little nervous," she says, thinking it's possible that if she shows some emotion and opens up to Jonathan, they'll forge some sort of connection.

It's a tactic that clearly doesn't work. He smiles sourly. "I'm sure you are."

She feels herself start to wilt but remembers one of Francis's columns from way back. It was one she memorized. *There are certain people who appreciate your vulnerability and certain people who will try to use it against you. But they can't if you don't let them.*

She takes a deep breath. "Is Howard in?" she asks, eager to see a friendlier face and to confirm once again that she has actually been given the job and this isn't all some strange hallucination.

"Let me see." Jonathan makes a show of looking at Howard's schedule on his computer and gives her an insincerely apologetic look. "It looks like he'll be taking meetings most of the day. He wanted me to bring you back to your office. He'll check on you later once you've gotten settled." He heaves himself up off his desk chair as though it requires a great amount of effort.

"That would be great." Alex smiles nervously. Jonathan stands up with a sigh and pockets his cell phone. Without another word to her, he spins on his heel as Alex scrambles to catch up with him. They cross the newsroom diagonally, winding through a grid of cubicles and turning heads to emerge near Howard Demetri's glass office. The door is shut tight, and the blinds closed today. Through the crack at the edge of the blinds Alex catches a quick glimpse of her new boss. He is standing rigidly, pressing a phone to his ear. Through the glass she can hear the muffled sound of his voice. It doesn't sound happy. But before she can try to decipher what he is saying, they've moved on.

She expects Jonathan to deposit her at one of the smaller glass-walled offices along the edge of the newsroom, but he keeps walking, leading her to the far end of the room. It looks as though Jonathan is bringing her straight into the wall, but as she reaches it she sees the slim doorway tucked between two tall filing cabinets, a sort of optical illusion where the wall between them is actually part of a hallway set farther back, invisible until you're standing right in front of it. Curious, she follows Jonathan as he ducks between the cabinets, turning off into the narrow hallway beyond. As soon as they step into it the atmosphere changes completely, the modern glass and concrete replaced with dark polished wood, cracked in places. And heavy closed doors that look as though they haven't been opened in a very long time. The overhead lights are encased in large glass shades in the shape of inverted tear-drops, buzzing above as they carry on.

"This must be the old part of the building?" she asks Jonathan's slim back even though the answer is obvious. This hallway makes her feel like they have stepped into a time capsule from a century ago.

"It is," he answers curtly without glancing at her. The area feels unused, closed off. Her nose wrinkles at the smell of dust and mildew as they pass several shut doors. She tries to imagine Francis Keen walking the same hall, her sleeves rolled up, ready to get to work. The thrill of it creeps up through her spine. And now here she is in the very same place, heading to her first day on the very same job.

Her stomach twists as they come to the very end of the hall and Jonathan stops in front of a large wooden door. For a moment Alex worries he is going to shove her into a storage closet, but then he inhales sharply and pulls it open. At once, cool natural light spills out into the hallway. She peers past him, her breath catching as she takes in a spacious corner office with massive paned glass windows that look out over Midtown. A solid wood desk, its finish wearing, sits to one side of the room, bare except for a computer monitor and an old-fashioned green-glass banker's lamp. She recognizes the office immediately as the place Francis's photo was taken. Jonathan moves aside and impatiently waves her through the doorway.

"Thank you, Jonathan," Alex says.

"Of course, just doing my job," he says in case she makes the mistake of thinking that he is showing her some special kindness. As she slips past him into the office, she notices his face is pale and peaked like he might be feeling sick.

"It's beautiful," she says. Turning around the spacious office, Alex is shocked to find that the two walls not dominated by windows are still hung with Francis's art. There is an old oil painting of the ocean with a tiny ship tilting on the waves; a yellowed art deco print of a woman smoking a cigarette from a long holder, her hip jutting confidently to the side; a large poster from a Francis Bacon exhibit at the MoMA, in which a man in a suit reclines against a drippy dark background, his face disturbed by streaks of paint.

She moves in closer to the wall, to better see some of the smaller personal photographs in black and white. One is of Francis leaning on the doorframe in front of the old entrance. She looks tiny and young, in an A-line dress and knee-high boots, dwarfed by the large art deco relief of the man with the book that now hangs in the lobby. Next to the photo is a framed newspaper clipping of the first column she ever wrote as Dear Constance, dated June 12, 1987. Alex remembers looking it up in an archive years ago. It is advice to a woman who is miserable in her career. She knows the reply without having to read it. *You are not miserable because of your job but rather because you have made it the whole focus of your life.*

Alex moves over to the window. To the left, the scalloped peak of the Chrysler Building cuts up into the skyline. To the right, the mirrored windows of the Excelsior Bank Building glimmer in the bright sunlight.

The high vantage point also gives the office a sort of secluded feeling, like being locked away in some forgotten turret of a castle. The traffic far below makes her dizzy and she steps away.

"And she really worked back here all alone?" She glances back at Jonathan, who hasn't moved from his spot by the door. He gives her an impatient nod, glancing behind him into the hallway before he answers.

"When they did the huge renovations about ten years ago, they had plans to move Francis's office into the modern part of the newsroom, near Howard's. But she insisted they keep her office back here, in the old part of the building. She always preferred it."

Alex runs her palm along the top of an old radiator under the window, collecting a handful of dust.

"Do you know why?" she asks, curious to know more about the inner mind of her hero.

"Francis said the only way she could really feel each person's struggles was to be alone with them," Jonathan says. "But if you would rather, I can see if we could get you a cubicle or something in the newsroom." He says the word *cubicle* derisively. Alex doesn't want to make the distinction between her and Francis so soon. She wants to like it back here, too, to live up to Francis's legacy.

Alex scrambles to clarify. "No, no. I was just asking. It's a beautiful office, I didn't mean to imply—" She spins back to the door, surprised to find that Jonathan is already backing out of the room. She notes the slight sheen that's sprung to his forehead.

"Well, I'll leave you to it." He claps his hands together. Then remembers something and reaches into his pocket for a small slip of paper.

"Here is the log-in to Francis's, um, the Dear Constance database so you can get started reading the letters right away. There should be quite a few of them after so long. You have your work cut out for you." With that, he shuts the door behind him with a click. She stands still, listening to his footsteps recede down the hallway. The subtext of his last line is unmistakable: *I don't think you can handle it.*

NINE

Alex carefully sits down at the desk. The springs of the wooden office chair squeak loudly and she cringes, feeling like an intruder. *This is where* she *sat,* Alex thinks, imagining Francis Keen in one of her trademark men's shirts, the sleeves pulled up to the elbows, typing her answers to all of life's important questions. Maybe when she gets paid, she'll look for an oversized white shirt of her own from one of the tiny boutiques she's always admiring along Madison Avenue.

She opens the top desk drawer. It has been emptied out of everything but a letter opener, brass with a handle inlaid with shell. She holds it in her hand like a priceless artifact, placing it carefully to one side. The bottom of the drawer still bears a constellation of old pencil marks on one side and a splotch of blue ink from a leaky pen soaked into the wood at the bottom. She runs her hand across the grooves where Francis's pens and pencils once lay, feeling herself well up. She's about to close the drawer when she notices something trapped on the edge, a piece of folded paper tucked into the seam of the wood. As she pries it loose, she finds that it's a matchbook. She holds it in her palm, marveling at the little relic left over from Francis's life. *The Nest*, it says in art deco–inspired font. The phone number is listed below in delicate gold embossing. Alex opens it and runs her fingers over the tight rows of matches, all unused. She places the matchbook back in the drawer. She'll keep it there as a little good-luck charm, a memento to remember her by.

She turns her focus to the computer monitor, which is brand-new. A thin film of plastic still clings to the front of it. Alex peels it back, feeling weirdly ashamed. Why couldn't they have left the old one? She rests her fingers lightly on the keyboard. Deep breath in. She takes the instructions that Jonathan has printed for her and logs into the *Herald*'s mail system.

Up until now this entire experience has all felt out of body, like she is watching it happen to someone else. But as she types in her temporary password, it all seems suddenly quite real and completely terrifying. She watches a solid wall of unread emails fill the screen. Messages about orientation and HR forms lost between rows and rows of subject lines begging her for help—*Desperately need you . . . Help me . . . Can you save my marriage?* The enormity of what she is supposed to do hits her all at once. She will have to show up for people the way Francis did. Alex scrolls down through what must be a thousand unread submissions. What if she has no idea how? What if the letters she wrote in the application were just a fluke? The feeling is both exhilarating and terrifying, like being at the top of a roller coaster. She exhales and clicks the first message open.

It's an incredibly strange feeling being able to peer into someone's most private life, to read about their shame and worries, to be told their deepest secrets. There is one message from a man who lost his daughter in a swimming accident and can't stop going out in the water looking for her even though he knows she isn't there; another from a woman whose husband is having an affair with her sister and thinks she doesn't know; there's a college-age girl who is lost and miserable at her Ivy League school; and on and on. . . . Alex's eyes burn from staring at them. She has been reading the letters for hours, but she has barely scraped the surface. And every time she returns to the inbox the list of unread messages has grown even longer, an unending stream of highlighted subject lines stacking on top of one another, all begging Dear Constance for help.

A ding. A new email appears at the top of the screen with the subject line *Please*.

Dear Constance,

Ha! Dear Constance, my ass. Whoever you are, you don't deserve to even have the same email address as Francis Keen. It's disgusting that Francis has been replaced so quickly and with someone so inexperienced. The Herald *has got to be absolutely joking if they think I'm going to trust you with my problems. You're a little twit, a hack, and you won't last. I give it a year before you lose your job. No one can compare with Francis. They shouldn't even have tried.*

Alex closes the email without finishing it. She wasn't expecting anger directed at her, though she realizes now that she probably should have. She'd been outraged herself when she found out about a possible replacement. She might not be the kind of person to write a nasty email, but she understands. *Deep breath*. Still, as she settles back in to read, a terrible feeling grips her. What if the person is right and she has no business reading these letters? What if she has no business being here at all?

TEN

The tapping is so soft that at first Alex doesn't notice it, her subconscious deciding it's some far-off dripping in the walls or pipes. It is only when it suddenly stops that she glances up from the message, her ears pricking.

She waits and, hearing nothing, clicks on another email. This one is from a woman whose wife is trying to convince her to have children, but she isn't sure she is ready. Alex settles in, getting immediately sucked into her life, when the tapping comes back louder. Now she realizes that someone has been knocking on her office door.

"Come in!" Alex calls out, embarrassed to have taken so long to answer. The door swings open slowly. Alex stands up, bracing for the mantis-like body of Howard Demetri. Instead, a young woman stands in the doorway.

"Oh, good, you're here already," she says, her voice bubbling over as she pushes her way into the room. "I was hoping you would be."

"Yes, I am," Alex says with a perplexed smile, trying to place her. The girl has round cheeks and circular wire-rimmed glasses perched on the end of a button nose. Her pale legs poke out from under a short, pleated skirt. Her entire body has a youthful fullness to it as though all of her edges have been smoothed over. All except for her hair, which is dyed nearly black and cut severely to her chin in a line so straight it must have been freshly put there by a razor blade.

The girl comes to stand in front of the desk, her round cheeks flushed with excitement. "I'm so glad you're here. And of course, I'm so happy to have a real job to do again. After Francis—" She pauses and frowns, swallowing uncomfortably at the memory. "Well, I've tried to help out in the mailroom, but it's mostly been a lot of waiting. And, you know, my mom always said idle minds and all that." She grimaces, sticking out her tongue theatrically.

"Sorry, who are you?" Alex says, doing her best not to sound rude. The girl's face falls.

"I'm Lucy Bentley." She presses her hand to her sweater, which Alex notices has an embroidery of a cat in the corner. "I'm your assistant. I was Francis's assistant for almost five years."

Alex scrambles to make her feel better. "To be fair, they have hardly told me anything. Jonathan just dropped me off here in her office a bit ago. I was thinking you were going to be Howard Demetri, actually. He's supposed to stop by, but then maybe he got sucked into something. I get the feeling everyone is spread a little thin?"

When she mentions Howard's name, Lucy glances back at the door as if she is worried he might be there. Up close, Alex realizes that Lucy can't be older than her midtwenties, though her clothes and demeanor make her seem like she's a teenager. "You read the vibe right. It's been pretty hard around here, honestly. The first and worst, obviously, was losing Francis, and then all the budget cuts. This place feels like it's barely holding on sometimes. I am so lucky they hired you when they did, or I bet I would have been out of a job."

"What exactly did Francis have you do for her?" Alex asks carefully. She had never imagined Francis as the type to have help on the job, and Alex doesn't want Lucy to know that she has no idea what to even do with an assistant. Having someone hovering over her makes her uneasy.

"Well, she had me run little errands for her, get coffee, make printouts, things like that. But most of my job is picking up and sorting all her letters from the mailroom."

"Letters from the mailroom?" Alex asks, her stomach clenching. "There are more letters?"

"Oh dear, you poor thing." Lucy tries to suppress a smile. "Did you think the only letters for you to read are the ones you get online?"

"No. I mean, yes? I guess I thought they were all digitized now. I don't know what I was thinking, really." Alex raises her eyebrows helplessly and shrugs.

Lucy grins, showing off two fang-like incisors that protrude farther than the rest of her teeth, giving her an oddly lupine quality. "No. I'm sorry. I shouldn't find it funny. It's just that there are a ton of people who still write in on paper." She laughs again. "The good news is that Francis always said that all the juiciest letters came from the mailroom and not by email."

"She did?" Alex tries to imagine the woman she thought she knew saying something like that and can't.

Lucy shrugs. "I think some people actually feel safer that way, more anonymous. It's harder to trace a piece of paper than an email address. Or maybe there is something to writing on a piece of paper and sending it." She pauses, her eyes getting a faraway look like she's remembering something.

Alex tries not to panic at the thought of all those letters just sitting there unopened. She'll have to read them all right away if she doesn't want to fall behind. "Right. That makes sense. Well, let's get to it, I guess! Can you show them to me?"

"Now?" Lucy looks startled. "Are you sure you don't want me to get you a coffee or something first?"

"I think I should get started. Maybe we could bring them up here?"

"Yes! Right. Good idea," Lucy says, looking around the office. "I *think* they'll all fit in this room."

ELEVEN

Lucy leads Alex out of the office and down the long hallway, occasionally glancing behind her. They pass the doorway that leads out into the newsroom and keep walking to the opposite end of the hall.

"I always take the stairs when I go between the newsroom and the mailroom. I hope you don't mind. I like the exercise," Lucy says, pushing open a heavy fire door at the end of the hall. It leads to the landing of an old stairwell with an elaborate wrought iron railing. The staircase wraps around an open atrium about twenty feet wide.

"This must still be the old part of the building?" Alex asks, trying to be conversational as they descend. She can feel the grooves in the marble stairs worn in the centers from decades of foot traffic.

"It is, yeah. Isn't it cool? Actually, this was once the building's main stairwell, but it was converted after the renovation." She glances back at Alex. "It's a shame it's not used much these days, because it's actually quite beautiful, I think."

Alex supposes she's right. With a bit of dusting and some better lighting, a coat of fresh paint on the chipped metalwork, it would be gorgeous. But as it is, the dank smell and the flickering yellow-green light make it more creepy than charming. Art deco flourishes embedded in the corners hold a coating of thick gray dust. The finish on the wrought iron banister is chipped in places, cracking away to reveal the raw metal below, like bones peeking through skin.

Alex leans over the railing to look down and gasps. Around the central space the loop of the staircase repeats for what feels like forever, ending a million miles below at the tiniest patch of checked tile floor.

"A little intense, huh? The history of this building is just so fascinating," Lucy says, continuing down the steps, her hand trailing lightly on the wood of the railing.

As she follows Lucy, Alex tries to imagine it bustling with people who worked here back in the early days. There would be lots of men in dark suits and hats. She pictures the heels of their polished shoes clicking quickly on the stairs as they rushed to deliver urgent copy to their editor or to go collect a story unfolding out in the world. There would have been women, though not nearly as many. They would likely have been kept in the realm of secretarial work.

Alex feels momentarily embarrassed that in her days of time-wasting research over the weekend, even after running out of things to google about Howard Demetri and his wife, it had not occurred to her to look up the history of the building itself.

"I just love history, don't you?" Lucy says, not waiting for a reply. "Did you know that the architect who made this place actually was petrified of the elevator? It was a new invention then, of course. He just straight up didn't trust it. That's why this stairwell is so nice."

"Interesting," Alex mumbles, looking over the edge.

Without slowing her pace, Lucy glances back, her cheeks glowing. "I'll never understand why he would kill himself by jumping from the top floor. That's never made sense to me."

Alex leaps back from the opening, pushing herself against the wall. The blood drains from her limbs as she imagines her own body falling through the space, dropping past the last forty-five floors and hitting the ground with a speed so violent it crushes her.

"You okay, Alex?" Lucy asks, her small face bunching up with concern.

"I'm fine," Alex says, her hand slick now as she guides it back to the banister. She wants to be out of there. She focuses on her feet, on placing each one in front of her and not falling.

"Ah, this is us," Lucy says finally, coming to a stop on a landing before a door with the number 42 nailed to it in an art deco font. She uses her full body weight to push it open. Alex lets out a long shaky breath as they emerge into an empty white hallway. Sickly fluorescent lighting buzzes overhead as they make their way down the hall, stopping at an off-white door stained with scuff marks.

"This is the mailroom, prepare to be dazzled," Lucy says wryly as she pulls a key on a coiled plastic cord from around her wrist, twisting it in the lock. It's a typical-looking mailroom, set up with a few metal tables in the center for sorting. One side of the room is orderly, a grid of nearly empty cubbies along the wall labeled with the names of different departments. But the opposite side of the room makes Alex gasp. A disorderly pile has formed in the corner. A mountain of letters joining into one heaving tower over the tops of three large roller bins. It is more mail than Alex has ever seen in one place. And she'll have to read it all.

"You might have already guessed that these are the Dear Constance letters. There are quite a few after eight months, obviously. We just haven't known what to do with them all and could never return them to sender." She chuckles. "That would be a bit like sending back letters to Santa from the North Pole."

"Didn't they know about Francis?" Alex asks. "You'd think that people would have stopped writing in." She approaches the pile tentatively, worried that any slight disturbance will send them toppling.

Lucy shrugs. "If anything, it seems like there have been more recently. I guess some people just didn't get the news."

Alex has begun mentally doing the math of how long it will take to read all of them. The long nights she'll have to put in to make sure she gets to each one. But it doesn't upset her. In fact, she feels herself eagerly looking forward to it. Lucy picks up a plastic bin from under the sorting table.

"Where do you want to start?" she asks.

"Which are the oldest?"

Lucy points to the bin farthest into the corner where the pile of letters is the highest. "I think those. But you'd have to get to the bottom of the pile."

"It only seems fair, doesn't it?" Alex says, then wobbles. "Or should I be answering those who have written in more recently, the ones I have more of a chance of helping?"

"Tell you what," Lucy says, so gently that she might think Alex is heading for a meltdown. "I can bring up some of these from each bin every day. That way you won't have to come down here and be overwhelmed by it all."

"That would be amazing," Alex says gratefully. It's not so bad having someone to walk her through her first day. Lucy being here is helping Alex feel a bit better about the whole situation. Though she'd still like to talk to Howard, see what her boss thinks about which to read first.

Lucy plunges her hands into the drift of letters. As she piles them into the bin, Alex thinks it must be hard for Lucy to be working with somebody new after all that time with Francis. It's got to be an intimate job, being someone's assistant. You'd know everything about them, from the ins and outs of their schedule down to what they like for lunch and how they take their coffee. Whether they came in early or liked to stay late. All of their habits and eccentricities. Alex could learn a lot about Francis from her, she thinks suddenly, a small thrill creeping up her spine. What amazing details could she tell Alex about Francis Keen's life?

"What was she like?" Alex asks cautiously.

"Who, Francis?" Lucy stops, resting one hand against her hip. "Well, she could be impatient at times. She suffered no fools, as my mom always says. But she also had this innate sense of wisdom. She never placated people. If someone was struggling, there was no pity, it was only empathy with Francis. And there's a big difference. You felt like she was in it with you." She gives a tight, pained smile, her eyes clouding. "I really loved her."

Alex smiles. "Funny, that's exactly how I imagined her to be. She sounds amazing." There is a tug of sadness in her chest that she was never able to meet Francis. Especially now that they share so much.

"Yeah, she was. Too bad you never got to meet her. I feel like you'd have a lot in common. It's honestly a bit hard for me to talk about her still. I'm sorry." Lucy turns away from her toward the piles of letters. Her shoulders slump as she pulls letters from the pile and continues stacking them in the small bin next to her. Alex wonders if she's upset Lucy. Maybe it was too much to ask. She leans over to help her, pulling out a handful of fresh envelopes stuck in the corner of one of the rolling bins and putting them into the smaller one.

"So, Francis really read every single one of these?" Alex asks.

Lucy's hair bounces around her face as she nods. "Oh yes. It was part of her belief system that everyone who shared something so special and secret was at least heard out."

"Did you ever help her read?" Alex asks.

"I offered pretty much daily, but she never would let me. Francis was very stubborn. Too proud not to do all the dirty work herself." She pauses. "There is a system for keeping the already read letters. Most of them are shredded eventually, but there are certain letters that Francis kept. She always wanted to make sure that she saved any letters from people who could possibly be a danger to themselves or others."

"Oh?" Alex tugs at the edges of her sleeves. "What did she do with those?"

"I'm not sure, honestly. I think she kept them at her beach house for some reason. All I know is that if someone wrote to her in need, there is no way she would get rid of the letter."

"Great," Alex says weakly, dropping an envelope and watching it flutter into the bin. The piles of letters are making her feel claustrophobic. It is almost as though she can hear the voices coming from each of them, crying out. The overhead lighting keeps flickering. She steps back from the bins and tries to take it all in, to fit the massive pile into her brain. She wonders if she will be able to handle it all. There are so many people out there struggling. Will she be able to truly help a single one of them?

TWELVE

When Alex looks up from reading, the light at the windows has shifted, throwing the office into the shadow of the surrounding buildings. Alex glances at the clock affixed to the wall above the door. Its gold hands and roman numerals show that it is already well past 8 p.m. It is easy to lose track of time back here, she thinks. Alex has been so engrossed in the letters she's nearly forgotten where she is. She yawns, extending her arms into the air and looking around the room.

Her stomach feels sour and empty. She should eat something. Just one more letter first. There is something thrilling about being allowed into a complete stranger's deepest thoughts and desires, being let into their inner life. She is quickly finding the letters addictive. Alex reaches across the desk and pulls the dangling chain on the green-glassed banker's lamp, but it remains dark. She fishes for the cord and finds it dangling below the desk unplugged.

She drops to her hands and knees on the worn Turkish carpet, dragging herself into the small space under her desk. She can feel the dust working into her palms as she crawls back to the outlet, hidden cleverly in a brass panel in the floor. As she plugs the lamp in, sending a dim beam of light behind her, she sees a shadow of something below the heavy wooden leg. It is a book, its pages bent and unfurling, wedged against the floor. It must have slid off the top of the desk and

gotten stuck there. She twists it out, pulling it with her as she shim-
mies backward out of the space. The lamp casts a yellowy glow onto
the book, a collection of poems by William Butler Yeats.

It is an old copy without a dust jacket. She delicately flips through
the first pages, sending out a cloud of dust that makes her nose run.
It's a first edition, she notes on the copyright page, probably quite a
valuable book. Strange it should have been forgotten.

On the dedication page is a note, hand-scrawled in black with darker
splatters of ink, like it came from a leaking fountain pen.

To Francis. Hearts are not had as a gift, but hearts are earned.

As she lowers the book to her desk, something flutters to the ground
from between the pages. Alex bends down and picks up a rectangular
piece of pale-green cardstock. It's heavy, the kind that you buy in a
stationery store to write proper thank-you notes on, with a delicate
gold line embossed around the border. There is a note on one side;
this handwriting is a far cry from the inky stain in the dedication. It is
neat, tilted script straight across the center, precise as if done with a
ruler. It says simply:

I know.

She flips it over, but the back of the card is unmarked.

There's a knock on the door, and Alex slips the note into the pocket
of her skirt and slides the book into her desk drawer, embarrassed that
she's allowed herself to become so distracted, especially on her first day.
She wants Howard Demetri's first image of her to be Alex Marks, hard at
work, not Alex Marks, covered in dust with her nose in a book of poetry.

"Come in," she calls out, her voice catching. But instead of Howard,
it is Lucy who pops her head once again around the side of the door.

"I'm going to go home now, if that's okay with you." She's wearing
a tote bag from the Strand bookshop and holds a thermos in her hand.
Alex realizes that she doesn't know where Lucy even works. Does she

have a desk somewhere, or does she just exist in the strange in-between of the mailroom and Alex's office?

"Thanks so much for your help today." Lucy beams. She is so young-looking it's hard for Alex to believe she was Francis's assistant for more than five years. "Truly, you've been a lifesaver. I don't know what I would have done here all on my own. I haven't seen Howard all day and I don't think Jonathan likes me very much," she admits.

"Don't even thank me, it's my job. I'm happy to help," Lucy says, surveying the unopened pile of letters on her desk. "You're sure you don't need help going through these? I can stay late if you need me to."

"I'll be fine," Alex says definitively. She's used to being alone. And she feels a tug of pride. She wants to be independent the way Francis was. "You haven't seen Howard around, have you?"

Lucy shakes her head. "He may have gone home for the day."

Alex tries to hide her disappointment.

"Did you need something?"

"No, I mean, he was going to stop by, he said." Had he just forgotten her there? All day she's listened for him in the hall, expecting his long-limbed figure at the door. She notices a flash of anxiety on Lucy's face at the mention of Howard. She glances behind her as though eager to leave. "It's fine. You go."

"Okay then. See you tomorrow, Alex." Lucy gives her a little wave and a strained smile.

Everyone seems a little on edge here, Alex thinks, remembering the sickly sheen on Jonathan's face earlier. What is it about this place? She opens a letter and begins to read a plea from a woman who wants help fixing her ailing marriage, but then puts it down, distracted.

Alex goes to the window, chewing on the inside of her cheek. The sky outside has gone dark denim blue. The last flares of an orange sunset streak the sky. She presses her forehead to the cool glass and looks down. Far below are lines of white and red light, traffic crawling across Midtown. Now that she's not reading, Alex feels her ears ringing from the quiet of her office. The silence agitates her. A little break from this room will be good. She wants to be out there, in the real world. She watches a crowd of people gather at the corner, their bodies moving as one through the crosswalk when the light changes, all heading home from work or out to dinner. She can see the lights from a coffee shop spilling out onto the street. Suddenly she wants to be down there with all of them, to leave the sterile chill of the *Herald*'s giant air-conditioning system and walk out into that wallop of heat.

THIRTEEN

The hallway feels even more strange and isolated, knowing that everyone has left for the day. She hurries down it and comes into the main newsroom.

The overhead lights have been dimmed for the night. The office looks as though it has been suddenly abandoned. Half-full coffee cups left on desks. Sweaters draped over the backs of chairs. Inside one of the cubicles a shadow moves slowly. She steps closer, her heart hammering as she catches sight of the thin cord dangling from the ceiling. It leads all the way down into one of the cubicles where a large shape sways very gently back and forth. Her heart thuds. She nearly screams until it bends, catching the fading light from the window, and she realizes it is actually a sign hanging from a piece of crepe paper, remnants from a sad office birthday celebration. The sound of Alex's startled laugh bounces around the empty room.

She continues through the newsroom, surprised to see a yellow glow coming from behind the blinds in Howard's office. His shape is barely visible moving behind the blinds. He is pacing, his limbs long and jerky like a shadow puppet. His muffled voice rises angrily from inside.

Curious, Alex moves toward the glass wall where there is a thin space between the sides of the blinds. Now she can see Howard. His jacket is off, his cuffs rolled up. He presses his phone to his ear. Alex watches his fingers clench as he speaks. "What can I possibly do about it?" she hears him say, the anger in his voice barely constrained. His hand runs through his hair, gripping it nervously. She moves closer, putting her face nearly up to the glass. His desk is in disarray, papers scattered across it. A mug sits on top. He picks it up and tilts it to his mouth, gulping from it.

"I don't know. I just don't know." His voice drops, the anger receding into a helpless monotone. Alex holds her breath trying to hear him. "Isn't there anything you can do?"

Suddenly he spins toward her. Alex clamps her hand over her mouth and jumps quickly away. She prays he hasn't seen her there. She draws back into the shadows, her heart pounding, then ducks into a cubicle, pressing herself into the fabric-covered partition as she hears him come out of his office.

"Hello? Is someone there?"

She keeps her hand over her mouth to prevent herself from making a sound. *Just what everyone needs on their first day of work, to be caught spying on their boss,* she scolds herself.

"Sorry, I thought I heard something," he says in a lower voice, to the person on the phone. When she is sure he's back in his office, she dashes as quickly as she can to the elevators.

FOURTEEN

The coffee shop across from the *Herald* is bright and buzzy, but at 9 p.m. Alex is the only customer. Canned pop music plays from the speakers as a man begins to mop the floor behind her, eager to close for the night. At the counter she orders an Americano from a bored-looking barista. She hasn't eaten since this morning's bagel, she realizes, suddenly famished.

"What's that?" she asks, pointing at the last thing in the food case, an unidentifiable beige baked good wrapped in plastic.

"Chocolate chip muffin," the woman mumbles. Behind her the door to the shop opens and closes. Out of the corner of her eye she sees a man walk up behind her. She can feel the impatient shuffle of his feet as he waits to order.

"Sure. I'll take it." Her streak of eating terrible food is ridiculous, but she's going to need fuel to get through all the letters in the bin. The thought of it piled high with envelopes makes her throat go dry. She can already feel the pressure mounting behind her eyelids as she anticipates another night of little to no sleep. And that isn't even the worst of it.

Reading them all is one thing, but she isn't even close to choosing a letter to answer. Sure, she's found a few possibilities and set them aside. She's beginning to wonder if it isn't the fear of failure that's holding her back now more than anything. She imagines herself finishing the column and turning it in. The disappointment in Howard Demetri's eyes as he tells her he has to fire her. It would hurt at first, but would part of her also be relieved?

She takes her purchases to the side counter and removes the lid of her coffee. As she reaches for the creamer a hand shoots out and intercepts her, a set of large fingers taking hold of the pitcher and snatching it away.

"Oh—" She looks up, startled, as the man obliviously tips it into his coffee. He's wearing a light-gray suit, perfectly cut to his frame, which is slender with broad shoulders. His hair is combed over to one side, though it looks a bit ruffled, like he's recently run his fingers through it. And the top button of his shirt is undone, his tie loose around his neck. He looks almost old-fashioned, like an extra from a movie set about Wall Street back in the day. The only thing that ruins the image is a set of puffy red headphones clamped onto his head. He stirs the creamer into his cup, his eyes flickering with focus on whatever he is listening to. When he is done he places the creamer at the far side of the counter where she can't reach it. She starts to say something but remembers the other day, the man at the restaurant. Alex doesn't need any more unsettling conflicts with strange men. Annoyed, she moves to the other side of the counter. Now he turns to look at her, pulling down the headphones so they dangle around his neck. He points at the creamer. "Sorry, were you going to use this? I thought you were done."

"I was about to. It's no big deal," she assures him, shaking off some residual irritation. Why do men always fill in all the space around them?

"No, really. I'm sorry. I shouldn't wear these things out in public." He smiles, revealing a deep dimple in his left cheek. "I'm a menace. Completely in my own world." He hands her the pitcher, and she forgives him internally without even meaning to.

"What are you listening to?" she asks, finding she's actually curious.

"*Great Expectations*," he says casually as he rips open a packet of sugar and dumps it into his cup.

"You're listening to an audiobook?" Alex says with true disbelief as she replaces the lid on her coffee.

"I like to put them on while I work. It passes the time between extremely stressful phone calls I couldn't care less about."

She looks at him suspiciously. What thirtysomething man listens to *Great Expectations* at work? "And are you enjoying it?" Alex doesn't know why she is drawing out the conversation. Maybe she isn't quite ready to return to the tomb-like quiet of the office. Or maybe it is the honey brown of his eyes sparkling down at her. It has been a long time since she has even met a man she was attracted to. *Dangerous, Alex.*

"It's a great story. I mean, I've read it before in school probably, but these voice actors are really something. Though I have to say I don't know why Miss Havisham is so sad about being stood up. It's a dodged bullet, if you ask me. I keep wishing I could go visit her—maybe I could have talked her out of years and years of misery."

"Oh, I doubt it," Alex says quickly. "The thing with people like her is they want to suffer. She was addicted to the pain of it, basically. If it wasn't her marriage, it probably would have been something else. There's nothing you could have done."

He looks at her with obvious surprise. Then his eyes wrinkle at the corners. "You sound just like my therapist." Alex's own smile wavers. "That's a good thing, she's quite intelligent." He nods at her small bag containing the muffin. "Chocolate chip muffin? I've been there before." He winces. "Desperate dinner of those behind on work. You're staying late at the office, too, I take it?"

"Yeah, trying to catch up," she says, suddenly too aware of her face and the way her mouth is moving. "I mean, this is actually my first week, so trying to get started actually."

"Oh yeah? Congratulations on the new gig." He looks at her for a beat longer than she is used to. She feels her ears getting hot.

"You're at the *Herald* too?" Alex asks, knowing from his clothes that he isn't. No journalist wears an actual suit anymore and this guy is dressed well. He reminds her of Gregory Peck in the very old movie version of *To Kill a Mockingbird*.

"No, I work directly across from it, over there." He rocks back on his heels and gestures with his coffee cup at the brightly lit gray marble exterior of the Excelsior Bank Building. "Boring money stuff, nothing as fun or interesting as journalism."

"Well, I guess somebody's got to do it," she says, not entirely sure that is true. All right, maybe not Gregory Peck.

"Yeah, sometimes I wonder." He laughs a bit sheepishly. "So, what do you do over at the paper? Are you a reporter?"

"Sort of. Something like that." Alex takes a sip of her coffee so she doesn't have to elaborate any further and winces as it scalds the back of her throat. It's too early to be sharing her new position with anyone, not when she hasn't even turned her column in yet. The column. Her stomach drops at the thought of all those letters she still has to read. She's promised herself she'll stay late enough tonight to finish all of the ones left on her desk. "Speaking of that, I should get back to it."

"Right, right. Me too."

They start for the door at the same time and there is an awkward moment where they nearly collide. He stops and steps back, motioning for her to go ahead. "After you," he says.

"Thanks." They lock eyes for a moment, and she feels a sharp fizzle of electricity between them.

"The least I can do after holding the creamer hostage."

"That's true," Alex says, smiling.

"Well, have a good night," he says. "Oh, I'm Tom, by the way. Maybe I'll run into you again. We are work neighbors after all."

I'd like that, she thinks, surprising herself. "I'm Alex. I'm sure I'll see you around."

As she walks across the street and into the lobby of the Herald Building, she finds a smile spreading across her face.

The light is still on in Howard's office when she tiptoes back through the newsroom. Through the cracks at the edge of the blinds she can see a slice of his back as he sits at his desk. His computer monitor is dark, his phone face down on his desk. He isn't moving. For a horrifying moment she thinks something terrible has happened to him, that he has had a stroke or a heart attack. But then she sees the slight quiver of his shoulders and the movement of his fingers through his hair as he buries his head in his hands.

Dear Constance,

For the very first time I have a real boyfriend. It's crazy to me that if I hadn't taken the job at the hardware store, I would never have met Brian. Who knows what would have happened then?

I can tell that Sam doesn't love Brian stopping by, but I don't know why. Brian is nothing but polite to him. Still, it bothers me. Sam is not someone who is normally rude to people. But when Brian comes into the store, Sam barely looks at him, never gives him the big smile he is normally so generous with.

"Doesn't he have his own job to get to?" Sam asked, watching through the window as he got into his truck and drove off.

"He's going there now," I said, feeling defensive.

"If you ask me, he's got a little too much time on his hands," Sam said in his slow way.

"I didn't," I said to Sam, my heart pounding fast. I don't ever talk back to Sam. He just blinked at me and walked away.

Brian came back when I was done with my shift. I ran out and hopped into his pickup. "How was work?" He pulled me toward him and gave me a kiss, looking into my eyes. All my worry dissolved in that moment. It is like that with us. Like we are in our own little world. Brian says we have something special, and he wouldn't let anything or anyone touch it.

"It was fine." I didn't tell him about what Sam said. I'm not sure who I'm trying to protect exactly. I get the feeling that the two of them should stay far apart. I haven't introduced Brian to my mom yet or to any of my friends, not that I see them that often anyway. I was so jealous of my friend Amanda when she left for college, and I stayed behind to work. Now I'd like for her to see me riding around in the passenger seat with a handsome architect. The idea of us together makes me feel proud, like I've done something more with my life than barely graduate from high school.

"What are we doing?" I asked, looking out the window. Brian

was taking us on a different route than we normally go on to get to his place.

"I thought we could cook at my apartment tonight," he said, pulling off to go to the grocery store.

"Oh, did you?" I was happy that he wanted to do something so homey. This feeling of total bliss came over me as we walked around the grocery store. Maybe it's silly that something so simple made me feel so happy. It's hard to describe, but for the first time maybe ever, I felt normal. Like this is what it is like to be a couple. To have another person waiting there with a grocery cart at the end of the aisle.

Back at his apartment we looked up a recipe for some sort of salmon and rice. He was good in the kitchen. He poured me a glass of wine and I sat at the counter while he cooked. I felt like an adult, like I could suddenly see more to life than just Sam's Hardware and dealing with my mom's boyfriend.

There was music on, some mix of old French music that I'd never heard before. It had the feeling like it was Christmas morning. The fluttery happiness. Like I wanted to store the feeling up so I can revisit it whenever I want.

After dinner we were curled up together on the couch with the fireplace on and he took my chin very gently and tilted it up toward him.

"What do you think about moving in?" he asked me.

"Here?" My chest swelled up at the thought of it. I looked behind him at the shiny new kitchen and the big views over the park. Was he really saying that this could be mine too? I pulled back to look at him better. Was he joking? But his eyes were calm and serious.

"It's fast, I know." He took my hands in his. "But listen, I feel so happy having you here. More than I've ever felt with anyone. Look at me, I can barely think about anything else."

I gave in and rolled toward him, saying yes as he pulled my top off and picked me up off the couch, carrying me into the bedroom.

I felt like I was watching myself from above. Like this whole thing wasn't happening to me but to some other girl. Someone who is actually worthy of it.

I texted my mom before I went to sleep and told her I was moving out and coming to live with Brian. I watched as she started to reply, the little gray text bubble appearing and disappearing. And then finally going away completely without her sending me anything. I think she's probably angry or maybe even jealous that things are working out for me.

I woke up in a panic, sitting straight up in bed gulping for air, my heart pounding like I'd forgotten something. Why does it seem like the people I'm closest to aren't happy for me? It makes me feel like I've done something wrong. I should just ignore them, right? Brian is wonderful. Maybe the best thing that ever happened to me. I hope you read this. I need someone to tell me that it is going to be okay. Why do I have the strangest feeling that it is not?

Please help,
Lost Girl

FIFTEEN

"So, how's it going up there at the *Herald*?" Raymond asks suspiciously as Alex slides onto her stool on Tuesday morning. The sky is heavy with clouds today, trapping the hot air, pulling it down like a blanket over the city where it steams up the front windows of the Bluebird.

"Oh, leave her alone," Janice scolds as she drops off Alex's coffee. "She hasn't even sat down yet. Usual?"

Alex nods. "To go today, Janice." She catches the worried glance between Janice and Raymond. "I have to catch up on work," she explains.

"Look at you, already putting in overtime," Raymond says.

"Just don't make it a regular thing," Janice says, turning to put the order in. "We sit, we eat, we talk here. This isn't a McDonald's."

Raymond leans toward her, toast in hand. "So, what's it like up there?"

"It's interesting. Her—*my* office is down this long hallway. Apparently Francis liked the old part of the building. But it's nearly empty, so it's really quiet back there," Alex says slowly, taking a sip of coffee. "But it's good."

"You don't sound so sure," Raymond says. Alex frowns. *Doesn't she?* Maybe that is because she's not. Alex still feels like she is in a sort of limbo. Maybe it's because she hasn't started the week's column, or maybe it's because she still hasn't spoken to Howard Demetri since the interview. The last image she has of him, his head buried in his hands, his shoulders convulsing, is not one that she wants to linger on. Or her feeling may be due to the fact that she is afraid that she might be tragically inadequate. Even though the job is all she's ever dreamed of, it is hard not to feel like an interloper in the sanctity of Francis Keen's office.

"I'm just very behind already. There are so many letters. Piles of them. More than you could possibly imagine. But I have an assistant," she says, trying to tell him the good parts. *This is a good thing, after all,* she reminds herself. "And a very large desk overlooking the city."

"Ooh, someone's hit the big time." Janice grins and rubs her palms together.

Raymond yawns theatrically, flipping to the next page in the *Daily* where there is a photograph of a bikini-clad woman lounging on the deck of a yacht under the headline *Headless Corpse Was Once Senator's Mistress.*

"Oh, and look, I found something strange in a book of her poetry." Alex digs into her purse, looking for the notecard.

"What poet?" Janice asks, surprising everyone. It's out of character and it makes both of them put their coffee down to stare at her.

"Keats, I think?" Alex says.

"Oh, I love Keats," Janice says. "I had a boyfriend who used to read it to me in bed. *Seasons of mist and mellow fruitiness,*" she begins with a faraway look in her eyes.

"Someone put me out of my misery," Raymond moans.

Alex's hand closes around the smooth edge of the card and she draws it out of her bag, placing it on the table. "Anyway, I found this inside the book." Raymond looks up from his paper, his curiosity suddenly piqued.

"What is it?" Janice cranes her neck to read upside down.

"I'm not sure," Alex admits.

Janice picks it up. "*I know*? What does that mean? What do they know?"

She passes it back to Alex with a smear of syrup on the corner. Raymond intercepts, snatches it from her hand. He takes his reading glasses from his pocket, his fingers shaking as he pushes them onto his face.

"It's probably nothing," Alex speculates as Raymond holds the note out from himself, turning it this way and that with his fingertips as though it might be explosive.

"It's a threat," Raymond barks, startling them both.

"Oh, Raymond, I don't know," Alex says. "It could be anything."

Janice rolls her eyes. "You know how he gets. It's all the crap he reads in the *Daily*. Always some scandal or somebody getting dismembered. It gets into your head."

"Maybe it's a love letter," Alex says. "Like, I know you better than anyone could ever know you."

"Or maybe she wrote it to herself, as some sort of reminder," Janice speculates.

"It's a letter that says *I know* on the desk of a dead woman," Raymond says, exasperated. He is looking intently at Alex now. "Was there anything else? Something tucked into the book maybe? Another note?" His eyes are sharp as daggers. He must have been a terror in the interrogation room back in the day.

Alex swallows. "No—I mean, there's the dedication. But it's in different handwriting than the notecard. She probably just stuck it in there to use as a bookmark or something."

"How could they have missed it?" Raymond mutters, still gazing at her over the half-moons of his reading glasses. "Now you are right there, right in the thick of it. This is something to take very seriously. A threatening letter is admissible evidence, Alexis."

Alex's chest tightens. She takes the card back from Raymond.

Even Janice seems to be considering this. "It wasn't written in a hurry, that's for sure."

"No, it is quite deliberate," Alex agrees, staring down at the perfect curve of the penmanship. "But I'm not sure I want to start getting paranoid."

"It's not paranoia. It's evidence." Raymond slams his palm down on the counter, sending a ripple of plates rattling. "Did you ever think that it could have been given to Francis as a threat?" he shouts, ignoring the glares of several diners at the other end of the counter. "Hell, it may have even been written by her killer." His face is getting red.

"Ray, even if it was, what would I do with it?" Alex protests, looking around. She isn't interested in the entire diner knowing her business. But there is a part of her that is wondering if he's right. Now that it's out in the open, she feels obligated to address the possibility that the notecard is more ominous than at first glance. "Should I take it to the police?"

"Forget it!" Raymond shakes his head. "That detective what's-his-name." He snaps his fingers, trying to remember. "That fucking Delfonte. He will drop it into some file somewhere and no one will give it a second look. He should never have been attached to the case. It's way above his pay grade."

"Then what do I do?" Alex says helplessly. She doesn't have time for this. She has a column to write and about three hundred letters left to read by Friday. "Can I just forget it for right now?"

"No!" Janice and Raymond both yell in unison. Raymond points a finger at her.

"Now, listen to me, Alexis. I want you to find a sample of Francis Keen's handwriting so we can rule her out as the writer. And be careful with this." He hands back the card, carefully holding the edges. "This is admissible evidence, so don't mess with it."

It's hard to take him seriously with the amount of toast crumbs on his T-shirt, but Alex nods as stoically as she can. She has more to worry about than playing detective. If she doesn't figure out her column soon, she won't even have her job come Friday.

"I think you have to find out who wrote it, Alex," Janice says.

"I have to go." Alex puts the card in her purse and slides off her stool. She makes a beeline for the door, wishing she hadn't brought any of it up. Now if there is even the slightest connection between the notecard and Francis's murder, she will feel responsible for it.

"Bagel! Alex!" Janice calls, waving a paper bag at her.

"Oh, right, thanks!" Alex turns back and grabs the bag, tucking it into her purse. She remembers something. "Actually, I think the book of poems was Yeats."

"Oh, well, then the note was definitely threatening," Janice says, crossing her arms over her apron.

Raymond's basset-hound eyes follow her warily. "You are involved now, Alexis, whether you like it or not."

SIXTEEN

At the office she settles herself back into Francis's old desk. How long will it take for it to feel like her own? Maybe once she has successfully written a column? Or perhaps once she has been here a month? Or possibly never, Alex thinks, dumping the latest bin of envelopes out onto the desk and pawing through them.

What Lucy said about the actual letters being the juicy ones is true. Alex has already read so many shocking admissions she is nearly numb, from cheating spouses to secret debts; there are things in the pages on her desk that could end marriages and ruin careers and put more than a few people into serious legal trouble. Still, she completely understands why they do it. There is something sacred about being able to put all of your worries, all the struggles and sadness, down on a piece of paper and sending it off to somebody anonymously. Something nearly ritualistic, like burning a photo of your ex or a scrap of paper at New Year's.

The downside to this is that she can't help everyone. What can Alex say to ease the guilt of someone who wasn't there when a loved one died, or to soothe a woman who has lost her baby? All she wants to do is fix everything for them, to give them back their sparks for life, to ease their guilt.

———————

The room has gone dark except from the light of her desk lamp. It catches the glass of the photos up on the wall. In one, Francis is perched on the edge of a table in the newsroom. She holds up a newspaper and points down at her column, smiling. Alex wonders how Francis managed to take it all in day after day, year after year. Did the struggles and suffering weigh on her? Or, after so long, was she able to push their voices aside to live her own life?

That isn't the point, she reminds herself, thinking back on an old interview with Francis she'd read. "Do you feel bad you can't help them all?" the interviewer had asked, to which Francis replied, "Of course, but the point of the column is for everyone to see that part of it is in their own control, that it always has been. A bit like Dorothy's ruby slippers."

Alex had started reading Francis's columns so many years ago when she truly needed them. Even if the problems in the published letters were nothing like her own, the advice was always something she could use. And beyond that, it was a reminder that we are all struggling, that no one has a monopoly on suffering. There are still so many snippets of Francis's answers interspersed in Alex's consciousness, mantras she tells herself when things get hard.

She takes a random envelope from the pile and begins to read a letter from a person who became obsessed with having it all. The letter tells a story of someone who had everything they ever wanted but lost it because they wanted even more—a perfect apartment, designer clothes, invitations to every social event—going into debt in the process and eventually losing everything. An interesting topic, but Alex can tell the person is not self-aware enough to change, so it feels like a response might be in vain. She puts it in the pile for Lucy to take away. She will have to keep reading. The longer it takes to find the right letter to answer, the more anxiety builds inside her.

She pulls a fresh letter out of the bin and slides a crisply folded sheet of paper from the envelope. The actual letter is only a few sentences long. She has to unfold the page to find the words there, in the very middle, indented and slightly off-center as though written on an old typewriter. As she reads, a chasm opens up in her chest.

Dear Constance,

I know who you are. You are hiding something, aren't you? Soon everyone else will know it too. If you aren't careful you are going to end up just like Francis.

SEVENTEEN

Alex stares at the words, not moving, not breathing. What do they mean, *hiding something*? They couldn't possibly know that. Not unless . . . No, Alex can't let herself go there. *It's nothing,* she tells herself, though the panic is making her feel dizzy. She takes a deep breath. It's just someone who doesn't want her taking over for Francis trying to scare her. She can handle it. If she has any chance of keeping this job, she'll have to. Alex only has three days left to find the perfect letter and write her first column. She can't let herself get distracted with empty threats from cowardly people who know absolutely nothing about her. She puts the letter into her drawer and closes it, picking a new envelope from the pile.

Dear Constance,

I need your help—

Her body buzzes unpleasantly and the words blur on the page as she loses focus. What if the letter isn't just some random person trying to scare her? She remembers Raymond's warning about the notecard. This is even more explicit. She can imagine what he'd say about it. A menacing letter mailed to the desk of a murdered woman. What if Francis got a letter as well before she died? Alex worries, her heart twisting. She puts the unread letter down. What if Francis got a letter like this one and dismissed it as something random and harmless from someone who was not a fan of her work? She imagines Francis going to her summer home and being confronted, a knife plunged into her chest.

There is a scraping sound in the hallway, the tap of footsteps, slow at first and then faster and louder. Someone coming toward her office. With Lucy already gone for the day, Alex stands anxiously. She waits for a knock on the door. When nothing comes, she looks around the office for something to defend herself with. Her eyes settle on the letter opener. She snatches it off the desk. The shell handle is cool against her palm. She holds the surprisingly heavy blade out in front of her, her hand trembling. Now another sound comes from the hall—quieter than before, a slow creaking of a shoe on the floor.

"Hello," she says in a voice barely loud enough to carry.

She creeps to the door, her heart roaring in her ears. Her breathing rattles loudly as she places a hand on the knob. The footsteps start again, pounding down the hall as she struggles to turn the handle and pull the door one-handed. By the time she has wrested the door open, the hallway is still and silent. She stands in the doorway, the letter opener wavering in her hand. Her chest rises and falls. She tries to tell herself it was her imagination, but the hall buzzes with a weird kinetic energy and she can nearly feel that someone has just been here.

She pulls the door shut, wishing there were a lock and a deadbolt like the ones in her apartment. She forces herself back to her desk and tries to read, but she is feeling anxious now. The words of the threatening letter cycle though her head. She rises and paces her office. The lights have come on in the Excelsior Building. She thinks about Tom. Maybe she should go get another coffee. But the chances of running into him this late are slim. She glances at her phone: 9:23. The coffee shop is closed already anyway. She remembers seeing an office kitchen off the newsroom.

Howard's office is dark tonight, the blinds open. He'll be home now with Regina, Alex thinks, imagining the two of them in their marble-

I NEED YOU TO READ THIS

countered kitchen pouring a glass of wine to go with some tastefully plated meal. Alex's stomach growls. She's been living on muffins and bagels. And coffee.

She turns on a light in the kitchenette and puts a pod into the coffee maker, trying to figure out the buttons. As she waits for it to brew, she looks at the corkboard on the wall. There are several notes about keeping things in the fridge, a few upcoming events, an invitation to a book party for a staff writer. A few newspaper clippings, one about a cow that escaped captivity by going incognito with a pack of wild bison. Tacked right in the center is Francis Keen's obituary. It is curling a bit on the edges, the paper darkening eight months out. It's amazing how fast newsprint ages. She looks at the photo of Francis, slightly blurry from the offset printing, standing behind what is now Alex's desk, her white shirtsleeves rolled up. As the coffee brews mechanically behind her, she looks into the eyes of Francis Keen. They are soft and happy. What would Francis think of all of this?

Alex leans in, trying to make out the objects on top of her desk as if she will be able to see more by being closer, but the picture just goes grainy and her eyes blur with the effort. Francis looks so lively, so wise. She was a voice of calm and reason to so many people, a stand-in mother, a wise aunt to those who didn't have one. She thinks of what it must have been like being alone in her house. Did she see her killer before the knife came down on her? Did she recognize them? Alex brushes her finger over the photograph.

What happened to you? Who would want to kill a woman who only tried to help people?

Behind her the coffee maker dings. She collects her cup and carries it back toward her office. The newsroom is silent, except for the background hum of electricity and forced air that keep a giant skyscraper's ecosystem going. She pauses, looking at the bank of huge windows across the newsroom. The last bit of sunset has just snuffed out, leaving all the windows black and scattered with yellow spots of lights from other buildings.

What an incredibly odd feeling to be standing here all alone, when a week ago she had never even dreamed of working at the *Herald*. She continues toward her office, trying to push thoughts of Francis's murder from her mind. It's a dream come true working here, she reminds herself as she passes through the doorway between the filing cabinets. She stops abruptly as she turns into the old part of the building. Her heart jerks violently in her chest at the sight of a tall figure far down the hall, standing right by her office door.

EIGHTEEN

"Alex! You're still here," Howard says, attempting to make his voice casual. He raises a hand in greeting, but his eyes flutter wide open under his glasses. Like he's been caught, Alex thinks, swallowing anxiously.

His tie is pulled loose around his neck, the top buttons of his shirt undone. He starts toward her, his legs shooting out in jerky movements, and she fights the urge to run.

"Yes, I've been staying late, you know, to finish up all the letters. There are a lot of them." She stumbles over her words, still recovering from the shock as she wipes coffee that's splattered on her hand onto the leg of her jeans.

"I'm glad you've been settling in all right." He comes to stand awkwardly next to her. He looks garish under the fluorescent lights. There are bags under his eyes she hadn't noticed before, a gray paleness to his skin that makes him look like he may be getting sick. Alex wishes she could tell him about the threatening letter. Ask him if Francis ever received one. But doing so would put her in a negative light, she thinks. She doesn't want him to think she's already causing problems, or that she can't handle it.

"Yes, Lucy has been a big help." He gives her a funny look, one she can't quite read. She thinks he might be angry. Maybe this is it, the moment she gets fired.

Instead, he apologizes. "Alex, I'm so sorry I haven't come by to see you sooner. I know I said I would. Time just got away from me."

"It's okay, I'm sure you're busy with *real* news," Alex says. "There is a lot going on in the world." She glances down the hall, acutely aware that they are the only two people in the office. In the whole building, as far as she knows. Anything could happen and no one would be here to see.

He gives a little snort and waves his hand in front of him. "Please. Real news these days is always the same. Bad. Your column, that's the important thing. That's what our readers want."

Alex doesn't know what to say. "It's fine. Really, I'm doing just fine. It's only been a couple of days anyway." She suddenly wants this uncomfortable exchange to be over.

"No. It's no excuse." He shakes his head, disgusted with himself. "I always make sure I give my best to my staff. I want you to know that this is not typical of me."

"I'm sure. I remember reading about how much Francis respected you," Alex says diplomatically. It's true. In every interview Alex had read while Francis was alive, she'd mentioned Howard's name. *A great editor*, she called him. *A moral compass.* What would she think of the man sneaking around by her office after hours? Was this his normal behavior? Alex looks at the man before her and tries to see him as a moral compass but just can't.

Howard's face goes slack at the mention of Francis's name. His legs waver and he reaches a hand out to steady himself against the wall, but he stumbles and falls toward her. Alex winces, closing her eyes as his hand flies toward her face. His palm lands flat against the wall just next to her head.

As she carefully opens her eyes, she notices the pale stripe on his ring finger. The indentation where his wedding band had been. What has happened? Alex thinks of the beautiful woman from the photos. Now she can see the strain in his eyes. Is that what she has been witnessing this week, the end of Howard Demetri's marriage?

"Oh, my goodness, look at me! Long day and I completely missed lunch," he says in nearly a whisper, pushing himself back upright. And then she smells it. Something sharp and familiar on his breath. *Whiskey.* She draws away from him, against the wall. He doesn't seem to notice.

"Francis always had a way of finding the right letter," he says suddenly, his posture straightening.

"What was that?" Alex asks, trying to keep her voice from shaking.

He frowns. "She always said that she would answer the first one in a week that made her cry."

"Thank you," Alex says, her heart thudding. She eyes him carefully. But he turns away from her now, swaying as he goes back toward the newsroom, the scent of whiskey trailing him down the hallway.

She feels a shiver at her back as she starts down the hall in the opposite direction. As jarring as the exchange was for her, Alex can tell that Howard hadn't expected to see her either. Which makes her question, if he wasn't coming to see her, what was he doing there?

Dear Constance,

Ever since I graduated from high school, I've never let myself think too hard about what I might want. That kind of thing has always felt like a recipe for making myself miserable. It's not like I have many options. But lately I have been thinking a lot about who I might want to be.

It's still hard for me to think of the apartment as mine. It's so modern. There is no clutter, no sign that anyone really lives here at all. The things I brought with me easily fit into a couple of drawers in the bedroom.

"Where is all your stuff?" I asked Brian once when I first was there.

"What do you mean?" he said, looking around. "It's right here."

I followed his eyes to the square cement coffee table and the sleek black credenza. I'd looked when he was in the other room and there was nothing inside it.

"No, I mean like your pictures, your books, papers, that sort of thing."

"I like to keep things clean. I don't need all that junk."

"Maybe we could buy a few paintings or something for the walls," I said, starting to imagine the ways I'd fix the place up, the colorful curtains, some flowers in vases around the apartment.

"Why would we do that? Isn't this good enough for you?" Brian said, his eyes narrowing. It was just a flash of annoyance, and then his face cleared and it was gone, but it gave me a sinking feeling like this place wasn't really mine.

We spend most of our evenings at his apartment drinking wine. We drink a lot of wine, too much for me a lot of the time. I try to hide it when I feel like my head spins, but Brian seems to think it's cute when I act a little drunk.

I was laying with my head on his chest. "You are the smartest woman I know. You could do anything you set your mind to." No one calls me smart. His fingers ran through my hair.

"You know, you could quit that place," he said, surprising me.

"Sam's?"

"Yeah. I don't like it," he said, pulling himself up on his elbow to look at me. "You know, I've seen the old man watching you through the window when I pick you up after work. It's weird."

I've known Sam a long time, ever since I was a little kid. And Brian is right, he has been acting strange lately. But he's not a bad person. I didn't say anything though. I didn't want to spoil the perfect moment we were having. His hand playing with my hair.

"All I'm saying is you could do something different," he said, flopping onto his back. I swallowed, not knowing what that would be but realizing that he was right. I could do something else.

As I lay there my old dream of going to school started to resurface. I pictured myself walking to classes in cute new clothes, a bag slung over my shoulder, talking to my friends as we walked to class. "I thought I might go to school. Maybe for art or psychology," I whispered, afraid of it, worried about what he might say. I held my breath as I waited for his reply.

"Yes, I think you should quit," he said again, so sharply I had to look at him to make sure he wasn't joking, but he had the serious look he got when he made up his mind about something. "Then you can have time to go to school. I'll even help you."

"Really?" I asked him, my heart racing.

"Really," he said. "You know I love you."

"I love you, too," I found myself saying, my throat thick with emotion. Things are changing, moving so fast it makes my head spin. Maybe that is just what happens when you take charge of your own life. Sometimes I worry that this is all in my imagination, that one day I will wake up back in my own room at home with no hope or future at all. I have to make myself look around, to recognize that this is all real. And it is mine. I don't know how I got so lucky, Constance.

Now that Brian is on board with school, I am going to do it. I am going to quit my job at Sam's and start my life fresh just like I've always wanted. It might not be far away, like I dreamed, but that doesn't mean it can't be good. I don't know why I'm so nervous. I feel like I finally am making my own life, like I have choices. I just hope I make the right ones. How do you know what you are meant to be doing with your life, Constance? How do you learn to trust yourself?

Sincerely,
Lost Girl

NINETEEN

The mailroom is dark, and Alex can't find the switch. She wanders in anyway, following the slim patch of light from the hallway. It illuminates the ragged edges of the bins. They have grown exponentially since she last saw them. They tower with letters now, masses and masses of them, piled so high they bow out overhead, threatening to topple. How are there so many? She hears something, a small voice, muffled by paper, calling for help. Is someone trapped inside the piles? She plunges a hand into the stack, trying to help. The voice calls out again. Clearer this time. *Please,* it says. *Please help.* It is frail and light, like the voice of a child. She begins to pull the letters away. But each time she stops and tries to orient herself, the pile has grown larger. It swells before her eyes, hitting the ceiling and bulging against the walls. She sees now that the letters are an organism, and this person is being slowly digested. She braces herself with her feet as she pushes her hand deeper; finally her fingers brush up against the hard warmth of a body. "I've got you," she calls out just as the letters begin to fall. They are beautiful at first, like a gentle snow, but soon they are toppling, suffocating her, slicing at her face and arms. Now invisible hands clamp down on her wrists. But they are not the small fingers of a child. They are coarse and strong. She screams as the fingers grab her amidst the blur of white. The hands are at her neck, squeezing.

They are familiar, and she knows they won't stop until they extinguish every last breath—

Alex jolts awake in the dark with a shuddering gasp as she struggles to fill her lungs with air. The blankets are twisted around her, pinning her legs down. She thrashes against them wildly until the familiar ceiling fan and dark curtains of the window in the corner reassure her that she is in her own bedroom. Heart still thrumming in her chest, she slowly untangles herself and sits up. It is unbearably hot in her apartment and her throat is parched.

Alex drags herself out of bed, making her way into the kitchen to get a glass of water. She goes to the windows, still rattled from the dream, and checks the locks. Across the street the Bluebird is dark inside. She scans the sidewalk, reassuring herself that there is no one there she recognizes. Only a young couple clinging to each other, stumbling a little on their way home from a nearby Irish pub. Their laughter echoes up into her apartment.

It's not normal to be like this, Alex thinks. She has been so isolated for so long. Ready to pack up and leave at a moment's notice. She has done so much to escape what happened to her all those years ago now, but it is still with her. She is still locking doors and hiding. Will she ever be able to free herself from it, or will it lurk forever in her subconscious waiting to step out and torment her just when things seem to be going okay for a change? The job is a step in the right direction. She can no longer hide in her apartment. More and more she wonders if anyone is even looking for her, or if it is all in her mind. Maybe she exaggerated the entire thing. Either way, she realizes now, looking out onto the empty street, she can't run anymore. Someday soon she'll have to stop and look behind her.

TWENTY

Alex is still rattled when she goes into the Bluebird on Friday morning. She hasn't slept well since the start of the week. Her eyes feel bloodshot and heavy.

"Looking rough, kid," Raymond says.

"Thanks, Raymond," Alex answers sarcastically, pulling a coffee toward her and taking a large gulp.

"They've got you working too hard up there," he says, munching on some toast.

"I don't know. I feel like I actually might not be working hard enough. I haven't come up with my column yet and it's due today." As she says it, her stomach turns.

"Cutting it close." Raymond whistles.

"Oh God, Ray. You really know how to make someone feel better, don't you?" Janice says, disgusted, dropping off their breakfasts. "You'll be great, Alex. Don't listen."

"I don't know. I just keep thinking I'm going to choose the wrong one and everyone will hate it."

"You just have to believe in yourself. What other option do you have?" Janice says. Alex smiles weakly, wishing that it were all so simple.

"Oh, but look. I wanted to show you both what I found." She pulls out a small sample of Francis's handwriting that she found in the kitchen cupboard—a Post-it, clinging to a box of expired peppermint tea: *Francis's! Please ask if you want one, you lovely thieves.*

Raymond pushes his plate away and runs his napkin over the counter. "Let me see the other one, the note." Alex retrieves the little notecard from her purse and hands it to him. He places the two paper squares on the counter next to one another and takes out his reading glasses.

"See how this one is more loopy? And this one is shorter, the *w* is more angular." It is already clear to Alex that they were not written by the same person, but she nods politely, listening to Raymond's impressions.

"Oh yeah, those are totally different," Janice says, barely pausing to glance as she passes with a tray full of omelets. "Doesn't take a detective to see it." Raymond glares up at her as Alex pulls the notes back, tucking them into her bag.

"So that rules out Francis as the one who wrote the note to herself," Alex says.

"Yes, I believe it does," Raymond agrees. Alex takes a sip of coffee. "Like I told you before, I would treat it as a threat."

"I didn't want to worry you, Ray, but I got something a little off in the mail bin."

"Show it to me."

Alex pulls out the typewritten letter, cringing as he bends over to look at it. His face goes slack with worry. She already knows what he'll say.

"This is not good, Alexis. Not good at all. Could it be from before, something written to someone else before you got the job?"

"I'm not sure. I didn't even think of that," Alex says, feeling stupid.

"What's the postmark say?" Janice reaches across the counter and picks up the envelope, holding it up to her face to see the details of the stamp on the corner.

"This was only mailed a week ago, from New York looks like," Janice says. "Sorry, lady, but this is for you."

Alex's heart sinks. She'd been hoping these two would help ease her mind, but they care for her. They're not going to lie.

"You are not safe until we know who is writing these," Raymond says emphatically. "You have to be vigilant up there. Pay attention to everyone around you. Nobody is innocent until we catch this guy. You hear me?"

"Yes, Raymond." Alex rolls her eyes and stands to leave, regretting sharing this new information with them. How can she be vigilant in an office building? The idea is absurd. How can she protect herself from a piece of paper?

TWENTY-ONE

It's the solstice and the summer heat has settled in, covering the city with a sticky film, turning people's tempers up, obliterating their patience. As Alex walks to work she can see the hot air wiggle up from the pavement, distorting everything around her. Her throat is parched by the time she drags herself onto Sixth Avenue. All she can think about is a glass of water, full of ice, something cold to take away the grime and discomfort that have already enveloped her.

As Alex approaches the Herald Building a large black town car with tinted windows passes her, swerving to a stop in front of the revolving doors. Howard Demetri emerges from the back seat, extending one long leg at a time onto the sidewalk. Something about seeing him there makes her step back, her heart thumping. She pulls her sunglasses down over her face, wiping a line of sweat from the top of her lip.

In the bright daylight Howard is less intimidating than he was in the hallway. He looks hungover, his face pale and gaunt. The sour smell of whiskey on his breath last night has cured her of the desire to have him stop by her office. She doesn't love the idea of being trapped in the elevator with him and she suspects he isn't looking to make awkward conversation with her right now either. She ducks toward the side of the building, waiting for him to go inside before her.

"Alex," a voice calls from behind her, startling her out of her thoughts. She turns to see Tom standing there obliviously. His headphones hang around his neck. She is surprised by how happy she is to see him.

"Hiding from someone?" He nods at Howard's back as he hurries toward the entrance.

"Kind of," she admits. "My boss."

"Oh, well, that makes sense. Who wants to be stuck making small talk with their boss first thing?" Tom says as they watch him go. Alex breathes a sigh of relief as Howard disappears through the revolving glass doors. "He looks familiar, actually."

"You've probably heard of him. Howard Demetri. He's kind of a big deal, if you're into newspapers." She feels her hair sticking to her forehead. This heat isn't making her feel exactly attractive. She can feel her skin growing slick beneath her shirtdress. Her hair clings uncomfortably to her neck. Tom, on the other hand, is wearing some sort of lightweight blue suit and doesn't appear to have broken a sweat despite the sidewalk feeling a lot like the surface of the sun.

Tom shakes his head. "Afraid I can't handle the heavy stuff. I'm far too sensitive for the real world. I prefer fictional problems."

"What's today's, then?" Alex asks, nodding to the headset around his neck.

"Well, I'm so glad you asked. Currently I am escaping into the troubled lives of Jo, Beth, Meg, and, of course, Amy."

"You're listening to *Little Women*?" Alex says incredulously. He has to be kidding. A banker in his midthirties wearing a suit could not possibly be interested in Louisa May Alcott.

"You don't believe me? Well, fine, have a listen!" He pulls the headphones off his neck and holds them out. She leans in tentatively, until she can hear the dim voice of a woman reading.

I don't pretend to be wise, but I am observing, and I see a great deal more than you'd imagine. I'm interested in other people's experiences and inconsistencies, and, though I can't explain, I remember and use them for my own benefit.

Their heads bend together listening, and Alex feels a sharp fizzle of electricity move between them. The whole scene is so implausible, the two of them out on the street listening to *Little Women* and sharing headphones like teenagers, that she straightens up and pulls herself away.

"I should go in," she says. "I have so much to do."

"Right. Well, I'll let you know how it ends. See you around, then," he says. She's only walked a few paces when she hears him call back to her.

"Hey, Alex!" She turns back. He stands in the middle of the sidewalk squinting into the morning sun. His jacket flaps slightly in the hot breeze. "Do you want to get dinner sometime?"

He looks so earnest, his head tilted to one side, waiting for her response. She thinks of one of Francis's letters. *You have to allow yourself to be vulnerable if you want to receive anything good this world has to offer.*

"Sure," she says, even as she feels her chest clamp up at the idea of going on a date.

He holds out his phone. "Can I have your number?"

She hesitates. "Why don't you give me yours?"

"Fair enough," he says. He digs around in his bag and finds a pen and a napkin. Before she knows it, he is leaning against the window scribbling down his number. Her palms are clammy as he hands it to her. She notices the expectation in his eyes. She tucks it into the pocket of her shirtdress and gives him a smile. "Great, thanks. I'll send you a text," Alex says, not sure if she means it.

"Great." He grins. "In the meantime, I'll look for your name in the paper."

He smiles, that one-sided dimple flashing at her before he turns away, pulling his headphones over his ears. As she glances back, she sees him duck into the Excelsior Bank Building, and an unfamiliar flutter rises up into her chest. She fights hard to extinguish it, but as she rides up to the forty-ninth floor, she imagines meeting Tom for dinner at one of the cafés nearby, talking into the night at one of the tables that spill out onto the street. The ones she always walks past alone.

TWENTY-TWO

"Well, that's nearly everything from one bin!" Lucy chirps. Alex gives her a weak smile. Her fingers are covered in paper cuts and her eyes throb from reading all of the letters on her desk, a full-on mountain of them but nothing that is right for her first column.

"Thanks," Alex says. As Lucy begins to stack fresh envelopes on her desk, the basket of letters tips, spilling all over her office floor.

"Shit. I'm so sorry," Lucy says, dropping to the floor and scrambling to gather the letters, stacking them in neat piles.

"It's okay, really." She joins Lucy on her hands and knees. "This is probably not in the job description you imagined for yourself when you applied here."

Lucy rocks back onto her heels, blowing a piece of hair out of her face. "I don't mind this at all. Truly. I'm from a small town. I never dreamed I'd get to work in an office like this, at a place everyone recognizes when I go back home for Thanksgiving. Even if they might not all like the *Herald,* they respect it. It means something. This job has been such a good experience for me. I like being an assistant. It's better here than where I'm from. There's nothing there." Her face darkens with some memory of it. Alex swallows. She can relate.

"Have you found *the one* yet?" Lucy asks.

"For this week? No, not yet. It's making me a bit nervous, honestly.

There are a few here that I feel so connected to, but so far nothing that seems just perfect. And I really want this first one to be the best I can make it." Alex is tempted to ask her assistant more about Francis. Did she ever have trouble choosing her column each week? Did she just reach in and pick one, or was she more deliberate, more calculating? But she remembers the grief that transformed Lucy's features when she spoke about her former boss. She should tread lightly.

"Maybe I'm overthinking it," she says instead.

"It must be a lot of pressure," Lucy says. "Big shoes to fill and all. But I'm sure you'll find something soon. I believe in you."

"Thanks, Lucy," Alex says, not feeling certain at all. The tapping of footsteps in the hall makes them both pause and look to the door until the sound recedes. "Every time I hear something out there, I keep thinking it's Howard Demetri."

Her assistant glances back at the door. She's gone pale, Alex notices, at the mention of Howard. "Lucy? Is there something wrong?"

"No. Nothing at all," Lucy says quickly, then stands up and brushes herself off. "I should go get some more letters for us! I'll come back up later and see if you need anything."

She gives Alex a bright smile as she leaves. Does it seem a bit forced? Alex wonders as Lucy backs out of the office, glancing along the hall before letting the door close behind her.

She turns back to the letters, now stacked in precise rows on her desk. She selects one from the top of her pile and slides out the single page.

Dear Constance,

I don't know where the years have gone. When I look back it is hard to remember them all. I had a bit of a life before, at least I think I did. But I let it lapse, to roll over day after day into a blur of sameness. Once I had a woman I loved dearly. I was afraid that if I chose her, I'd be giving up on everything else, all the other dreams I had and ways I saw myself, that all those exciting doors would close to me. I haven't ever been to Italy like I always promised her. I had many things I said I'd do one day, many plans for the future, and somehow here I am, sixty-five years old. I don't even know if I would go to Italy now given the chance, but I would have married Hazel. I guess that's how it all goes in this life, and I shouldn't feel sorry for myself. But I wake up each day with a deep well of regret that nothing around me can fill. And now I realize that I'd rather have been standing in a hallway of closed doors all this time with her than all alone with all the options in the world. It is far too late for Hazel and me. But I don't want to live like this anymore. Nothing was ever good enough for me to commit to, and now that I've committed to nothing, I have nothing.

Something made me wake up recently and realize that things could be different. I guess what I want to know is how do I live the rest of my years without this ache of regret consuming me whole?

I'll wait for your answer. I hope I have time.
Misgivings

TWENTY-THREE

Alex's skin prickles with goose bumps. She rereads the letter quickly and then, before she can lose confidence, she begins to type a response.

Dear Misgivings,

Regret can come in many forms.

Once she has committed, the words come fast. Everything else falls away and she disappears into a sort of trance. Alex is back in the same place she went to just a couple of weeks ago, sitting on her living room floor, writing the answers to the application in her sweatpants. As she writes, her eyes sting with tears. There is so much she wants to say to Misgivings. She becomes immersed in their problem, completely transfixed by the solution as it unspools before her on the screen. She watches the words land on the page as though by divine intervention. She thinks that this must be the feeling writers talk about, where something that almost feels outside of yourself takes over. The writing feels urgent and necessary, and as she nears the end of her response, she realizes that the advice is something she needs to hear too.

We can never get back time—it's one of life's biggest tragedies but also one of its greatest motivators. If things were not finite, there would be no need to ever evaluate what is most important to us. You thought you were being true to yourself by keeping your options open, but all that time you were living in fear. If you are not mindful, you can spend a whole lifetime weighing your options. Commitment to anything, let alone another person, takes bravery.

She sits back, her chair creaking, and drops her hands from her keyboard. Her body is stiff from spending so long in deep concentration. It's amazing the way this feeling overtakes her when she writes. She spent so long in life not knowing that writing was so transportive. She is oddly calm now. She can tell she wrote it well. She looks over the letter, rereading it carefully and correcting any small typos she made in the rush to get it onto the page. Then attaches it to an email to Howard Demetri. She presses Send and sighs with relief.

When she finally looks up, the sky has cleared into a crystal blue after days of oppressive smog. The afternoon sun sparkles warmly in the glass of the skyscrapers. She glances at the Excelsior Building, remembering Tom. It wouldn't be so terrible to go out and have a nice dinner, would it? She remembers the dimple in his cheek, the way he bobbed his head a bit when he asked her out. She feels like the letter she answered was trying to heal her as well. Maybe she just needs to be brave enough to trust her own message.

Before she can talk herself out of it, she picks up her phone and texts the number Tom gave her.

Dinner tonight? I'm suddenly free.

Immediately after she sends it her chest tightens anxiously. It is unlikely that he'll be free last-minute anyway, she thinks, trying to distract herself by cleaning up her desk, sweeping aside the already-read letters, and straightening the others in their neat pile. But less than a minute later the screen of her phone lights up.

I'm up for it! Let me find us a reservation somewhere. 7pm?

As Alex looks down at the screen, she can't tell if she's thrilled or terrified. Probably a mixture of both.

Perfect!

TWENTY-FOUR

The restaurant Tom chooses is tucked away on one of the shortest streets in Little Italy. With all of Alex's aimless walking over the past seven years, it is rare for a place to be new to her. Glowing string lights crisscross the narrow street lined on both sides with little mom-and-pop Italian restaurants. People sit at tables along the sidewalk, talking and drinking wine over red-checked tablecloths as scents of garlic and oregano and freshly baked bread waft from the open doorways. Alex stumbles down the sidewalk transported. She's so charmed by it all she almost doesn't see that Tom is already waiting for her, sitting on the steps in front of a small church next to the restaurant. When he sees her, he grins and stands up, brushing off the front of his pants. He's wearing a jacket despite the warm weather, a crisp blue shirt buttoned up underneath.

Alex is glad that she ran home after they texted, showering and changing into a long-sleeved white linen dress that is just a little too short with a cutout along the collarbone. She'd pulled out the only pair of heels she owns, a pair of nude slides that were an impulse buy she had yet to wear outside of her apartment. She'd gotten dressed and stood teetering on the edge of the bathtub to see herself in the bathroom mirror as the pigeons watched her warily from the window. *Don't worry, it's just one date,* she'd found herself saying, as much to herself as to Mildred.

Now she's glad she made the effort as Tom walks down the steps of the church, looking at her appreciatively.

"Wow," he says when he gets close enough. "You look great."

"I'm not always dressed like a writer on deadline," she says, the compliment making her cheeks flush. "Usually, though."

"Ready?" Tom gestures for her to go ahead of him through a small red-painted doorway. Inside, the place is not one of the new modern Italian restaurants she often passes while out for walks in her neighborhood, the ones with the polished cement bars and people in the window eating tiny portions off massive plates. This is a proper Italian bistro, with an arched brick ceiling and bouquets of breadsticks teetering in cups in the center of the tables. A waiter brings them back to a small table set against the wall. A candle flickers invitingly, some of its wax already collecting on the checkered tablecloth below. The overt date vibes of the place make them both a little shy and they decide to order a bottle of wine. It's an optimistic gesture, Alex thinks. A sign that they are anticipating the date going well.

"Any preference on style?" He looks at her over the plastic-coated menu.

"Red? Good-tasting?" Alex shrugs and he laughs. As much as she loves to drink it, she's never been much of a wine snob. She tends to forget much beyond the very basics.

"I think we can probably do that." She watches him deliberate with the sommelier about bottles. It's been a long time since she's had this kind of feeling about a person, the kind of comfortable chemistry where just watching them do something mundane is attractive.

"So—" they both start to say, and then stop and laugh, each waiting for the other to continue.

"I hope you like it here," he says, looking around the cozy brick-lined room.

"It's so lovely," she says. "There's something very comforting about it."

He nods. "It's one of my favorite restaurants in the city. Reminds me of my grandparents."

"They were Italian?" Alex asks.

"Irish," he says, and she bursts out laughing. He gives her a crooked grin, pleased with himself for inadvertently making such a funny joke. "But my granddad worked as a line cook in Philly. Was his first job off the boat, so our family dinners were decidedly very Italian American, with a potato or two thrown in." Alex likes the way his eyes crinkle and the slightly shy duck of his head. *Keep your shit together,* she tells herself. *No need to lose it because this is your first date in eight years.*

"I would have thought you came from a long line of bankers," she jokes.

"God, no. My whole family is blue-collar. I mean, they've done good for themselves, but no one has ever had any desire to work on Wall Street. Myself included."

"You went into banking accidentally?"

"Kind of. I actually have no idea how I got into it. A friend of mine in college, his dad worked high up at Excelsior, and I just kind of glommed on, summer internship, first-year job. I kind of hate it, to be honest. I don't think anyone understands why I do it to myself. The hours are terrible. They'd be happier if I found a nice girl to marry and took over the family restaurant." Embarrassed, he clears his throat, his eyes jumping down to his menu. "What about you? Do you have a big family?"

Talking about her early life makes her skin prickle nervously. Under the table she tugs at her sleeves. It's not that it's a secret, but somehow bringing up the time before New York feels dangerous. The truth is, she is ashamed of what happened back then. And of the recluse she has let herself become. "No, I—" A waiter comes to the table, giving Alex a much-needed reprieve. He drops off two heaping plates of pasta flecked with basil and shavings of Parmesan and a bowl of some sort of salad with perfectly in-season sliced peaches, an orb of burrata nestled in the center.

"This looks delicious," Alex says, thrilled to be looking at real food for the first time all week. Tom scoops up a bite of linguine, expertly twirling it around his fork and taking a bite. He closes his eyes, enjoying the flavors. Alex watches him, intrigued. She wonders if he is always so appreciative of things.

"Well, it's no nine p.m. chocolate chip muffin." He puts his fork down and smiles at her. "Now, I was hoping you could tell me what the name of your column is, because I've been reading the *Herald* all week and I can't find it for the life of me."

She weighs her options. She can't keep everything from him. Plus, she is starting to suspect that she might truly like Tom. Which means she'll have to open up to him. This realization makes her stomach flip. She takes another sip of wine.

"I feel almost bizarre telling you this, because it barely feels real to me. I was hired just a week ago to be the new Dear Constance."

She watches him put it together. His eyes get big. "The advice columnist?"

She nods.

"The one who—"

She nods again, hoping that he won't focus on the sad part of her job. She realizes with some heaviness that her job will always be linked to Francis's murder. That telling people will always have them scratching their heads and asking whether they'd ever found the person who killed her, and watching their eyes widen when she says no.

"That's great, Alex. Amazing, really. What a cool job," he says. And she smiles, relieved.

"I actually turned in my first column today," she admits. "It's why I texted you. I felt like I could finally relax a tiny bit."

"Wow. I can't wait to read it. I'm honored to celebrate with you," he says. "Truly. What an accomplishment. I have no doubt you'll be amazing at it. There is something about you, something I noticed right away—I hope you don't mind me saying it. I think you make people feel comfortable."

She reaches her wineglass to his, a tingling in her chest as the glasses ding together. Alex *has* heard this before. She's always been the kind of person who people feel at ease around, who they'd tell things to. Back in the before times, she used to joke that if someone had committed a murder, they'd probably tell her about it. She wonders if that is still true.

There is a pause in their conversation as they eat. The wine has made her warm inside. Tom smiles at her over the candle. She holds his gaze. There's no ducking away this time, no awkwardness. It is the first time in as long as she can remember that she has felt this calm. And then he puts down his fork, pats his mouth with the white napkin, and leans back.

"So, your boss is *the* Howard Demetri?" he asks.

"The one and only!" She expects him to be impressed, but instead Tom looks down into his lap. "Why?" she asks, confused. He hesitates, like he's not sure he wants to tell her now.

"Well, when I said I recognized him earlier, it wasn't the way you might think. I mean, now that you say it, of course I know his name. And I thought he had a familiar look to him. But there is something else I wasn't sure I should bring up."

"And now?" She feels her skin prickle.

"Now I've had half a bottle of this fabulous pinot and I am losing my ability to keep this extremely tantalizing gossip from you."

Alex leans in. She raises her eyebrows at him, trying to ignore the anxious flutter that's started in her stomach. "Tell me."

"Okay, I know this is going to sound kind of weird, but I think his office window is directly across from mine. I've seen him in there at night . . ." He trails off.

"You spy on him?" Alex narrows her eyes at the stranger across the table. His cheeks flush and he holds his palms out to her, pleading innocence.

"No! I mean, not on purpose. My desk points right toward the *Herald*. When it's dark out, those big windows are practically lit up like television screens."

"Are you sure it's him?" Alex asks, her elbows on the table. She is afraid of what he's about to say, and she's not sure if it is because of what it will reveal about Howard or what it already tells her about Tom.

He nods. "After seeing him outside the other day, I'm positive.

I can't see too many details, but I know it's him. You can't exactly mistake him for someone else with that height and that thick JFK hair of his and all."

It's true, Alex thinks. The shape of Howard Demetri is so striking that it would be almost impossible not to pick him out of a lineup. "So, what have you seen?"

His finger traces the top of his empty wineglass. "I hope what I'm about to tell you doesn't make me sound creepy."

"I hope not, too," she says with a laugh, but her hands have gone slick as she tugs on her sleeves under the table.

"I don't normally watch people at night through the window, you have to understand. But there was a while there where I was working on a big project for the bank and I was staying late, even later than normal. And let's just say that, at least during that time, Mr. Howard Demetri had a semiregular nightly visitor, and it was very friendly."

It takes her a second to understand what he's referring to. "What! You mean they were having sex? In his office?" Alex asks, scandalized. "Did you see her?"

Tom blushes. "Not really. Just her back. They were, um, on the desk."

"Wow. I would not have expected that."

"I know. It was so wildly inappropriate I couldn't tear my eyes away," he says. "Anyway, sorry, this is not the most date-friendly topic."

"I mean, it is kind of a shock, honestly. But he did stop wearing his wedding band right after I got there, so maybe it shouldn't be."

"Maybe it's all aboveboard then?"

Alex shakes her head, feeling sad. "I don't know why people do that to their partners. Fragile egos, I guess. I just can't imagine that kind of thing even feeling good. Not long-term. The stress of it."

"No. I mean, I don't even think it's about the women for so many of them. It's like getting an expensive car, more about how you view yourself than anything else. Plus, someone like Howard Demetri is probably used to the rush of excitement from his work. Maybe this is just an extension of that." Tom is watching her intently, a crease between his brows. "You really admire him?"

Alex nods. "It is a bit disappointing, though it probably shouldn't be. This is what powerful men always do, isn't it?"

"Too many of them," Tom says, still looking right at her. She is unused to this kind of direct attention and is relieved when the waiter interrupts, bringing them dessert menus. "But not all of them. Some just use their powers to order multiple desserts. What do you think about tiramisu?" Tom smiles and Alex laughs, nodding in agreement.

After dinner they linger on the sidewalk outside the restaurant. Tom tilts his head down to look at her and they lock eyes. There it is, that buzzy feeling again, that energy crackling between them like static electricity.

"Thanks for dinner," she says, allowing herself to lean into him slightly. Alex can smell the bite of garlic and wine on his breath. It isn't bad. She actually finds it weirdly intoxicating. He is so close that the pattern on his shirt blurs in front of her eyes and she can smell his laundry detergent. The scent of it reminds her of her childhood home, of the laundry room off the kitchen with the big tubs of powdered detergent her mom bought on sale. He doesn't come from money, she realizes suddenly. The thought fills her with empathy. He feels comfortable, like someone she's known for years and years. For a moment she thinks he might kiss her.

"Should I get a car?" Registering the surprise on her face, Tom pulls back and clears his throat. "I mean for you to get home in."

Alex exhales, both relieved and disappointed. She isn't ready for that. Not yet. At least, she doesn't think she is. She punches her information into his phone and lets him order her an Uber.

"Thank you for dinner. I loved that place."

"Anytime," he says.

The wine has made her sleepy and happy, and she leans back in the seat on the way home and watches the city pass in a blur of lights and people, some of them stumbling to bars or out into the street as the car brings her uptown.

It isn't until she has gotten home and bolted the door behind her that she hears the cheerful *ding* of an incoming text and realizes what she has done. She looks down at her phone, her stomach already turning. It glows in her hand. A text from Tom reads:

> I see you are home! Tracked it on the app. Hope you have a good sleep. Oh, and, Alex, I had a really nice time tonight. Hope you did too.

She leans her back against the door feeling dizzy. She wasn't being careful. It was the wine and the almost-kissing that threw her. And now he knows where she lives. Alex checks the locks again on the door, then the windows. She looks out onto the street. The diner lights are out for the night. A few dark figures rush past. One stops and loiters there. It's probably fine. Alex realizes she doesn't even know Tom yet. She should have ordered her own car home but was stupidly swept up in the chivalry of all of it. Drunk on the attention. It was sloppy of her.

And yet Alex knows she will have to let go of all this fear if she wants to let anything in. She is done running. If not for the stupid threatening letter, she would almost be ready to believe that no one is chasing her anymore. Another text comes in.

> I hope I didn't freak you out with all of my talk about your boss.

He hadn't, not at the time, but now she wonders if it isn't a little strange to sit there in your office and spy on people through the window while they are having sex.

He'd had a nice time though, that was what he wrote. Alex had had a nice time too. The thought is startling, foreign to her. A nice time on a date. It's almost like she is a normal woman. *Things are okay,* she tells herself. She remembers the words from one of Francis's columns. It was one from years ago about a man on the precipice of starting his life over. She can't remember all of the details, but she remembers one line: *Sometimes it is easy to mistake hope for fear.*

Dear Constance,

Everything has changed. It's what I wanted, right? I felt so terrible when I told Sam I wouldn't be coming back to work next week. I wanted to make a clean start, I said when he mumbled something about giving two weeks' notice. It is better that way.

Sam looked concerned, which was strange because he always seems laid-back, not the worrying type like I am.

"I'm glad you're going to school though. You are a smart cookie. Don't let anyone tell you otherwise. You hear?" He looked at me like he was waiting for me to give him a sign, that he could talk about Brian, warn me or something. But I wouldn't let him. And Brian also thinks that I'm smart, so I knew Sam was wrong about him.

"Yessir," I said, and I hugged his big barrel chest. And even though things have been a little weird between us lately had, I felt myself getting all choked up. Sam has always been so nice to me. He is the only man who I have ever felt cared about me at all. Before Brian anyway.

I said goodbye and walked all the way down to the community college. It was full of people my age and I imagined myself walking around with them, a cool tote bag over my arm full of notebooks, feeling like I had my whole future in front of me. I took a course catalog with me and flipped through it when I got back to the apartment. It felt like a Choose Your Own Adventure book. I could be an accountant or a graphic designer or even an interior decorator. There were so many options it made my head spin. I spent the afternoon imagining each of them.

"What is that?" Brian asked when he got home.

"The college catalog," I told him, excited, holding it out for him to see the cover. "I finally quit Sam's." I expected him to be happy that I'd done what he'd told me to. I thought maybe he'd even look at the classes with me and help me pick, but instead he threw his stuff down on the counter.

"Brian?" I called out. I was already starting to feel nervous. I'd expected him to smile at the very least, but he seemed angry, slamming

things around in the refrigerator and finally pulling out a can of Coke and opening it. "Are you okay?" I asked him as he guzzled from the can. When he finally put it down, he looked at me in disgust.

"How are you going to go to college?" he said, and the floor dropped out from below me.

"But I thought you said you'd help me?" My voice was shaking. I stood up. "You told me to quit my job."

"I said quit your job, sure. But I never said anything about college," he scoffed. "What are you going to put on the application? That you worked in a hardware store? That you graduated from high school three years ago?" He picked up the catalog and opened the lid of the garbage can, tossing it inside. I just stood there, totally numb. I felt like the world had stopped spinning. What was even happening? And then he just walked into the bathroom and shut the door.

I stood there frozen in place while he went and took a shower. As the water ran, I tiptoed into the kitchen and opened the trash can. I felt my heart beating inside my throat as I considered fishing it out. I listened for the water to stop. For the sound of the bathroom door. Instead, I very quietly closed the lid.

We didn't talk much after that. He even started acting more normal, making dinner for us. I questioned whether it had happened at all. It's hard to trust my memory now. I wish there was someone else in the room who could tell me I'm not going crazy, to put things in perspective. But there is no one to guide me, no one to tell me what is real. There is only Brian. Just us alone together in this apartment where I feel I can't take a step without it possibly being in the wrong direction.

I wish you'd write back, Constance. I feel like something is very wrong, and I don't know who to turn to. I think I've made a terrible mistake. I'm afraid this horrible feeling in my chest might open up and swallow me for good.

Please, read this. I need you.
Lost Girl

TWENTY-FIVE

The morning air is hot already in Alex's apartment, a layer of humidity coating her skin, making her feel sticky and uncomfortable as her eyes flutter open. It feels at first like any other hot summer morning in New York. But then she remembers.

Today is the day that Alex becomes a published writer.

With a quiver of nervous energy, she tosses the sheet off her legs. The sun beats in around the edges of the privacy curtains. She pulls them up, letting the hot summer light spill onto her bare walls.

She rushes to the shower. "Morning, Mildred, Percy," she says to her pigeons. They swivel and bob their heads at her from the bathroom window. The date still lingers with her, and as she steps into the shower, she swears she can smell Tom on her skin even though they haven't so much as kissed. Not yet. When she thinks about him, she can still feel the electrical charge between them. After all this time it feels good to be near someone again. As much as she doesn't want to let herself hope for anything more than that, not yet, Alex can't help herself.

A car swerves around the corner, laying on the horn as Alex crosses the street to the Bluebird. She rolls her eyes at the sound of summer road rage. It happens this way every year as soon as the heat becomes a weighted blanket. Across Manhattan the changeover is happening from early summer to deep hot summer. Every rich person will have fled by now to their home in the Hamptons, their month in the Greek islands, their grandfather's rustic cottage in Maine. It is only the people who are working hard, those who are struggling, and those who are new that are left wandering around the city dodging the tourists with aggravation in their bellies.

The air is humid and thick with cooking oil as Alex makes her way to the back corner of the Bluebird. Raymond is sitting in his usual spot, the crown of his head barely visible over the newspaper in his hands. As she gets closer, she sees that instead of his usual tabloid-sized *Daily* he is holding up a copy of the *Herald*. Her heart thuds. Her column must be in there. It's hard for her to even believe.

"There she is," Raymond says. "Our famous neighborhood advice columnist." He swivels the paper to show her the column printed with a small illustration of her face next to it. Alex looks in wonder at the words, *her* words printed on the page for the whole city, the whole country to see.

"He bought his own copy, that's how excited he was," Janice says.

"You did a great job, Alexis," Raymond says. His wide hand pats her on the shoulder as she sits down next to him. "I don't know how you did it. I could never have that kind of patience or insight. I would have just told them to stop whining and get over themselves."

"It was beautiful," Janice agrees. "He had tears in his eyes."

"That was from the toast burning." Raymond dismisses her with a wave. "Practically smoked us all out."

"Well, that's because someone likes it extra crispy." Janice clears her throat, glancing at the black crumbs left on Raymond's plate, then says to Alex, "Usual?"

Alex's stomach rumbles. She can feel last night's slight wine hangover behind her eyes. "Actually, I'll have what he's having," she says, pointing at Raymond's mushroom and cheese omelet. Janice's tattooed eyebrows shoot up her forehead, but she writes it on a slip and passes it back through the window to the kitchen.

"What's different about her?" Janice says, putting down a fresh mug of coffee in front of Alex. "Besides her adventurous order."

Raymond also turns to stare. "You're right, there is something. Maybe it's just her sudden fame?"

"Is that it?" Janice asks. They both stare until Alex breaks.

"Fine, stop torturing me. I went on a date!" Alex admits, covering her face with her hands as soon as she says it.

"I knew it!" Raymond slaps the paper against the counter.

"No, you didn't," Janice says, grinning. "*I* knew it. Didn't I say?"

"I did, I did. I just couldn't put my finger on it."

"A date? Alex! How could you have kept this new development from us?" Janice asks. "Who is he?"

"He works at the building across from the *Herald*," Alex says quietly, already wishing she hadn't told them. "We met at the coffee shop across the street. He was working late too."

"A banker?" Janice scrunches up her nose. "I never liked those finance types. You think they're just boring but they're actually depraved."

"Who's paranoid now?" Raymond coughs. As usual, his T-shirt is covered with toast crumbs. "Nothing wrong with having a nice normal job."

Alex leans over the counter, blocking them from starting one of their arguments. "Yeah, he works at Excelsior Bank, but I get the feeling he doesn't like it. He did tell me something interesting about Howard Demetri though. Something potentially damaging."

"Oh, really?" Raymond says. Both of them bend toward her to hear.

"What did you find out?" Janice asks.

A man far down the counter waves a hand at Janice. "Hey! Are you going to take our order?"

She returns his request with a look of death. "I said I'll be right there. So how does he know Howard?"

"Well, he doesn't. Not really. But his office is right across from Howard's office and apparently he's seen Howard in there when he's working late."

"So the man works hard? That's to be admired," Raymond says.

"*With* someone," Alex says meaningfully.

"And?" Raymond is not getting the hint.

"I think she means the man is having sex in his office, Ray," Janice hisses loudly enough for the rest of the diner to tune in. Raymond's toast stops halfway to his mouth.

"Yes, he says he saw Howard and a woman on his desk. And it wasn't just once."

"Very interesting. Did he see who the woman was?"

"No, he couldn't see her very well. But I don't think it was Regina—Howard's wife."

"So, he's having an affair. That's a very interesting development. Maybe you could get your friend to stay late again, and he could find out who it is. We could stake out the place—"

"No, absolutely not, Ray. I am not involving Tom."

"Oh, his name is Tommmm." Janice's eyebrows waggle.

"Just because your new boyfriend saw something by accident doesn't mean he isn't involved now. He can be helpful to us, Alexis." Raymond pushes his plate to the edge of the counter. "More toast please, Janice."

"Wait, what did you just say?" Alex asks, her heart suddenly thumping.

"More toast?" Raymond looks confused.

"No, before that." Something laps at the edge of Alex's brain.

"He stumbled on someone having sex by accident?" Raymond asks, still confused.

"Yes, exactly," Alex says, thinking of the indentation on Howard's ring finger and the angry late-night phone call she'd overheard. The thought fills her with anxiety. Maybe it wasn't some disgruntled recipient of one of her columns who killed Francis Keen after all. Could she have seen something at the office, something she wasn't supposed to?

"What if Francis stayed late in the office one night, reading through those stacks of letters . . . ?" Alex begins.

"And somehow stumbled upon Howard having an affair," Janice finishes, tapping her pen against her chin.

"Exactly."

"Then we'd have a motive," Raymond says. "Can you even believe it? Maybe the main suspect has been sitting up there this whole time in the editor in chief's office." His voice rises with excitement.

"All you need to do is find proof," Janice says. "You need an ally, someone who's been there for a while who can give you more evidence."

"You guys, I really don't want to lose my job," Alex protests.

"And you'll have to be able to give them something, too, in exchange for information," Raymond says, drumming his fingers on the counter. "These things never come free."

TWENTY-SIX

When Alex walks into the *Herald* on Monday morning, something in the air of the office has shifted. The first difference is Jonathan, who actually lifts his head from his phone to look at her, an inscrutable expression on his face. He's not the only one. The sounds of keyboards and chatter stop as soon as she enters the newsroom. People's heads snap up from their monitors. She watches, confused, as colleagues she's never spoken to, who have kept their distance since she started working to the point where Alex felt nearly invisible, follow her with their eyes as she walks toward her office.

Her anxiety grows as she walks past them. Do they know something she doesn't? Jonathan rushes through the newsroom after her. "Howard wants to talk to you later," he says breathlessly. "Is it all right if I send him to your office?"

"Of course," Alex says, very anxious now. *He's going to fire me,* she thinks with sudden clarity as she continues through the newsroom. *The reception for the column was terrible.* For the first time she feels relieved to disappear into the isolated hallway and to shut herself in her remote office.

She hasn't even sat down at her desk when her office door swings open.

"Congratulations on your first column, Alex," Lucy says, letting herself in. Before Alex can get irritated that Lucy didn't knock, she notices that she's holding two paper cups from the café across the street. "Americano, right? With a splash of half-and-half?"

"How did you know?" Alex takes the coffee from her and sits down.

"Us assistants have our sources." Lucy smiles mischievously. "Oh, and I got you a muffin too. Chocolate chip." Alex cringes inwardly. She must have seen the sad remnants of her dinner last week and thought it was something Alex actually enjoyed.

"Thank you so much, Lucy. So thoughtful."

"You must be so happy that's it's done so well," Lucy says.

"What? It has?"

"I mean, I think so, it's everywhere. All over social. I've had people who don't even know I work with you post about it."

"You have?" Alex says, hiding her discomfort by taking a sip of coffee. The whole thing should have adrenaline surging through her, but instead she feels a strange flatness. Maybe she is just too tired to fully appreciate it. Alex knows that there is something else too. There is a larger part of her that worries that it was just a fluke. That she won't be able to sustain it week after week and, if she's lucky, year after year. That eventually she'll be found out.

"Anything else I can do for you before I take these rejects down into storage?" Lucy asks, picking up a bin of discarded envelopes.

"No, you've done so much already, Lucy. I really appreciate it."

There is a noise in the hall, the tap of shoes on the linoleum drawing closer.

"Do you think that's Howard?" Lucy says, her eyes wide.

"It could be. He said he wanted to stop by."

"Why didn't you tell me?" she hisses. Alex can see the rapid rise and fall of Lucy's chest.

It's a strange thing to say, Alex thinks. Why should it matter what Alex tells her? But Lucy is turning around the office looking for another way out. "Are you okay?" Alex asks.

There is a knock on the door. Howard's voice, low and distinctive: "Alex! May I come in?"

"Alex, please. I don't want him to see me." Lucy's voice is brittle, panicked. At the last second Alex moves her legs out of the space under her desk. *What the hell is going on?*

Alex doesn't have time to make sense of it. Whatever the reason, her assistant is terrified of Howard Demetri.

"Quick, under here," she whispers. Lucy drops to the ground, curling up under the desk.

Thank you, she mouths.

"Yes, of course," Alex calls out as Howard slowly opens her office door. He steps inside, looking around as if he expects someone else to be there. Alex makes a show of looking up from her computer and giving him her most natural fake smile.

"May I?" he asks, and without waiting for an answer, he takes the chair from the corner and pulls it to the front of Alex's desk. He sits and crosses one long leg over the other. If Howard has any embarrassment about cornering her in the hallway the other night, he makes no sign of it. Maybe he doesn't even remember he was there. She thinks of the smell of whiskey, the way he could barely keep himself upright. She glances at his hand. The ring finger is still bare.

Howard clears his throat, settling back into the chair and giving her a secretive smile. "Do you know how many people have read your first column, Alex?"

She shakes her head.

"Your first Dear Constance letter has been viewed more than a hundred thousand times since yesterday. This puts it in the top five articles on the whole website. It's being shared with people in countries all around the world."

"Wow, that's great."

"Congratulations, Alex. You've done a remarkable job with the first column. Already well on your way to making your mark at the *Herald*." He breaks into a rare grin. He's truly a handsome man. She wonders if he is able to lure women in with that smile.

"Thank you, sir," she says uncomfortably.

"Are you all right, Alex?" He studies her. "You don't look particularly pleased. I would think this would be a relief to you." The truth is that Alex doesn't feel relieved. She feels exposed. Between the strange threatening letters and Howard's erratic behavior, and now Lucy quivering under her desk, this job is causing her more stress than she thought possible when she signed on.

But she shakes the frown from her face. "I'm thrilled. Really. I'm just worried about keeping it up." She looks him in the eyes deliberately as she continues. "I care so much about Francis's legacy. I want to do right by her."

He gives her a tight smile. "If your next letter is anything like your first, I don't think that's a worry. Off to a great start, Alex. Francis would be proud."

In her peripheral lower vision, she can see Lucy's hands clasped around her legs. Her tights today are printed with little multicolored stars. She is so young. So vulnerable. Alex looks back across her desk at Howard, her heart pounding, wondering suddenly if it is possible that Lucy's fear and Howard's affair are connected.

"Thank you for giving me the opportunity," Alex says. "I know so many women weren't so lucky."

"Well, I'll leave you to it." Howard slaps his thighs and stands up. "Oh, and Alex, take some time to relish this success. You don't need to burn the candle at both ends." He nods at the two coffee cups sitting on top of her desk. Alex flinches. "It's important to have you well rested. Francis always said that nothing good comes from staying late."

Alex looks at him, alarmed, but she doesn't have time to dissect that last comment. As soon as the door closes behind him, Lucy lets out a sob.

TWENTY-SEVEN

"Lucy! Oh my God. What's wrong?" Alex ducks down, kneeling next to her assistant. But Lucy's face is buried in her knees. Her shoulders quiver. "Please tell me."

"I'm sorry, Alex," she sniffles. "I know I must seem insane."

"No. You just seem upset. I want to know what's going on. Lucy, what happened between you and Howard?"

"Nothing, I—" Lucy finally looks up, her face swollen from crying. Trails of gray mascara cling to her cheeks. Lucy doesn't just look upset, she looks terrified.

"What is it?" Alex asks, a knot forming in her stomach. She reaches out and puts her hand awkwardly on her shoulder. "Please, you can tell me."

Lucy pulls herself out of the cavity and stands up, looking to make sure the door is shut. She turns back to Alex and says nearly in a whisper, "It's just that Howard Demetri isn't the great guy you might think he is."

"In what way?" Alex asks. She thinks about the angry phone call and the clenched fist she saw through the crack in the blinds. The weaving drunk Howard she ran into in the hallway at night. There was also what Tom told her about the woman.

Lucy leans forward, her eyes looking impossibly large and round. "He has another side to him, one that is—" She glances once more at the door, her face twisted in fear. She lowers her voice. "Dangerous. For women, you know?"

A shiver starts in the back of Alex's skull and spreads up through her hair. Could it be true? But she knows that of course it could be. Look at all of the powerful men who by all accounts seemed fine, even like exemplary leaders, but who were predators in secret. Is there anything to say that Howard Demetri couldn't be one of them?

"What has he done?" Alex asks, a sinking feeling in her chest.

Lucy's voice is so quiet Alex has to lean over her desk to hear it. "He came to visit me, down in the mailroom. He . . . made a pass at me. I didn't feel like I could turn him down, Alex. There's no one down there, you know? He said I would lose my job."

Alex realizes she's been holding her breath. She slowly releases it. "That's so terrible. To feel threatened at work. I'm so sorry, Lucy, I had no idea." But maybe she is being naive. It happens all the time like this, doesn't it? Powerful men taking advantage.

"I'm not the only one," Lucy says darkly. She's stopped crying now but her voice is still raw. "There was another girl in the mailroom, Veronica. Howard would go down there and pay her visits when she was all alone. This was a while ago, back when I was new here. Before I knew."

"What happened to her? Is she okay?" Alex can feel Lucy's fear.

"I don't know. Only a week or two later she didn't show up to work. No one knows where she went."

"That's too much for anyone to have to go through. I am so sorry, Lucy. There has to be something we can do."

A sob escapes Lucy's throat. "Oh God, please do not tell anyone about this. It would ruin me. I can't lose this job." Alex is alarmed by the outburst. She goes around her desk and puts an arm around Lucy's small shoulders.

The idea of Howard getting away with something like that infuriates her. "I'm sure they wouldn't fire you if you went to HR and explained to them—"

"No!" Lucy draws back and looks at Alex, panicked. "No. I cannot go to HR. And you can't either. You have to promise me. Oh my God."

Her chest rises and falls so rapidly that Alex worries she might start to hyperventilate.

"Okay, no, I won't, Lucy. I promise. Here." She reaches for a water bottle she'd taken from the break room earlier. Lucy takes it from her and drinks noisily. "I'll make sure to warn you if I see him," Alex says, feeling helpless. It isn't enough, not nearly. But Lucy nods gratefully.

"Thanks, Alex. I'm so glad you're here. It's been such a hard time at the office since Francis." She drinks several more gulps of water and coughs. The girl is obviously traumatized by her boss dying, and now this. It is too much for someone so young to deal with. Lucy pulls away, giving a loud sniffle and dabbing at her eyes.

"But can you be sure to tell me if anything else happens that I should know about? And will you promise to go to HR if he does anything else to you?"

Lucy glances once more toward the door. "Of course," she says, not very convincingly. "I should get going."

"Of course." Alex watches Lucy's back as she disappears into the hallway. She seems so young, so vulnerable, that Alex finds a lump forming in her own throat. She can relate to Lucy. There is a kind of bravery that you must possess to come to this city with nothing and no one, a certain amount of having nothing to lose.

Dear Constance,

Brian and I went to a movie last night. It started off good. I wore a dress he bought me. It's red and short and I knew it would make me cold in the theater, but it was worth it, I thought, for those few minutes while we were getting ready in front of the mirror together. I put on my full makeup. Then I stood there and watched him shave, using some sort of good-smelling shaving cream out of a fancy bottle. When he was done, he stopped and admired us. "People will think that's an attractive couple," he murmured, pulling me tight to him. "They'll be so jealous."

He'd told me to buy the movie tickets. I was trying to impress him so I picked the one that just came out by some edgy director I thought he'd like, even though the Sense and Sensibility *remake would have been my actual choice. I didn't realize until it had started that the movie was about a woman who cheats on her husband.*

"Why did you want to see that?" he asked me right afterward, not trying to hide his disgust.

"I'm sorry, I thought you'd like it," I insisted. All I'd known before was that it was some sort of thriller, and I know Brian likes them. But on our way out of the theater he was quiet like he was annoyed with me. We walked toward the parking lot in the dark and he wasn't talking, and he'd put his hands into his pockets instead of holding mine. He asked me again why I would want to go see a movie like that.

"Do you want to cheat on me?" he asked, his eyes on the street in front of him.

"No, Brian. God, no. I didn't even know what the movie was about," I said, pulling on his arm, like I could make him snap out of it and bring him back to the person I know. But he just stared straight ahead like he didn't believe me. He shook me off and started walking so fast that I had to run to keep up with him. He ducked around the corner. It was dark on the street, and I was

afraid if he went too far ahead, I'd lose him. Or that he'd get to the car and drive off without me, leaving me downtown with no way to get home.

"Brian," I yelled out, begging him to stop and talk to me. I was panicking, thinking that I made a mistake, that I'd hurt his feelings or unknowingly told him something I didn't mean to. He was being a giant baby, I thought, but I didn't say anything. How could I when he was so hurt? Finally, he stopped dead in his tracks and turned back to me.

"What?" He said it like he hated me. I didn't say anything after that. I just followed him to the car. He was mad at me all night. We picked up takeout on the way home and he would barely look at me. "I just don't get it," he said once, slamming his hands on the steering wheel. I watched the headlights hit his face and wondered what had happened.

I just let my head rest on the seat belt and watched the town that I grew up in flash past the window. I tried to make myself small until it passed.

Did I do something wrong? Was I really not being sensitive to his needs? Selfish? It was just a movie, but now I am questioning everything. If I knew things were okay, I could rest. But I can't. It chews on my insides and makes it so I can't sleep.

I waited awake in bed until morning. But this time, instead of making breakfast and putting on the radio like he normally does, he drove off in his truck, leaving me here for I don't know how long.

I feel so alone. I need him to tell me it's going to be okay, but he won't. He won't even look at me. And now that we live together, I feel like things are miserable and somehow they are all my fault. If you are reading this at all, please send me some sort of sign. I have no one to talk to. Constance, I'm begging you.

Please read this,
Lost Girl

TWENTY-EIGHT

The text from Tom comes in the afternoon.

Shakespeare in the Park? They're doing Macbeth.

Alex has been distracted all day, replaying the situation with Lucy. She has avoided the newsroom today, not wanting to see Howard at his desk pretending to be some upstanding moral leader.

But she's been wondering when Tom would text her again. A part of her has been hoping he wouldn't, that their date was a one-off and her life will remain simple, uncluttered by the complications of a relationship. But the nonlogical, less-thinking force in her brain has been waiting for his message, has craved nothing more since their very first meeting than to just be near him again.

She hesitates. A second date with Tom means moving toward something else, something she can't come back from, something she worries she won't want to.

When? she replies, her heart beating faster as the bubble appears on her screen, starting and stopping several times.

Tonight?

Is it too brazen to suggest something so last-minute, or is it just spontaneous? She isn't sure. It doesn't matter, she decides, remembering the electricity she felt when they said good night. The way their lips nearly brushed as the lights from the restaurant played on their faces is all that is on her mind when she replies, quickly and without thinking:

Sure.

Again, Tom is already there when she arrives, leaning casually against a stone gate at the edge of Central Park. He's wearing one of his suits in a textured navy linen, cut slim. His white shirt is unbuttoned at the neck, which suggests he removed his tie before coming to meet her. They embrace quickly.

"I came straight from work," he says as he pulls away, glancing down at his clothes.

"You look good in a suit," she replies, fighting the urge to reach out and touch him. "I've never been here before."

He looks at her, surprised. "I would have thought a cultured woman like you would have been to Shakespeare in the Park before, especially as you live so close. It's such a New York institution."

"There are quite a few New York things I haven't done," Alex says, feeling slightly embarrassed. "I guess I've let some of the things I always wanted to do here slide. I've just been focused on work." *And staying out of sight.* She glances around nervously as they join the crowd moving toward the amphitheater. People look relaxed and glowy, happy to be in New York City on a beautiful summer evening. She allows herself to get swept down the path with them, to appreciate participating. "I've actually never seen *Macbeth* at all. I just read it in high school English," she admits.

"Honestly, when I was younger, I always thought Shakespeare was unbelievably boring. I felt like the people who said they liked his plays must be pretending."

She laughs. "What changed your mind?"

"Would you laugh if I told you it was all those audiobooks?" He glances sideways at her, a crooked smile appearing on his face.

"Maybe?" She smiles back.

"When I listen to the classics, I don't know, it's like I can hear them in a way I could never read them. Scenes and people appear in my mind. There is a melody to it. I can close my eyes and see it. Obviously just the way Shakespeare intended." He laughs.

"Oh, I don't know. He's pretty lucky to still be relevant, if you ask me," she says.

He grins. They've come around to the entrance to the stage.

"Here we are." He shows a barcode to the attendant. How different Tom is, Alex thinks again. His seemingly recent interest in old literature. His curiosity about, well, everything. Including her boss. She tries to push the dark cloud of Howard Demetri and his affairs from her mind. Tonight, for once in her life, she wants to just be Alex Marks, a normal, successful woman on a date with an attractive and interesting man who, she notes as the usher shows them to their row in the front of the theater. She sits down, feeling excited about having a new experience for a change. She feels for the first time like she has made it.

She glances behind her at the rows and rows of people, their faces illuminated by the house lights. So many faces, she can't take them all in. Down here, anyone could be watching her. As she looks at them, everything dims and enthusiastic voices fade to a ripple of murmurs and then silence. She begins to relax.

It's a bleak play, the story more morbid than she'd ever picked up on back in school. Intense and surprisingly engaging.

Their proximity to the stage means that she is able to see each actor's changing expressions. It's incredible watching a person get absorbed into a role, Alex thinks, mesmerized. Actors are such amazing liars; they must have to convince even themselves.

The sky beyond the stage has gone electric cobalt blue as the sun drops beyond the edge of the amphitheater. She glances at Tom. The angular planes of his face lit by the glow of the stage. He is rapt with interest as he follows along, trailing the movements of the actors. She is distracted from it all by her proximity to him. It's been so long since she's sat quietly next to someone. Why has she waited so long? What has she been so afraid of? Even as she tries not to stare at him, she notices the rise and fall of his chest beneath his shirt. His hand rests in his lap. She imagines herself reaching for it, their fingers entwining. It makes her shiver. He glances at her now, and she smiles at him and forces her eyes back to the actors onstage. The ones being paid to pretend.

Macbeth crosses the stage. His eyes are empty when he scans the crowd.

> *Infected be the air whereon they ride,*
> *And damned all those that trust them.*

The sky is a deep nighttime blue when they emerge from the amphitheater, the walkway in shadow. The crowd thins as they cut across the park, away from the entrance. They are talking and she pays no attention to where they are going until the path grows black under her feet and the trees start to knot above them. She is walking closer to Tom now as the trail in front of them narrows. They are no longer talking, their heavy breathing audible from the climb up the path. Their fingertips brush in the dark. He's taken her a way she doesn't know. Normally she tries to stay off the smaller paths. There can be strange people, unpleasant surprises or worse. She can't see his face anymore. She can't quell the cold hammering of her heart as she realizes how little she knows about Tom. Alex has tried not to ingest the stories of women murdered in the park, but they are bubbling up now. The bodies found in the woods. She can see it now on the front page of the *Daily*: the woman who got murdered on a second date.

The brush to one side recedes and they come to a clearing next to the pond. The full sky of city lights reflects in its surface, a magnificent sparkling city above and below that makes her breath catch. There is the footbridge all lit up; it spans the pond. Above the tree line the lights of the buildings that fringe the park. All of it reflects in the water below.

His hand reaches for hers, their fingers firmly interlace. She turns away from the lights toward him. The fear melts away. How many nights has she lain awake wishing her life was exactly this? She has spent enough time running from the past. She wants to be here now, to stake her claim on this glorious city.

She doesn't try to stop him. His other hand is at her face, drawing her toward him. She completely gives in to the feeling of it, letting him pull her closer. His hand is firm but gentle against the nape of her neck. She bends her neck back as their lips meet, slowly at first and then faster. The thrill of it warms her body, makes the dangers dissolve. And when they finally draw away from each other and begin walking down the path toward the bright lights of Columbus Circle, she can't remember being afraid at all.

TWENTY-NINE

The date with Tom did a good job of distracting her, almost eclipsing all of the office drama. But as soon as the elevator doors seal shut behind her on Tuesday morning, it returns. All of her anxiety rushes back as she steps into the office. Howard and his disgusting advances on her poor assistant, the threatening letter, and then, of course, humming ominously in the background, Francis Keen's murder. Alex isn't sure she can keep her head down and continue working, given what she now knows about Howard.

Alex stops dead in her tracks when she sees the woman standing in front of Jonathan's desk. She takes in the haughty straightness of her spine, the flowy white pants that hang elegantly from a thin snakeskin belt about her thin hips. Her white-blond hair is as thick and straight as one of Alex's childhood Barbie dolls. The Chanel slingbacks on her narrow feet tap impatiently. Beyond her, standing rigidly at the reception desk, Jonathan's face pales.

"Regina! It's so good to see you," he says with terror in his eyes.

"Oh, is it, Jonathan?" Regina responds, her tone terrifyingly cold.

"What can I help you with?" he asks primly. His eyes fall on Alex now. For the first time he doesn't look disappointed to see her there. He looks almost relieved.

"I'm here to see my husband," she says, taking her jacket off. More

Chanel from the look of it, Alex thinks. Jonathan looks confused. Why is Regina at the office asking after her own husband?

"He hasn't been in yet today. I can let him know you stopped by—"

Regina ignores him. Alex watches as she steps past the desk toward the newsroom.

"Well, if you don't mind, I'll just go wait in his office for him to return," she says. Her voice remains light, but there is an underlying threat that is impossible to ignore.

"Wouldn't you be more comfortable waiting out here, or maybe in the café across the street?" Jonathan asks hopefully.

Regina continues her march around the front desk toward the newsroom. "Oh, and I'll have a coffee," she calls over her shoulder. "A latte, with oat milk."

Jonathan turns to Alex panicked. "I have no idea where Howard is," he hisses at her. "What the hell am I supposed to do?" His eyes focus on Alex, and she sees it is all about to become her problem too.

"I'll make her a coffee," Alex offers, seizing this serendipitous opportunity to get on Jonathan's good side.

"You'd really do that?" he says. He looks like he might start to cry. "I need to go look for him. He'll hate that I've let her go back to his office while he isn't there."

"Of course I'll do it. Whatever you need," Alex says. Ingratiating herself with Jonathan in his time of need could have its perks, she realizes. Who else has access to Howard Demetri's planner? Who else could tell her where he goes and when? And, most importantly, *with whom*.

"Thank you, Alex. I owe you."

Yes, you do, Alex thinks, giving him a smile and turning toward the office kitchen.

THIRTY

Alex can't find any oat milk, but she does stumble on a box of something far back inside one of the kitchen cabinets that claims to be flavored like a French vanilla cappuccino. Regina will hate it, Alex is sure, but it will have to do. She puts a coffee pod in the machine and presses the button.

While she waits for it to brew, Alex walks back and forth across the tiny kitchen already overwhelmed by the morning she's had. On the bulletin board behind the coffeepot, Francis Keen looks out from her front-page obituary photo, a wry smile on her face.

Alex unpins the obit from the bulletin board. The newsprint is already fragile after less than a year. It's interesting about newspaper, how brittle it becomes. She flips the paper over, to look below the fold where Francis's obituary is written.

Alex hasn't read the obituary since it came out last year. Her chest is tight as she rereads the details of Francis's life: her devotion to the column, her love of gardening and animals and long walks. Alex feels a kinship with Francis all over again. She wishes that Francis were here now to help her through this. Of course, if Francis *were* here, Alex would be sitting at the Bluebird right now ready to drag herself back to her apartment to write copy for the drug company.

As she keeps reading, something makes her breath catch. She goes back to the beginning of a quote from Howard Demetri and rereads it: "Francis could be impatient at times. She suffered no fools, as my mom always says. But she also had this innate sense of wisdom. She really listened. It was never about placating. If someone was struggling, there was no pity; she always said pity was a waste. There was only empathy with Francis. You really felt like she was living your struggles with you."

She turns the words over inside her head. Didn't she just hear them somewhere? They are there, just over the horizon of her memory. If only she could see who was saying them.

"Alex," Jonathan hisses from the doorway, his eyes wide and panicked. "She's waiting."

"No luck finding Howard?" Alex says, hoping he doesn't notice as she quickly pins the obit back on the board. He shakes his head.

"I am one hundred percent fucked," he says, his eyelashes fluttering like he might pass out.

"Howard will understand," Alex assures him. "Besides, it's not like it's your fault he's missing. What are you supposed to do?"

"It's not Howard I'm worried about," he says, his eyes darting over his shoulder. "You know Regina's dad owns this whole company? This whole building! She could have me fired quicker than it takes for her to pick up that black pebble-leather Birkin."

Alex did not know this. She scrambles to fix the coffee now, for herself as much as for Jonathan, pouring it into a nicer cup and putting it on a saucer.

"Alex, can you just keep her company for a minute? While I go look for him, again?" He looks desperate.

"I don't think she'll really want to hang out with me, but I can try."

"Thank you, Alex. I don't want her digging around in his office and getting me into trouble." A sheen has started on his forehead. What is in Howard's office that could possibly get Jonathan in trouble? She gives him a quick nod. He looks like he might actually hug her for a second, but changes his mind and runs out into the newsroom to search for Howard.

When Alex brings the coffee to Howard's office, Regina is sitting in his chair, her legs stretched out in front of her. Makes sense now, Alex thinks, that she'd choose his chair and not the one facing his desk that's for visitors. No wonder Regina acts like she owns the place. She actually does.

Alex takes a deep breath, clenches her teeth into her most gracious smile, and pushes through the glass door. Regina's perfect face falls when Alex walks in, clearly disappointed she is not Howard or anyone important. "Are you new?" Regina asks derisively, giving Alex a curt once-over as she places the cup before her on the edge of Howard's desk. "I don't remember you."

"Yes, I'm Alex, the new Dear Constance columnist."

Regina's face snaps up now, studying Alex. "You're an interesting choice for a replacement," she says, leaning back in the chair and looking amused. Regina gestures to the chair across from Howard's desk. Her ring is hard to miss, a diamond cut to nearly the width of her finger, its facets cleaner and clearer than glass. Alex wonders if Regina knows her husband is no longer wearing his own wedding band.

Not wanting to, Alex drops into the chair. "Thank you?"

Regina narrows her wide-set eyes and gives Alex a tight smile. "You truly came out of nowhere, didn't you? You walked into this building and went straight to a corner office. Not exactly a conventional career path." Alex smiles uncomfortably. Regina reminds her of a snake, waiting and watching for her to make a wrong move so that she can strike.

"I wasn't sure what Howard was doing hiring you at first, but he seemed dead set on it. Strange, really." She laughs humorlessly. "I'm a bit envious, honestly. I've been pestering him to introduce me, and now here you are." She picks up the coffee and leans back, looking at Alex coolly.

"No. It's definitely not conventional," Alex admits, trying not to squirm. "But then again, I'm not sure an advice columnist ever has a very linear career path. I think Howard wanted someone with respect for the column, someone who could grow with it, who could start fresh."

"So new and with such insight into the mind of the editor in chief." She smirks like she knows something Alex doesn't. "You know my father has to approve everyone Howard hires. He's the reason Howard has this job at all."

Alex says nothing. Despite her new suspicions about her boss, she has seen glimmers of the man everyone else raves about. His career can't be entirely due to nepotism.

"It was quite the feat Howard pulled off, convincing my father you were the right one for the job. He didn't believe Howard that you'd be a good choice." She shakes her finger at Alex like she's teasing, but Alex can tell she is not. "You really can write, though. I'll give you that. Maybe better than Francis could. So far you've proven Daddy wrong."

"I'm so glad," Alex says humbly. Why is Regina power-tripping and praising her? This whole interaction is feeling like some sort of test. One she isn't sure she can pass.

Regina laughs bitterly. "Don't be. He hates to be proven wrong. But don't you worry. When you succeed, they'll find a way to take all the credit. That's just how men are."

Now her irises dart toward the newsroom, scanning for Howard. *She's nervous,* Alex realizes. She wonders how close of a tab Regina keeps on her husband. Is she trying to maintain control over something she's afraid she's lost? She probably isn't used to Howard not being right where she can find him. Regina regains her composure in an instant, becoming hard and confident again.

"My great-grandfather made this the greatest newspaper in the country," Regina says, glancing around the office smugly as if she had built it herself.

"That's quite the journalistic legacy for us all to live up to," Alex says carefully.

Regina snorts, a surprisingly unrefined sound coming out of her perfectly straight little nose. "Oh, please. It wasn't because he cared about journalism. This is a business first and foremost. He'd have sold it for scrap if he thought that would be more profitable to him, to our family. It's in our blood, business, negotiation. My husband has benefited from it, and now so have you." Regina crosses her long legs, leaning back in the chair, enjoying the power dynamic.

"You know, this was actually going to be my desk at one time," she says, running her hand along the polished mahogany. "At least, I thought it was what I was told."

"What happened? You seem like you'd be a very formidable boss," Alex says, surprised.

"Thank you," Regina says, clearly taking it as a compliment. Looking at her in that chair, who could deny that she has the look of someone destined for power? But there is something cold about her. Regina is too calculating to do much to inspire. And Alex gets the feeling it isn't bringing people the news that drives her.

"Daddy couldn't picture a woman overseeing a newspaper. He literally couldn't imagine it. He never actually said it that way, not out loud. Of course, this was back in the nineties." She smiles hollowly.

"That must have been hard," Alex says, feeling a tug of pity for Regina. All the money in the world couldn't buy her a father's approval, or a place at the head of the table where she clearly saw herself.

"Oh, I think I made out all right, don't you?" she snaps, clearly uncomfortable with Alex's sympathy. "Besides, that's why I married Howard. I knew he would do a good job. And he has. So I don't mind, most of the time. What's that old adage, 'behind every good man' and all that crap?" Is she saying she married Howard to keep the family business in the family?

"We all have to make our compromises, don't we, *Alex*?" she says, emphasizing the name. "Brave choice for a girl. Family name, I assume?" Regina feels vulnerable, Alex thinks. She has shared more than she wanted to—Alex has that effect on people. And now Regina is turning the tables on her once again. Still, Alex's throat goes dry as she tries to formulate a response. She is saved at the last second by Jonathan, who appears leading a chagrined-looking Howard Demetri hustling back toward his office.

Thank you, Jonathan mouths at Alex, who gives a grateful nod.

"Oh, look, here he is," Alex says eagerly, standing up. "I'll leave you to it. I'm sure you have a lot to sort out."

"Lovely," Regina says. She doesn't give Alex another glance as she too stands up, her fingers trailing along the desk as she moves to the other side, relinquishing Howard's chair.

As Howard approaches his office, Alex watches the color drain from his face.

THIRTY-ONE

Later there is a knock on her office door.

"Come in," she calls out, looking up from her computer, surprised to see Jonathan's face peer around the edge of the doorframe.

"Jonathan! Hi." She stands up.

"Can I talk to you?" Jonathan asks, looking sheepish.

"Yes, come in." Alex starts to move another chair closer to her desk, but Jonathan makes an uncomfortable face, glancing around the office and then averting his eyes.

"Would you mind somewhere else?" He gestures at the hallway.

"Of course." Alex follows him all the way down the hall until they reach the door to the old stairwell.

"This okay? There's no one ever back here."

"Sure," Alex says, swallowing her fear of the staircase and following Jonathan through the fire door. Once they are on the landing, he turns to her apologetically.

"I'm sorry. Her—your—office still makes me feel really strange. It seems too soon to be in there with someone else somehow. I know that isn't nice for you to hear probably, but every time I set foot in there, I feel like I'm going to have a panic attack." The admission doesn't make her feel bad; she's grateful to have Jonathan sharing anything with her.

"Were you and Francis close?" Alex asks. She hasn't ever considered

Jonathan's relationship to Francis, but working at the front desk, he would have seen her every day. She wonders what he might be able to tell her about Francis's last days.

"I loved her," he says quickly. "There was a time when I felt like nobody but her understood me. She cared for me, too, but honestly, it was more me needing her than her needing me. I think I felt almost betrayed when she died."

Alex reaches out and places a hand gently on his shoulder. He doesn't flinch.

"It's so hard to lose the people who care for us. Or to see them replaced?" she says meaningfully.

Jonathan gives her a crooked smile, knowing he's being called out. He leans over and crosses his arms on the banister.

"You tried to make things hard for me," Alex says, unsure she can trust him. "When I started here."

"Just a little." He scrunches up his nose. "She was my favorite person in the universe. And I didn't like how Howard did it—so publicly. I didn't think Francis would have liked that."

Jonathan has been mean to her out of loyalty to Francis? Even if it made her life harder, Alex can kind of understand that. She allows herself to lean against the banister next to him. "I know. I was angry about the whole thing, too, honestly. I didn't know her personally like you did, but it felt off to me. The entire reason I filled out the application was to see what kind of screening they were using to choose her replacement. Well, that and a bottle of wine," she admits.

"You hate-applied." He smirks.

"You know, I think I did." Their laughter bounces through the stairwell.

"I'm glad you're the one who got the job, Alex. I'm sorry for being a dick. She was like an aunt to me. It's why I had a hard time accepting you."

"I can imagine," Alex says, self-doubt blooming in her chest. "Even *I* have had a hard time accepting me as her replacement."

"You're doing great," Jonathan says. The unexpected kindness of him saying so makes her want to cry.

"I feel like a mess. Francis seemed so calm, so together. Whereas I'm a"—she gestures at herself helplessly—"a total disaster. Who am I to give advice?"

Jonathan shakes his head. "Oh, please. Whatever image you have in your head of Francis, please just erase it. She was so far from having it all together. She had a bad temper sometimes. She swore like a sailor. And she could be impossible." He smiles at the memory. "Living some perfect life wouldn't have made her good at her job though, Alex. Empathy. The ability to imagine yourself in anyone else's life. That's what you have in common. I didn't want to admit it, but I could tell even before you turned in that first column that you were going to be good at this."

Now Alex is tearing up. "Thank you."

"Don't mention it. Anyway, I owe you for earlier. In case you couldn't tell, Regina absolutely hates me."

"Yeah, what is up with her?" She wipes her eyes on the sleeve of her shirt.

He sighs and rests his head on his arms for a moment. "Well, there was this one time I really fucked up."

"You!" Alex says in mock horror.

"Yeah." He cringes, lowering his voice to a near whisper. "I know. This was bad though. It was last year, just before Francis . . . I was making a dinner reservation for him at one of his favorite places. It was at this old hotel bar he likes to go to that is still somehow impossible to get a table at, but I kept calling and pulling every string and I finally snagged a spot for two."

He leans toward her. "Well, a couple of days prior Regina had come up to the office to meet him. She was super dressed up, so I thought they were going to one of their gala things. I said, as she was leaving, 'Don't worry, I booked your reservation for Wednesday night.'

"I knew as soon as she whipped around to look at me I had done something unspeakable. '*Excuse me?*' she said. I had this crazy bolt of recognition then. The reservation wasn't for her."

"What did you do?"

"I tried to backpedal, naturally. I felt so terrible. But she is too smart, I could see her putting things together. I think there was something that added up to her then, something about Howard."

"That he was having an affair."

"So, you've heard the rumors too?" Jonathan sighs. He puts his head in his hands for a few seconds, like he is hiding from the truth of it.

"Do you know who it was?" She is so close to the information she needs that she can almost taste it.

"No. The thing about Howard is he's always very, very discreet," Jonathan says. "I assumed he'd put an end to it. But then a few months later, he started looking really bad. He lost weight and his skin got that waxy look to it. The way it does now most of the time. You've seen it."

"Like he's drinking a lot?" Alex ventures meekly.

He nods, looking miserably down into the stairwell.

"But he didn't stop wearing his wedding ring until recently. He had it on when he interviewed me a couple of weeks ago," Alex says, confused.

"I know. I'm not sure what happened. They must have been trying to make it work and it all just fell apart. It can't be easy to be married to Regina."

"No," Alex agrees. "Do you like working here, Jonathan?"

"I don't think anyone has ever asked me that. Except my boyfriend, who is constantly trying to get me to quit."

"He thinks it's bad for you?"

"Look, this place is in transition. You have to understand I was devoted to this job before. I always thought it would be the place I stayed forever. Back before Francis died I was happy with that. But there has been a real shift. The vibe has changed. Everything is different now, or at least feels different. I loved her, truly. It was her who kept me from getting fired during the whole Regina debacle. So to answer your question, yes and no."

"I wish I could have seen it then," Alex says.

"You would have liked it, I think." He looks down over the tops of his arms into the endless loop of the stairs. "So creepy back here, isn't it?"

"The architect died, apparently," Alex says, shuddering. A door opens and closes somewhere far below, echoing up through the opening.

"Oh God, how morbid. I never heard that." He straightens up and brushes the dust off his pant legs. "Well, duty calls, I suppose."

"No rest for the wicked," Alex says.

"Yes, I'm sure Regina would agree." He turns toward the door.

"Hey, Jonathan." Alex begins to follow him. "Where did you say you made the reservation for Howard?"

"I don't know why he always went to this place inside some old hotel." He makes a face. "I think the bar is called the Bird or the Wren or something."

"The Nest?" she asks, her heart pounding.

"Yeah, that's the one," he says as the door shuts behind him, echoing into the stairwell.

Before she follows him back into the hall, Alex pulls out her phone and texts Raymond.

Want to go out for a little fact-finding drink tonight?

THIRTY-TWO

Raymond is already standing on the corner of Eighty-Sixth Street when Alex gets there after work, rushing to arrive for their 8 p.m. meeting time. Instead of his typical T-shirt and jeans he's got on a dark-charcoal-colored suit. It is cut wide and boxy, a style that went out of fashion a good twenty years ago. He reminds her of the detectives in the eighties shows her mom would watch as reruns when she was little. The jacket is wrinkled and the shoulders bulge hollowly. She has a feeling from the way he shuffles back and forth that he's been there awhile already and his feet are getting tired. He lights up when he sees her approach.

"Is this some sort of a stakeout?" Raymond's eyes are sparkling.

"Kind of. More of a fact-finding mission," Alex says. "I heard from someone at work that Howard had a reservation at some old hotel bar with his mistress right before Francis died. And I found a matchbook inside Francis's desk with the same restaurant's name on the front."

"Ah, that is good deduction, Alexis." He rubs his palms together. "We're going to get to the bottom of it. And don't you worry, because I happen to be very good at this," Raymond assures her. Alex wonders if this was a bad idea. Behind them the lights of the Bluebird go off for the night.

"Good at what?" They turn around to find that Janice has slipped out of the diner and is standing in the doorway, a set of keys dangling from her finger.

"At getting information," Raymond says. "We're investigating something."

Alex interjects: "We are just going to ask some questions. But I have no idea if anything will come of it."

"Oh yeah? Where at?" Janice finishes locking the door.

"It's a bar inside the Temple Hotel. The Nest, it's called."

"I feel like I've heard of it." Raymond shakes his head.

"Oh, *I* know the Nest," Janice says cryptically.

"You do?" Alex is surprised.

"Yeah, was a very popular jazz bar back in the day. Used to be filled with celebrities. I knew a guy who worked as a server there. He used to sneak my sister and me in. Got wild in there."

"Wild?" Alex steps out into the street and raises her arm out into traffic to call a taxi.

"Oh, you know, drugs, sex, that sort of thing. Once I gave a tissue in the bathroom to a very famous actress whose boyfriend had broken up with her." She flaps a hand as if those are the types she always used to spend time with. "Best martini in the city though, and best jazz." She smiles at some secret memory of it. A cab screeches to a sudden stop in front of them.

"Well, good luck," Janice says a little sadly. Raymond grunts with the effort of getting himself into the back seat of the car. Janice watches from the curb, her apron dangling out of the side of her purse. "You know, the entrance to the Nest is almost impossible to find."

"Did you want to come with, Janice?" Alex asks. God help her. She's barely finished the invite before Janice is stepping into the street and hustling toward the open door of the taxi. "Okay, but only because the two of you clearly need all the help you can get."

She heaves herself into the car, slamming the door behind her. As they speed downtown a hard knot begins to form in Alex's stomach. Howard Demetri is her boss. She isn't sure she should be doing this at all, but the temptation to learn about Francis's last days is too strong.

She hopes that this will lead her somehow to the writer of her own threatening letter. That once she finds out who killed Francis, she will be free from the fear of it, able to move on in her work knowing that there is no connection.

"The Temple Hotel," Raymond calls to the driver.

"Now, tell me what we are trying to find out here," Janice says.

"We wonder if Francis caught Howard in an affair," Raymond says.

"Maybe he lured Francis to the hotel so he could threaten her some-place away from the *Herald*," Alex speculates. "He could have told her that her career was at stake."

"Or it could be that Francis found out that Howard was having a rendezvous at the hotel and confronted him there," Raymond continues.

On the other side of Alex, Janice digs in her purse and pulls out a shiny gold tube of the reddest lipstick Alex has ever seen.

"Do we have any clue who this younger woman is?" Janice asks.

Alex has been afraid that saying it out loud will make it more likely, and she desperately doesn't want it to be true. The thought of it all has been making her sick. She's had dreams about Howard cornering her in the hallway. Dreams that may have ended in something worse for those poor girls. "Apparently, he likes the girls in the mailroom."

"They're isolated there," Raymond says, shaking his head. "Easier to groom maybe."

"And to keep people from noticing," Janice says, blotting her lipstick on a tissue and putting it back into her bag.

"Good point," Alex says, thinking of her interaction with Regina that morning. Would she have known about these affairs? There was something about the anger in her that makes Alex think she might suspect something.

"We'll see what we can find," Raymond says, looking out the window as they drive down Broadway. She realizes that these two are quite comforting in their own strange ways. She wants them there with her. She might even need them.

THIRTY-THREE

They've been following Janice through the hotel for ages now, up flights of stairs and down marble hallways, past darkened conference rooms, until the crowds of tourists thin out and they are deep inside the hotel, walking quickly down a narrow hallway lined with gilded mirrors.

"Are we there yet?" Ray calls out, limping as he tries to catch up.

"You're sure it's way back here?" Alex asks as they weave around a row of potted palms. She is starting to get claustrophobic.

"This place is old-school, trust me. That's why it's called the Nest. They don't want just anyone finding it," Janice says without slowing her pace. "No interlopers. Or even worse, tourists. Ah-ha, this is the one," she calls back to them victoriously. They follow her up a small marble staircase and turn one last corner before emerging finally into a domed atrium. She takes them through an elaborately carved wooden wall into a soaring stone barroom. At the entrance they stop, gaping at the grand room.

"Whoa," Raymond says, taking in the human-sized granite fireplace that occupies nearly an entire wall. On the other end of the room a grand piano is being played by a man in a tuxedo. Between them is a long polished-mahogany bar, backed by a wall of windows through which the city lights glitter, blurred by hundreds of panes of beveled glass. There are only a few tables of people in the center. They sit in wingback club chairs, their drinks glowing warmly in front of them on small cocktail tables.

Alex has never seen anywhere like it. "I can't believe this is inside a hotel."

"Not so shabby, huh?" Janice says, obviously impressed with herself for finding it.

Raymond pulls on his jacket collar, straightening the front of his suit. He tries to seize control of the situation. "Listen, you two, we need a strategy. We get in. We get what we need. Then we get out."

Janice isn't paying attention. "Look, this is where my friend and I used to get the guys to order us drinks," she says, twirling in front of the bar. "We had no money to drink those Sazeracs and martinis, you know, so we had to resort to flirting with the rich guys. And this is where the dance floor used to be. Otherwise, it really hasn't changed much."

"Okay, long enough stroll down memory lane for you?" Raymond says. "We need to focus, you two. We're here on a mission."

"We have to at least order a drink," Alex says, eyeing a bright-green cocktail on one of the tables.

Janice nods. "Relax, Ray, it's a bar. Doesn't hurt to have a little fun while we're here." She pokes Alex in the ribcage and smiles conspiratorially. "How about a little ambience to set the mood? I'm going to see if that piano man takes requests." She charges away, beelining to the piano, a pep in her step Alex can't help but smile at.

"So, tell me what our main questions for this bartender are?"

"Okay, Ray. We need to find out what Howard was doing here before Francis died and who he was with." They settle onto two empty barstools.

"Look, it's like the Bluebird but with alcohol," Alex jokes. But Raymond's face is hard and vigilant, like he's on the job. His eyes follow the bartender as he stirs a dark drink with a long silver spoon, straining it into a glass with a single cube of ice. He twists an orange rind into it, so fresh that Alex can smell the spray of oils from the peel. He passes it to a server waiting with a silver tray.

"Can I help you?" the bartender asks, handing each of them a card with a list of cocktails. Alex and Raymond exchange a look.

"I'll have the Garden Gimlet," Alex says, hoping for the green drink she saw earlier.

"I'll do ... ah ... the ..." Ray flips over the bar menu. "Where's the beers on this thing?"

"He'll do the Stubborn Old-Fashioned," Alex reads from the menu. "Sound good?"

Raymond gives the bartender a nod and hands him the menu. "Smartass," Raymond mutters. Alex shrugs. They watch the bartender mix their drinks.

"We're here to see if you know anything about a guy," Ray says. The bartender doesn't look up as he pours a drink from a silver shaker through a strainer into a highball glass and finishes it with a sprig of rosemary.

"I wouldn't tell you if I did. Bartender's etiquette." He says it amiably enough, but Alex detects a sharpness to his voice. It makes her realize that directly questioning him is going to get them nowhere.

"He probably doesn't know him anyway," Alex says to Raymond loudly enough for the bartender to hear.

"Sure he does, he sees everyone who comes in here." Alex gives Raymond a meaningful look and he gets what she is trying to do. "You're right," he says, playing the part now. He leans back in his stool and turns toward her. "He wouldn't know Howard Demetri."

The bartender, who has been cutting the rind off a lemon with a paring knife, stops mid-slice. The tang of it hangs in the air as he gives them a long look.

"What name did you say?" He is acting different now, actually looking at them as he slides their finished drinks over the bar.

Raymond keeps his eyes on the man. "He was here the first week of October of last year. We think he was with a woman."

"We were hoping you could tell us who it was and what they were doing," Alex adds.

"Just one moment, please. Let me see what I can find out." He disappears around the side of the bar. She looks at Raymond and shrugs.

"You think he'll tell us?" Alex asks.

"I don't know. There's something off about him," Raymond says.

"I agree."

They sip their drinks. "How's yours?" Alex asks.

"Tastes like the man stirred potpourri into a vat of Lysol," he deadpans. Raymond looks more nervous than he has in the entire time she's known him. He pulls a packet of Tums from his breast pocket and drops a few into his mouth. He chews noisily and washes them down with his cocktail.

"Well, that was a bummer," Janice says, coming up behind them. "Can you believe it, he was offended? Said he doesn't *do* Taylor Swift." She shrugs. "Wouldn't know a classic if it bit him in the ass. What's going on here? Did we get what we need?"

"Not yet," Raymond says, eyeballing the entrance. "And I got a bad feeling about it."

The bartender comes out from around the back of the bar and they look up, watching as he is quickly followed by a giant cinder block of a man dressed in a black suit. As he moves toward them, Alex sees the wire loop around his ear.

"These are the patrons asking about some of our clientele," the bartender says, raising his eyebrows at them. Raymond's hand clenches on the edge of the bar. Alex is beginning to catch on. The larger man looms over them.

"What the hell is going on here?" Janice demands.

"Your friends have been overserved and need to leave."

"Nah, these two haven't had a drop. Look at them. They aren't even dancing."

The bartender leans forward onto the bar. "Why don't I call you a cab," he says firmly. His large forearms pulse on the bar between them.

"Back when Jimmy worked here, there is no way he would have let us get treated this way," Janice tells him. Alex cringes as the man looks down at her.

"I don't know a Jimmy, ma'am." The other man is stone-faced. "Why don't you all move along. Before I put in a call letting Mr. Demetri know you were here asking about him." Alex's mouth goes dry. She hadn't considered the effect saying Howard's name would have. She should have found a way to be more subtle.

"I will not. I have as much right to be here as anyone," Raymond says.

Janice chimes in: "Yeah, this is a public place. We've done nothing wrong." Janice's finger comes down square in the center of the man's giant chest. The man's hand moves toward his belt and Raymond steps back, spreading his arms out in surrender.

"No need to escalate things. I see where you are coming from."

"Let's go," Alex says. She feels the men's eyes boring into her back as she leads Janice and Raymond from the barroom. The upbeat tinkle of piano music follows them as they flee down the hallway.

"I don't remember this area," Alex says as they come into a small square atrium, its walls covered in stark abstract paintings.

"We must have gotten turned around." Janice stops and puts her finger to her lips, mumbling directions under her breath.

"Come on. Let's get out of here," Raymond says, uncomfortable.

"This looks right." Janice points them into another corridor. This one is darker than the others, lined with hotel rooms. The runner is plush beneath their feet as they follow it right, then left.

Raymond stops, peers back into the quiet hallway. "Do you two not hear anyone else?" he says. "I swear we're being tailed."

"Let's keep going," Alex says, distracted by worries of the large barman calling her boss. They take another turn. A maid's cart rolls into the hallway in front of them, blocking their path. They come to a sudden halt in front of it.

"Is that you, Ray?" A woman's voice comes from behind a pile of little travel bottles, a stack of individually wrapped hotel soaps.

"It is you." The woman is tiny and delicate. She is wearing a crisp red tunic and black pants, the uniform of Temple Hotel employees. "They said it was, but I didn't believe it. I didn't think you'd show your face here after everything." She eyeballs Alex and Janice.

"Evelyn?" Raymond gasps. "I didn't know you worked here."

She holds a squeegee out in front of her. "Well, got to do a lot more work to support the family now. Thanks to you."

Raymond stumbles backward, his trembling hands reaching back into space. Alex and Janice freeze, turning to watch the scene unfold.

"What's going on, Ray?" Janice hisses. "An old friend of yours?"

The woman gestures at Alex and Janice with the squeegee. "Who are your friends? Do they know what you did to Armond, to our family?"

Raymond looks helpless. "Please. I need you to know I never meant any of that to happen."

But she is having none of it. She advances on him. "Bullshit," she says, her delicate face screwing up into a venomous rage. "You're a disgrace."

"I'm sorry, Evelyn." Raymond's voice is hoarse. "You know I loved him."

She scoffs at this, waving the squeegee. The edge of it shakes in her hand as she points it toward the loose skin of his neck. "Then why did you let him die?" Her voice is a blade dropping through the air.

Raymond has gone pale. His mouth opens and closes. "Let's get out of here," he mutters, backing away.

"Oh yeah, run away. Just like you always do. You coward!" she shouts. He retreats, eyes watering as she bears down on him, a tiny woman with a squeegee but she has put the fear of God into Raymond. It is easy to see in his face. This doesn't faze the woman, who continues toward him muttering what Alex is sure are obscenities under her breath. Alex and Janice watch dumbstruck as Raymond's foot comes up against a potted palm, and he stumbles backward, his hands flailing, fingers grasping at the air behind him. He falls hard onto his back on the carpet.

"Raymond!" Alex yells, fearing she's let this go on for too long. She dashes to her friend who is lying there, pale and winded, on the hallway carpeting.

"I'm sorry," he says. "I'm sorry. I'm sorry."

"Ray, come on. It's okay," Janice whispers as they pull Raymond to his feet.

Evelyn watches them, her face a mask of anger. She is over her outburst. Her tiny chest rises and falls. It reminds Alex of an injured bird's. "Run away, you coward. That's what you do best."

Grief will make a person do desperate things, Alex thinks, watching the woman's chin tremble. The loss of someone you love can transform you into something else entirely, someone you don't even recognize.

"Don't you come back here," Evelyn yells at their backs. "You're not welcome."

They move through the maze of the hotel, Janice leading them into a large dark conference room. Raymond looks on the verge of tears. "How do I get out of this damn place?" he cries out.

"I don't know, this is a different way than we came in." Janice is doubled over from the exertion, her hands on her knees as she tries to catch her breath. Alex can feel them starting to unravel. She realizes that she has to seize control of the situation before everyone loses it.

"This way," Alex says, spotting a fire door. She pushes through it, bringing them onto a metal stairwell. They clamber down it. Alex's knees shake as they descend. Finally, they burst outside. They are in some kind of short alleyway, standing on the edge of a loading dock. They gulp in the hot nighttime air.

"Who was that?" Janice explodes as soon as they are on the street. But Raymond doesn't stop to rest. Grunting with effort, he lowers himself off the edge, dropping down into the street. He takes off at a fast pace, stumbling away from the hotel as fast as he can. Janice and Alex leap onto the pavement behind him, scampering to keep up. He ducks onto the sidewalk in front of the hotel and walks quickly to the curb, glancing back anxiously at the hotel's gleaming entrance. Alex glances back too. There is no sign that anyone's followed them out.

"You okay, Ray?" she asks. In all these years, she's never seen Raymond this out of sorts. She doesn't ask him what she really wants to know, which is what happened to Armond.

Raymond doesn't answer her. He steps off the curb, his hand shaking violently as he raises it out into traffic.

THIRTY-FOUR

They are introspective as the taxi crawls its way uptown. This whole expedition was a waste, Alex realizes, feeling heavy. She is no closer to figuring out what happened with Francis, nor does she have a clue who wrote the threatening note. All she has managed to do is traumatize everyone around her. And for what?

Alex is beginning to think that there is no logical order to any of it. It is quite possible that everything happening is completely random. What if, instead of it being a premeditated murder, Francis was in the wrong place at the wrong time, stabbed by someone who happened to be passing by her house with a random urge to kill someone? As for the letters, they were vague enough that really anyone could have written them. Maybe this is all just a distraction, a way for her to avoid thinking about her own failings.

She gives Raymond a concerned glance. He hasn't spoken a word since leaving the hotel. His eyes look hollow. They pass by the billboards of Times Square. Alex watches the colored lights hitting the origami-fold planes of his face. The taxi stops at a light, and a mass of people swarm the car as they cross Broadway.

"Look at this hellscape," Janice mutters, dabbing at her forehead with a monogrammed napkin from the Nest as they pass by rows of bad pizza shops and brightly lit stores selling touristy T-shirts and plaster replicas of the Statue of Liberty. "No self-respecting New Yorker would ever."

They make a right, heading east across town. The foot traffic starts to thin out as they pass Lexington, cutting uptown on Third Avenue.

"Stop the car," Raymond barks suddenly to the driver. "Right here. Pull over. That's it." The taxi swerves to a stop next to a low brick building covered in scaffolding. Raymond thrusts the fare at the driver and fumbles to pull the car door open. Alex thinks that he is going to leave them there, but he stops and peers back at them, gripping the edge of the car door.

"You coming?" he asks gruffly. Alex looks at Janice. She nods, and they scoot out of the back seat. It isn't until they are out of the cab that Alex sees the subterranean dive bar peeking out over the sidewalk. A neon sign for Budweiser shines out from a clouded window at shin level. They follow Raymond down a short set of steps into the partially submerged first floor of a dilapidated brick building. ATTILA'S BAR reads the rusted black lettering above the frosted-glass door.

Raymond hustles down the steps, into the bar. Alex and Janice follow him. Alex glances back at the steps as she pushes through the door.

The place is small, a low-ceilinged box with a small bar to the right and a pool table in back. The yellow lighting is not there to do anyone any favors, Alex thinks, looking around at the weathered assortment of characters who inhabit the place. All of whom turn to look as the three of them make their way to the bar.

"Are those people actually smoking?" Janice hisses at her. "So retro." Alex glances around at a large bald man in a leather vest who holds a fat cigar glowing between his fingers. The man gives her a glare and she turns away quickly, not wanting to cause any trouble for them.

"Yep."

Raymond seems not to have noticed, pushing himself up against the bar and calling out to the bartender, "A whiskey, Michter's. Neat."

"What about these two?" The bartender, a man with arms as big as fire hydrants, points at Alex and Janice.

"Do you have any pineapple juice—" Janice starts to say, but Alex gives her a look.

"We'll do three whiskeys," Alex says. The bartender grunts his approval, lining up three smudged shot glasses on the bar.

"So, this is where you come in your spare time," Janice says, looking around the dimly lit room. "Fun-looking group of people."

Two men look up at them from the end of the bar. Alex braces herself, glancing at the door. She could run if she had to, but what about these two? Her companions are not exactly agile.

One of them nods familiarly, giving Raymond a little wave. "Former Hell's Angels," Raymond says under his breath. "Those guys did some informant work for me a while back."

The bartender slides the shots across the bar. Raymond's hands are shaking so badly that he struggles to pick up his glass. When he finally gets a grip on it, he throws the entirety back into his mouth, shuddering after. Janice raises her whiskey and gives Alex a look. Alex takes a sip of hers and sets it down, the memory of Howard's breath in the hall making her stomach roil.

Janice turns toward Raymond. "Okay, now are you going to tell us what the hell happened back there?"

"What did that woman mean?" Alex asks him carefully.

Raymond brings his hands to his face, pressing his thumbs into his eye sockets. "She was the wife of someone I used to work with," he says quietly.

"An enemy?" Janice speculates.

"No. A friend." Raymond's voice tears. He looks away from them, out the window.

Alex can tell that he wasn't just an acquaintance.

"Why did she say that?"

Raymond stares down at the bar for a beat. Just when Alex thinks he might start to cry, his eyes harden. His knuckles grow white against the empty glass.

"You have to forgive me. All this time." His voice is ragged. "I've been lying."

THIRTY-FIVE

He sighs deeply, rattling his entire body and ending with something like a moan. "I didn't retire. Not on purpose anyway. I was kicked off the force."

"No! Ray?" Janice puts a hand to her chest.

"There was a guy we'd been looking for. He was real bad. Used to send little kids out as drug runners for him. Two of them even died. This guy wasn't an idiot like some of them though. He had a few brain cells on him. I had been trying to pin him for years, but he never did anything risky enough for me to catch him. We didn't want to bring him in on something small. We needed him to fuck up big so we could put him away. It's harder to get these guys than you'd think. You have to see them moving massive quantities of the stuff, and even then. But he never touched it himself. He was too smart for that."

"What happened?" Alex says.

"Well, we watched him. We were patient. It took, like, a year, but finally we got a wire on him. We got word from this kid that we be-friended that a shipment was coming in. We were ready to move in on him. *We got him,* I said to my partner the night before. I was so confident that we were going to be able to do the right thing then. We were so close."

He picks up his glass and tilts it toward the bar, nodding to the bartender for another. When he gets his full glass back, his hand is shaking so hard, whiskey sloshes over the edge as he draws it toward himself.

"The plan was for Armond to go in the front, and I would circle around to the back of the house and wait for his text. It was dark out already when we got there, which was great. I crept around back to this dilapidated screened-in porch. All the blinds were drawn in the house, but I could see through the window. I eased up to the door. I could see the guy in there. Huge guy. Face like a fighter. Broken nose. He was talking to his friends. Armond's text came through on my phone. It just said *go*. Then it was like slow motion. I saw him go in through the front door." He shivers and throws back the whiskey.

"When I heard the first shots, I had, like, PTSD or something. I had a panic attack. I am telling my body to go but it won't. And he is in there and I can see him. He is looking for me through the window, but he can't see me. I couldn't move. I see this look on his face right before they got him. He was afraid, sure, but beyond that. It was just pure disappointed."

"Oh, Ray, you didn't want it to happen," Janice said.

But Raymond shakes his head violently. "It doesn't matter. I basically killed my own partner. I wasn't brave enough. I fucked up. I ended his life, ruined his family in one stupid moment. Do you know how many times I've replayed it all in my head, trying to go back there to make myself move?" He grips the shot glass.

"You can't take that all on," Alex insists. "Not for your whole life, Ray." She puts a hand on his arm. It feels thin and knobby beneath the jacket.

"I can. I will. It's the least I can do." Raymond jerks his shoulder away from her. He's not angry with Alex, she knows that. He's mad at himself, frustrated with the utter impossibility of taking back a wrong. It's hard to live with regret. Alex understands the way you can relive something that happened to you, turning it over and over, polishing it like rock until its edges lose their definition and you can no longer even remember it clearly. "Doesn't matter if I meant to or not," Raymond continues, his voice quiet. "All that matters is that he died and that I wasn't brave enough or smart enough to help him."

He gets up from his stool abruptly. "Ray!" Alex calls as he heads for the door.

Janice's hand lands on her shoulder. "He'll be okay, Alex. You gotta just let him go walk it off. Trust me. Guys like that, they weren't trained to talk about their feelings."

They watch the shape of him grow faint against the glass as he takes the stairs. Through the glow of the neon sign his brown shoes drag sadly past the window and disappear into the night.

"I had no idea that happened, did you?" Alex asks, rattled.

Janice shakes her head. "There are a lot of lonely people who come to the diner, but there was something about Ray that always felt different. No friends, no family he ever talked about. I always thought he was hiding something."

"But he never mentioned Armond before?"

"No, never. But that isn't a surprise. Ray and I didn't used to talk much," Janice says.

"Oh really? For some reason I thought you two were old friends."

"Not at all. He sat there at the counter for years before we said more than a few words to one another."

"What changed?"

Janice sips from her glass. "Well, you showed up."

The admission startles Alex. She tries to think back on her earliest days in the city, but all she can remember is the way things are now. The two of them, the pillars, and herself as the interloper. She has never thought of herself as someone who brings people together.

"It must be so hard for him—being so proud of being a detective was his whole life, and then something so tragic happens and ends it all just like that."

"Think of his partner's poor family." Janice whistles. "How could you forgive something like that? He just let him die."

They sit silently, Raymond's admission heavy on them. Part of Alex feels guilty about how the night progressed. She shouldn't have gone down this path at all, shouldn't have brought them into her work drama. She looks down into her whiskey, her stomach turning.

Janice claps her hands loudly, jolting Alex from her spiral. "Oh, I almost forgot! I got some good intel in the bar. From the guy playing piano."

Alex leans in. "You did? Wait, what? What did he say?"

"He remembered Howard because he dropped a fifty-dollar bill into his tip jar and when he looked up, he recognized him as a famous newspaper editor."

"He's hard to miss," Alex agrees. "Was he with anyone?"

"Yes, he said there was a woman with him, sixtysomething. Graying hair. And, get this, she was wearing a white men's shirt, rolled up at the sleeves. He said they were arguing about something."

"Francis," Alex says, her stomach sinking. "Did he hear what they were talking about? Did he say anything else?"

"Only that she left first, looking upset," Janice says.

"Men." They look down into their drinks, commiserating over this statement.

"You two have a good night," the bartender calls out as they stand to leave. It reminds Alex that danger is not always to be found in the places that seem most predisposed to it, that it often can be found in the places you least expect it.

When she gets home, Alex's apartment is dark and still. She locks all three locks and taps them with her finger just to be sure. She slides off her sandals and leaves them next to the door. The heat from the day still radiates off the hardwood floor as she steps across the tiny apartment and falls into her bed.

She is exhausted but knows she won't be able to sleep, not yet. Her mind is whirring with activity. She is thinking about Raymond and the heartbroken woman working at the hotel who lost her husband. Her mind travels through the byzantine maze of the hotel to the Nest. Why would Francis have met Howard there when they could just as easily have met at the office? Unless she wanted to be somewhere else? To confront him on neutral ground? Or perhaps he had been the one to ask her there. It was on his calendar after all. Maybe he wanted to tell her to leave him alone. Alex knows she must be missing something else, that one piece that would make the entire picture of what happened come clear.

She looks around at the little collection of rooms she's called home for so many years. She's always meant to make it cozier. To get a bedframe, for Christ's sake. But she doesn't have so much as a picture on the wall. She came close a few times, walking into furniture stores and trying things out. Imagining filling her space with objects and plants and comfort; but at the last minute something always stopped her, and she'd return to her flimsy desk and box spring on the floor. It's sad, she thinks. She never meant for things to be like this. She rolls over and looks at her phone.

Tom has texted. She opens her phone quickly, holding her breath as she reads it.

Hi Alex, how's your column going this week? I was hoping we could get dinner again soon.

She starts to type a message in reply—then stops, afraid she'll regret it in the morning. Instead, she pulls the sheet up over her, her head buzzing with whiskey and images of Francis Keen fleeing the Nest.

THIRTY-SIX

Alex jolts awake to her alarm beeping. It must have been going off for nearly an hour, a shock as Alex is a notoriously light sleeper. She leaps from bed, snatching a towel off the back of a chair. Her apartment has turned chaotic since she started the job. With no spare time, her clothes have become a mess, creeping across her bedroom on various surfaces. She chooses a blue shirt and a loose pair of pants from a pile of clean laundry on her table. Not her best outfit, but she doesn't have time to be picky. She rushes in the shower and the bottle of soap slides out of her hand, shattering into the bathtub.

"Damn it," she shouts, jumping out of the tub soaking wet so she doesn't cut herself. In the window Mildred flaps away, startled by the outburst. She watches with a sinking feeling as the expensive golden soap bubbles swirl down the drain.

This day is already not going the way she wanted it to. She throws her clothes on, brushing her wet hair into a low bun and putting on sunglasses to disguise the dark half-moons that have appeared under her eyes this past couple of weeks. She steps out onto the street. She needs just a moment to think, to catch up with her thoughts. But she won't find one. Not now. Since last night she's been replaying the Francis scenario different ways in her head. She still can't envision Howard actually murdering Francis. It seems too visceral, too crass. She thinks of the call she overheard the first day. His voice, angry on the phone: "What can I possibly do about it?" There was also the incident at the Nest, the implication that Howard Demetri had sway beyond the reach of a normal person. She wonders if he could have used some sort of service to dispose of Francis. A third party. The idea puts a cold metallic taste in Alex's mouth.

She avoids Howard's office as she comes in, purposefully walking the long way around the newsroom toward the old hallway. She imagines Francis walking down this same hallway, possibly with the knowledge that her boss was trying to get rid of her. By all accounts, Francis liked Howard. Alex had read only positive things that Francis said about him.

In the office she goes to one of the photographs of Francis on the wall. It's black and white, from decades ago. She is perched casually on the side of a desk; her hair is past her shoulders and wavy, parted in the middle. She is sitting between two men: one thin with a goofy smile and a bow tie; the other more serious, with a heavy brow and a round face. As she studies it, she is shocked to realize that the man on the left is Howard Demetri. He is almost unrecognizable in his younger years, hardly the dapper New York City social giant that he is now. The other man has something familiar about him as well, but she can't place it. Something about the face. It looks like someone. *Regina*, Alex realizes with a jolt. It must be her father.

There's a noise in the hall that jerks her attention away from the photograph. It sounds like something is running along the wall, the way a child might trail their fingers. As it comes closer, Alex reaches instinctively for the letter opener on her desk. She hides it in her palm and steps toward the door. She puts her hand on the door handle, already anticipating the empty hallway. How many times will she hear things in the hall and find nothing there? It is enough to make her stop trusting herself. But the noise grows louder, scraping against the wall now so close to the other side of the door that she holds her breath and pulls it open.

She screams when she sees the face right there on the other side.

"Lucy. God, you startled me," Alex pants, embarrassed. She looks at the bin of letters in Lucy's arms; one larger cardboard envelope sticks out from the bin and bends against the wall, explaining the scraping noise Alex was so afraid of.

"You okay, Alex?" Lucy looks concerned. "Just making a delivery. I thought I'd bring you a few extra letters, or a hundred, since you finished the others." Her smile disappears when she looks down and sees the letter opener clenched in Alex's fist. "I can come back."

"No, Lucy. I'm sorry, please." She tries to laugh it off, quickly setting the letter opener on the desk and stepping away from it. "Sometimes I get creeped out back here."

"It's okay, Alex. I know that this job can be a lot of pressure," Lucy says. "You need to make sure you're getting enough rest."

Her assistant is being too kind. Alex will be lucky if she doesn't march straight down to HR after this and warn them that their new advice columnist is walking around waving sharp objects at people for no good reason.

"Thank you for bringing these. I'm just—" Alex stops, unsure how to continue. *Just what?* she thinks. *Just unhinged? Paranoid? Trying to implicate my boss in a murder plot?*

"Exhausted," Lucy finishes for her. She gives Alex a sympathetic look. "Don't take this the wrong way, but I can tell. Can I get you anything else? A coffee maybe?"

"No, it's fine, I'll make one myself," Alex says, grateful for the distraction. She needs to calm down.

"Well, I'm here if you need me," Lucy says. "I'll come back up and check in later in case you do." She looks eager to escape the room. Could Alex blame her? she thinks as the door shuts again. She sighs. Right now, the best thing for her is to work. She has another column due.

Still feeling jumpy, she turns her attention to the letters, lifting one from the bin.

Dear Constance,

Every day I wake up with the feeling that I am not doing enough. My children and husband need near constant attention. I feel

that I can give and give, and it will never fulfill their endless
needs. At the same time, I can feel the life draining out of me.
The things I once enjoyed seem like such a distant memory that
I can no longer even remember what I liked about them. But the
way I'm living isn't tenable. How do I find myself while in survival
mode—

She puts the letter down, the answer beginning to take shape in her mind. But she can't stay focused. Alex finds her eyes wandering to another letter on top of the pile. Her heart twists in her chest at the sight of the familiar typewriter font on the front of the envelope. Alex unfolds it, and her chest clenches as she sees the short message in the center of the page. Just like the last one.

Dear Constance,

You are a fraud. You don't belong here. You have caused so much
trouble. I know who you are. You can't escape your past. I am
watching you.

Alex fumbles in her purse for the other letter. Her fingers tremble as she opens them side by side on the desk. The same font, same format. It is the same person who wrote the last letter, Alex has no doubt. She feels a shiver works its way up her back to her skull.

THIRTY-SEVEN

Shaken, Alex makes her way to the staff kitchen. The letters could be nothing still, she tells herself. It could be a very unfunny practical joke, or some messed-up fan of Francis trying to scare her. She pulls a mug down from the cupboard and starts the coffee maker.

She is considering eating an old piece of coffee cake sitting on a warped tin tray when Jonathan bustles into the room, his face flushed with excitement.

"Oh, thank God. There you are. I've been looking everywhere." He leans close to Alex and stage-whispers, "Did you see? It's back."

"What do you mean? What's back?" Alex says, trying to focus on what he is saying. Her mind is still on the letter.

"His ring. Go look, it's back on his finger," Jonathan says impatiently.

She leans past the doorway of the kitchen and peers into the newsroom. Nearby, Howard talks over a cubicle to one of the editors. After all that she has learned about her new boss, looking at him sends a sharp twist of anxiety through her stomach. Jonathan is right though. She can see it there, a stripe of gold sparkling against the partition. She watches him say something and smile amicably with the younger editor. *Did you kill Francis?*

"It's there, all right," Alex says pulling herself back in from the doorway.

"What do you think happened? They must be back together. Maybe it has something to do with Regina coming into the office. Do you think he begged her to take him back?" Jonathan asks, aghast. Alex thinks of what Regina had revealed about Howard's job.

"Regina told me that, originally, she was supposed to take over the *Herald*, but her father wouldn't let her. He wanted a man for the job."

"Can you imagine? What a terror." He laughs, starting the coffee maker as soon as she removes her cup.

Alex isn't sure. "Maybe she only seems mean because that's the only way she's been able to get people to listen to her." Jonathan looks skeptical. "No, really. If you never were taken seriously even by your own family, it could make you—"

"A raging bitch? I don't know, Alex." He shakes his head. "You haven't been here that long. Regina has been nasty pretty much forever. I think it's in her DNA. I love that you have sympathy for her though. You really are perfect for your job."

Alex looks down into her coffee cup, watching the swirl of milk dissolve as she stirs. She feels wrung out and exhausted. She thinks of the men who chased her out of the hotel last night. What if the letters aren't from her past at all but are from someone loyal to Howard? Someone who wants to stop her from digging.

"Are you okay?" Jonathan asks now, pausing to look at her more closely. "You seem off." He waves a hand at her wrinkled shirt.

"Did Francis ever get any threatening letters that you know of?"

"Oh, is that what's happening? The hate mail's already started? Ignore it. People are always going to get mad. Even if the advice is good, sometimes it isn't what people want to hear. But that's the world now, right? You try finding a single place online where there aren't people getting death threats. It's sick. You can't listen to that stuff, Alex. It'll drive you crazy if you let it in." He taps gently on her forehead.

"Very wise," she says, and laughs. But inside she wonders if Francis got anything threatening leading up to her death. The clock on the wall buzzes.

"Okay, I have to get back to work." He picks up his coffee.

"I should too." She finds herself eager to get back to her work, to let the piles of letters from strangers wash over her, to replace her worries with theirs.

"Back to the trenches," Jonathan says as he leads the way out into the newsroom, raising his mug in front of him. "The people need their content."

As she walks back to her office, Alex looks down at a text from Tom on her phone.

Dinner tonight?

Alex wants to see Tom. And even more, she wants to forget everything else. She wants to stop thinking about Francis dead on the floor of her house; she wants to forget the cryptic notes and the sleazy boss and the crushing problems she can't solve and the ominous letters. Her chest still buzzing with anxiety, she quickly replies.

How about drinks instead?

Dear Constance,

It's hard to believe that Brian is the same man I met all those months ago at Sam's Hardware. Sometimes I try to remember him the way he was back then, back when he first came into the store. The way he had that easy smile on his face, the nice things he said to me, how he held the door like I was someone who deserved to have the door opened for her. That man told me I was smart, I deserved the world, I think he said. Yeah, right.

I couldn't have imagined the Brian from back then breaking a TV remote or slamming a plate onto the ground. I couldn't have pictured the way his face would turn bright red and his jaw would vibrate from the way his teeth clenched below the skin. And yet. Here I am.

The person I was back then also seems very far in the distance, like an old relative I've lost touch with. Would I even recognize her anymore? Thinking of how much I've lost of myself in the past nine months makes me want to cry. Maybe I was miserable back at my mom and Sid's, but I wasn't trapped in this nothing. I had a plan to get out.

Suddenly I was furious. I looked around Brian's sterile apartment and wanted to break something. I imagined kicking in his expensive sound system, smashing the TV, dumping out all of his expensive skincare products, the ones he tells me not to use. I think of packing a bag and walking out on him. But where would I go? I sat there sobbing at the kitchen counter. And then my eyes landed on the refrigerator. I was hungry, Constance. So hungry and so tired and so lonely. I opened the refrigerator and saw his leftover macaroni and cheese in there and I thought, Screw you.

I put it into the oven until it was hot and bubbly. At first, I was going to only have a little bit of it, but I was starving. I ended up eating the whole thing.

I cleaned the container and put it away, hoping he would forget about it. He'd always said I could have some anyway, but the guilt of it prickled at my back as he walked in, dropping off his keys in a tray by the door. I saw him sniff the air like a bloodhound. He looked at me suspiciously and walked straight to the refrigerator.

I watched with my heart in my throat as he opened the door, shifting things around inside. He turned and looked at me like eating his macaroni was unforgivable. It was so ridiculous I wanted to laugh, but the expression on his face set me straight.

He slammed me against the wall.

"Ow. Brian!" I gasped.

"That doesn't belong to you," he said. His fingers were around my neck. "That wasn't yours, you understand?"

I was choking now, gasping for breath. All this time Brian had made me feel that I wasn't good enough. I never thought he'd do something to actually hurt me. But now I know that I have more to worry about than my self-esteem. For a few horrible seconds I was afraid he was going to kill me. Finally he let me go, turning away as though I'd disgusted him. And even though I am okay now, I can still feel his fingers at my neck. I flinch when he comes close to me.

I am lost, completely lost, and there's no way out.

Help,
Lost Girl

THIRTY-EIGHT

Alex wakes up to a window thrown wide open. The bright light stream-
ing into the unfamiliar room makes her body go rigid under the sheet.
She is naked, she realizes slowly. She reaches behind her on the bed
to where the warmth of another body makes her jerk away, pulling
the sheet with her. Tom is lying next to her. They had come back late,
drunk and laughing. It had seemed like a good idea at the time, she
remembers fuzzily. God, were they even singing something? She half
laughs, half cringes at the memory of it.

There was the other part too. She remembers clothes being pulled
off. She looks over the side of the bed and sees his suit crumpled next
to it. She sees her pants in the pile; her shirt is nowhere to be found.

Tom raises his head from the pillow and squints at her. His hair is
messy, his cheek red from where it was resting on his arm.

"Morning," he says, his voice thick. His hands reach for her under
the crisp white sheet. She lets him circle her waist, pulling her close to
him. She feels his lips on her shoulder blade. *Is this even happening,* she
wonders, her eyes on the bedroom curtains. They are a thin sage-green
fabric that catches the breeze and billows into the room. Now she can
see the tree-lined street beyond his window. It's so different from the
wide avenue she lives on with its truck exhaust and delivery drivers
honking. Alex has the realization that she doesn't know where she is.
The thought sends a short burst of terror through her.

"Can I make you some coffee?" Tom asks suddenly. He leaps from the bed. She watches from the corner of her eye as he slips into a pair of track shorts. His body is sturdier than it appeared in his suits, his chest broad and, she is surprised to see, somewhat muscular. He runs his hand through his hair, pushing it out of his eyes.

"That would be lovely," she says.

He kisses the top of her head. "I'll be right back."

She pulls the sheet up around her and sits up in bed, looking around the room again for her clothes.

"Stay in bed. I'll bring it back." Through the bedroom door she can see him walking around in the apartment's bright kitchen, measuring coffee into a contraption on the marble countertop. He seems so domestic it is kind of strange he isn't married, Alex thinks.

"Cream? Sugar?" he calls out to her.

"Half-and-half if you have it."

He chatters as the coffee brews, telling her about the apartment, his neighbors, one of whom has an aggressive corgi. She half listens, looking around the apartment for clues about who Tom really is. She's surprised to find it extremely cozy. There are houseplants in pots clustered around the bedroom window that appear to actually be thriving. The walls have real art: a framed poster of an exhibition in Berlin, a black-and-white photo of a couple kissing in a café in what looks like the fifties. She leans forward, scooting herself toward the edge of the bed to see a smaller framed photo. A boy and a young girl. They are holding up ice-cream cones on some sort of boardwalk. She's never asked him if he has any siblings, she realizes.

"My family used to go to the Jersey Shore every summer," Tom says. She hadn't heard him come into the room. "My grandma would take us."

"I've never been," she says.

"Oh. Maybe someday we should go. It's an easy drive." Her heart thumps. Making plans with her at this stage. It's too fast.

He is holding two mugs; he puts them on the bedside table and slides back into bed, and she rolls toward him.

"What's this from?" he asks quietly, his fingers tracing the inside of her wrist. *Oh God.* Her fingers tremble. She wasn't paying attention. She'd let herself forget about the scars entirely. *How very, very stupid.* She jerks her hands away from him, burying them under the sheet in front of her. She can feel her face throbbing. The humiliation of it all.

"It's okay, Alex." His voice being so kind makes her feel even worse. She is holding her breath as though by not taking another inhale she can somehow prevent herself from fully absorbing the sting of it all. She can feel them now; they itch at her wrists. How many times has she wished she could remove the skin there and with it every memory of how they got there?

"I should get to work," Alex says, suddenly standing up and yanking the sheet with her. Her rules for safety have gone completely out the window. She is panicking now. She flees the bedroom, the sheet trailing her.

"Alex? Are you okay?" Tom has stood up. Now he follows her into the living room, watches as she stumbles frantically around his apartment collecting her things. A strapless bra on the edge of the couch. Her underwear inexplicably on the coffee table. She doesn't look at Tom as she slips into each of these, furtively pulling them on underneath the sheet like she did back in the dressing room of her high school gym class. She would like nothing more than to shrivel up and disappear.

"Alex, really. It's nothing to be embarrassed about." But she can feel the prickly sting of tears in the back of her eyes.

"Have you seen my shirt?" she asks, her vision blurring. She feels herself beginning to have a breakdown. He points at a floor lamp, to which her shirt is somehow clinging, one arm reaching for the floor.

She yanks it off the lampshade and pulls it on quickly, fumbling with the top buttons, tears hazing her eyes. All of this was a mistake.

"I don't know what I did to make you so upset, but I promise you I understand," he says.

"You don't," Alex says. "You couldn't possibly."

"No?" he says. His voice has an edge to it now. "You don't think I have struggled? That I struggle?"

"I don't think you have any idea what I've gone through, Tom." She feels a flash of anger now, avoiding eye contact as she reaches down to collect her sandals from the kitchen floor. Heels. She'd nearly forgotten. What a dumb thing to wear. She glances at the door.

"Oh no?" His voice is getting impatient. "Maybe not, but I know you can't just escape the past."

Her breath catches in her throat. She turns slowly, her shoes dangling from her hand. "What did you just say?" She looks at him. This man, this stranger.

His chest rises and falls. "Oh, come on, Alex. It's obvious that you're hiding from something."

The first times they'd met flash in her memory, the coffee shop and then later on the street. Funny how it was always Tom approaching her. Almost as though he'd planned it that way. Was it all really just happenstance, or is there something more deliberate about the way Tom has inserted himself into her life? "Why did you ask me out, Tom?" Alex says, edging toward the door.

He steps toward her. "What do you mean? You just seemed interesting to me. I felt like we already knew each other somehow." But she no longer believes him. The words of the letter coming straight out of his mouth are too much of a coincidence. She snatches her phone off the counter, her heart hammering.

"Alex, please." He is pulling on a T-shirt, following her to the door. "Are you sure I can't make you breakfast? I have a very good French toast recipe." She almost wants to laugh at this.

"Alex," he calls out as she darts past him. "Please." But she doesn't dare look back. She can't trust him. She should never have allowed herself to go on the date to begin with.

THIRTY-NINE

The Bluebird is nearly empty when Alex ducks out of the office to meet Janice and Raymond for an "emergency summit," as Janice named it on their group text.

"Sit, Alex. You look exhausted," Janice says, guiding her to a booth in back instead of their usual corner at the counter. "Just wait here a minute. I'll be right back." She disappears into the kitchen and returns to the booth holding a tray aloft on her arm.

"Here we are, grilled cheeses and Cokes," she says, arranging everything on the Formica in front of them and settling herself heavily into the booth across from Alex.

"Thank you," Alex says. "No Raymond, huh?" He hadn't replied to the group chat and she hasn't seen him since the night at the hotel. She wishes he were here now. Even though he can be reactive, his advice has always made Alex feel safer, like someone is looking out for her.

"I haven't seen him at all since the other night."

She thinks of his shoulder, how fragile it felt under her hand. "Do you think he's okay?"

Janice waves a hand, brushing off her worry. "You know men, especially that generation. He probably just got embarrassed. I'm sure he'll be back." Alex watches the concern cloud her eyes. She isn't entirely sure. Janice's cheeks are pink after a long shift on her feet. "Eat. You need to eat something."

Alex's stomach has been turning at the idea of food, but she picks up her own grilled cheese and takes a bite to be polite. It is better than she expects. The outside crisp and salty, the cheese perfectly melted. It is, without exaggeration, the best thing she's ever tasted. Suddenly she is ravenous and has eaten half of the sandwich. Janice watches, a satisfied smile on her lips. "The key is a little mayo on the bread before you grill it," Janice whispers.

When they are both finished eating, Janice leans back and wipes her fingers on her apron. "So, you want to tell me what's going on?"

Alex tugs on the hems of her sleeves, tucking her hands inside. Alex doesn't want to divulge too much; she's afraid Janice will look at her differently when she knows what she's done. Or what a mess she left behind. And she can't tell Janice about what happened with Tom without opening herself up to all sorts of other questioning that will make her feel stupid for even going home with him in the first place. So she focuses on the other new piece of information.

"I found out something else about Howard I've been meaning to tell you. My assistant Lucy hid under my desk when he came into the room. She said he'd made a pass at her. And she wasn't the only one, according to her. She was hysterical."

"That sleazebag," Janice says, slurping angrily from her Coke. "So, he's a pedophile on top of everything else."

"Well, I believe the girls are in their twenties," Alex says. "So not minors."

"*Pfft.*" Janice rolls her eyes and flaps a hand through the air. "No one's brain is developed like an adult's until they are at least twenty-five. You can google it."

Alex tends to agree with her. "They do seem young, and honestly, when you factor in the power imbalance, there is something really awful about it." She can see how a young woman would be flattered by attention from a boss as magnetic as Howard, how she could be lured by the glamour of it all, not recognizing the tradeoff she's made until it is too late.

"Did you get the names of these other girls?" Janice asks.

"Just the first name of one, Veronica. I didn't ask for any others. Lucy seemed quite fragile. I didn't want to make her even more upset. She was afraid of losing her job. Apparently he threatened her career if she told anyone."

"And you think Francis Keen could have seen Howard with one of these young girls before, you know?" Janice makes a slight stabbing motion with her pickle. Alex nods. They look at each other across the table for a beat, silenced by the implications. Alex looks down into the patterns on the Formica. Her eyes blur with exhausted tears.

"Maybe I can't do this anymore," she says, her throat tight. "Maybe I should just turn the notes and everything I know in to the police and be done with it."

"You could," Janice says slowly, considering. "I just want to make sure if you go to the cops, they listen to you. Women have to go through a lot in order to be taken seriously in this city. I've seen people who died before the cops believed their spouse was abusing them. I don't want them to take the evidence you bring them and just ignore the danger you might be in. What would Raymond say?"

Alex lowers her voice to a deep grumble and pounds a fist gently on the table, smiling through a film of tears. "Probably that if you're going to go to the station, it needs to be with a credible threat, not some anonymous notes and a few unsubstantiated rumors. Oh, and more toast, Janice."

"There you go," Janice says. Her arm shoots out over the table, and she takes Alex's hand in her own, giving it a firm squeeze. "You can do this, Alex. You go back up there and find what you need to get this guy. Think of all the women you'll be helping. You can put this fucker away for good."

FORTY

"You've been gone awhile," Jonathan says when she steps out of the elevator onto the forty-ninth floor.

"Aw, you missed me?" Alex says.

Jonathan sticks his tongue out. "No, but I was getting a little worried about you, honestly. Thought maybe you decided it all was too much and you bailed."

"Not yet," Alex says. She'd do anything at this point to prevent returning to her previous life. "Besides, I have a column due."

"Good. We can't lose two columnists in a year." The joke lands between them heavier than he intends. Jonathan clears his throat uncomfortably. "Right."

"Well, have a good afternoon. I'll be in my office," Alex says.

"Go get 'em. I'll be out here scheduling meetings if you need anything."

Alex opens the door to her office. The sky outside is dark with an impending summer squall. She switches the desk lamp on. There is something comforting about the piles of letters waiting to be read. As she sits, anticipating the squeak of the chair, she realizes that for the first time ever the office feels like her own. She picks up the half-read letter from yesterday, the one from the person who was having trouble balancing the demands of their family with the desire to stop and take stock of what they need in life. Alex lets her mind relax and starts to write.

Dear Without a Compass,

It can be hard to find an anchor when you are constantly being tugged in different directions. Sometimes it feels like it will be easier on us to move along with the current, to take care of each person as their needs arise. But one day you will wake up and you will be far downstream without knowing exactly how you got there or even if you agreed to go in the first place. Sometimes what seems like the path of least resistance is actually the one that gets us into the most trouble. You need to be deliberate if you want to stay afloat.

When she is finally finished with her answer, the office is dark and shadowy. A bank of clouds presses in on the city; she watches them billowing in, enveloping whole buildings. There is something almost comforting about it, Alex thinks, her face next to the glass, something she likes about nature being in charge. The window goes gray. The rain finally hits, going from a light patter to a heavy squall in a matter of seconds. The buildings around the *Herald* are only fuzzy outlines through the rain. She'll have to wait until the storm passes to leave for the night. She creeps out into the hall as a rattle of thunder shakes the building. She wonders how often lightning hits skyscrapers. They are basically giant tuning forks.

The newsroom is dark except for the emergency lights illuminating the exits. A crack of thunder and a gust of wind, and Alex swears she can feel the building shift around her. She stops in front of Howard's office. The blinds are all the way up, the overhead light still on. His desk is uncharacteristically tidy, his chair spun to the side haphazardly from the last time he stood up. He has been going home early since Regina showed up and the ring mysteriously appeared back on his finger. A desperate ploy to save his marriage from collapse, it would seem.

She pushes her fingers against the door, half expecting it to be locked, but it swings easily inward. She glances back at the empty newsroom before she steps inside. The rain assails the outer window as she goes to stand behind his desk. Alex isn't sure what she is looking for. A notecard perhaps, with a threatening memo. She stands in the stillness of the office and looks out over the city. The desk. This is where he brought the young girl he cheated on his wife with, Alex thinks, her stomach turning. She wonders what he promised these girls to convince them to sleep with him. Higher positions? Bylines? Or did he just tell them they were beautiful, irresistible in fact, and afterward that if they told anyone he would fire them?

A deafening crack of thunder comes from the other side of the building. She spins back toward the newsroom, and watches through the far bank of windows as lightning tears through the sky. How would she explain herself, barging into Howard Demetri's office at 10 p.m.? If anyone were there to see what she was doing, she'd be out of a job immediately.

She isn't sure what makes rummaging around in her boss's desk worth the risk except for her aching need to finish what she has begun, to put something to rest that has been eating the *Herald* away from the inside. The death of Francis Keen. Alex won't feel safe until she knows what happened.

She opens a desk drawer. She's always seen Howard as someone orderly and meticulous, so she is shocked to find his things in chaos. A tangle of papers, books, pens without caps. What is she looking for?

She slides the drawers open one at a time, pulling out crimped pages of articles about Russia, the presidential primaries, scrawled lists of potential op-eds. In her days of research, she'd read somewhere that Howard still did all of his edits by hand. She looks at his scrawled penciled notes in the margins of a piece about an oil pipeline expansion and is amazed he is able to read them.

As Alex pulls open the bottom drawer, something clinks far back behind a row of file folders. She pulls the folders forward, and three empty whiskey bottles fall over into the bottom of the drawer. So, that time she saw him in the hall wasn't a one-off. Alex's heart sinks. She wonders what Howard is trying to numb. She closes that drawer and slides open the last, a narrow drawer that stretches along the top of the desk.

Pushed into the back corner she finds a flat piece of leather. Alex pulls it forward and picks it up. It's heavy. A fold of leather with an inscription embossed in gold along the edge. She turns it over to read it.

For Howard, to keep you sharp.

As she turns it over, putting her finger into the stiff loop, she realizes she is looking at a sheath. Her hands tremble. Where is the knife? She opens the drawer farther, looking for the glint of a blade deeper in the drawer, but finds only a box of pens and a slew of uncontained paper clips.

The *ding* of an incoming text startles her and she drops the sheath back into the drawer, slamming it shut. The screen of her phone is lit up on Howard's desk. Her fingers tremble as she slides it toward her.

What kind of trouble are you getting into Alex?

The skin on her neck prickles as she stands and turns toward the outside window. As she approaches her reflection in the rain-flecked glass, she remembers what he said: *I've seen him in there at night . . .* As an afterthought, she leans over to the light switch, hitting it. The office goes dark, and now she can easily see a brightly lit window in the Excelsior Building and the outline of a dark figure standing at it. She gasps. Across the expanse, Tom stares back at her.

Dear Constance,

I'm terrified of even writing the words down on paper. Afraid he'll be able to see the memory of the pen on the page. I think Brian could read invisible ink if he wanted. He tricks you so that one moment you feel safe and the next he has taken something you've said and twisted it into something else completely. He is so aware of everything happening, so quick to anger that being around him feels like walking across shards of broken glass and just waiting for one of them to pierce the skin.

I hate even the smell of him now. It feels oppressive, disgusting. That cologne he wears tears at the back of my throat when he comes close. I don't think he feels good about me either. He makes comments about my body sometimes. "You know, you could be an eight if you tried harder," he says.

I want to leave him, Constance. I just don't know how. I have money from the hardware store in my savings account. Brian doesn't know about it. I could leave if there were any way out. I have no car. No friends to take me to the airport or help me with a ticket. Not now that Brian has made sure it is only the two of us.

My old friends feel like a long way away now, even though they only live a couple of miles away. I remember Amanda and how she was going to start college in the fall. I haven't texted her in forever, I realize. I am completely cut off. Sometimes I get a pang of longing so intense that I can hardly breathe. I want to go home. I think it to myself over and over again. And then my throat catches. I don't know where home is.

The truth is, Constance, I feel ashamed. I am embarrassed that I have gotten myself into this nightmare. I can't believe I let this happen. It feels like my fault, like I should have known better. I never believed him when he said all of those nice things to me, not really. Just like I never quite trusted him when he said he loved me. There was a part of it that always seemed like he was making it all up or saying the words just to get a reaction. And maybe in some ways I was acting, too, wanting so badly for my life to get better. But what does it mean if the only person who ever said he loved me was lying? How can I ever feel okay about another man? How can I ever feel okay about myself?

I won't write you again. I think that you don't do what you say, that you don't read these letters. It's unfair, me pouring my heart out week after week to a stranger and getting nothing in return. And I don't need anyone else in this life breaking my heart.

The Herald *promises that you read every single one of these. I really hope that's true. If you have any goodness in you, tell me what to do. I feel like I'm falling. Please write back. You are the only person can help me. I hope you're listening.*

Please,
Lost Girl

FORTY-ONE

When Alex arrives bleary-eyed and shaken at the *Herald* the next morning, Tom is sitting on a long couch in the big glass-walled atrium waiting area.

"Alex!" He leaps up when he sees her. "I'm sorry about last night. I was worried that I scared you. I didn't mean to."

He isn't wearing his headphones, she notices. His neck looks nearly naked without them as he rushes toward her, thwarted by the arrangement of long sectional couches in the lobby. Her palms go damp as she continues through the atrium past him. She doesn't slow down. She doesn't have time for this.

"Alex, wait! I've been wanting to talk to you, and, well, as you know you haven't been answering my texts since the other night and I didn't know how else to contact you."

She squeezes her eyes shut. A hot wave of shame rushes over her. She does not want to think about the other night. Not now. She should not have gotten involved with this man she doesn't know. It was careless of her.

"What happened? Alex?" His forehead creases with worry. "I must have done something to make you react that way; I would love to know what."

Alex is so tired. She wants so badly to believe that he has nothing to do with what is happening to her. She imagines collapsing into one of the seats of the sectional and letting him pull her to his chest and telling him everything, but there is too much about Tom that doesn't add up: the spying, the strange run-ins, and mostly those words, the ones that still make her chest clamp up when she thinks of them. *You can't escape the past.*

He leaps over the couch awkwardly, landing right in front of her just before she reaches the turnstiles. She is forced to stop, to look at him there. His face looks more haggard than she's ever seen it. There is stubble growing in on his cheeks.

"What are you doing, Tom?" She narrows her eyes.

"What am I—?" He looks taken aback. "I told you, I just wanted to talk to you, Alex." But Alex doesn't have time to explain the letters. And besides, she isn't sure she believes him. It all still seems a little too convenient. A quirky handsome man who listens to audiobooks, *Little Women*, for Christ's sake, just happens to run into her again and again? All this coinciding with a slew of threatening notes, one of which he happens to quote. No, it doesn't add up, but Alex doesn't have the time or the energy to figure it out right now. Not with all that's going on. She has to keep herself safe. And if doing so means staying away from Tom, then so be it.

"Alex!" he says again, more softly.

"You spy on people, Tom. You've insinuated yourself into my life when I never asked you to. You are out there watching; I never know if you are doing something bad or you are just strange, but it's too much. I don't know if you're bad or good. All I know is you're scaring me."

"Please, Alex. You're right." He puts his palms out to her. "It has nothing to do with you. Maybe I shouldn't look out the window so much, but you try working in banking. It's horrible. I just hate my job. I'm so bored I'll do anything to preoccupy myself. I swear it was never meant to be creepy. I am so truly sorry that I scared you."

"And what about the thing you said?" She still has no idea why he said it, but it terrified her. "You don't know anything about my past."

"Alex, I'm sorry for using some generic aphorism about life. I can tell it freaked you out, but I promise you I don't know what is happening. If you explained to me what is going on exactly, I could maybe have some idea of what you're talking about. And then I could reassure you that I have nothing to do with it."

The closeness of their time together still clings to her, coating her in a weird film of embarrassment. She hadn't wanted to make herself so vulnerable. Her stomach turns as she remembers him looking at her scars. She should never have given in to him, shouldn't have allowed herself to get caught up in the image of her and him together. What did she think was going to happen? That they'd become a perfect little couple? Alex knows better than that. It was reckless of her. Stupid. She looks away from him.

"Let me go," Alex demands, her heart pumping quickly. "I don't know what you're doing, but you need to leave."

He moves aside abruptly, hurt creasing his face. "Of course. God. I would never try to stop you." He steps back, clearing her path to the elevators. "Alex, I'm so sorry. I'm just really confused. If you ever want to tell me what happened, I would love to know."

Alex passes by him, walking as quickly as she can to the turnstiles, her fingers trembling as she scans her ID. She heads for the elevators, not letting herself turn back, relieved as she hears the whisk of the glass partitions shutting behind her.

FORTY-TWO

She sinks into her desk chair still upset from her run-in with Tom. What right did he have to show up at her office? She wants desperately to be left alone. To just disappear into her job. She is surprised to find that she is looking forward to work, that it is possibly the only thing she wants to do. She craves the escape of the letters. She wants to dissolve into other people's worlds, into problems unlike her own, ones that she might actually have a chance of helping people solve.

But despite her best efforts, she can't focus. Her mind is still circling with thoughts of Howard and Tom and the young girls and the missing knife. Wondering if there is anything she should do, if there is anything that can be done. Absently Alex pulls the next letter from the bin. She doesn't pay attention to the lack of writing on the front, the absence of any postmark, as she slides the blade of the letter opener through the fold and withdraws the contents. There are two sheets of paper folded together. The first is clean and white, like a fresh piece of printer paper. It holds only two lines of text, printed like the others in the center of the page.

You aren't taking me seriously.
It seems I need to prove to you that I am not joking.

Alex stops breathing as her fingers grope for the second sheet of paper. It is lined, yellowed slightly with age. Alex unfolds it carefully, her fingers weak with fear. Her brain tries to make sense of the handwriting, fast and sloppy across the page. The letter is written with one of those glitter pens young people like to use. The kind used to love.

Dear Constance,

He'll be back now at any moment. I know that he'll be angry. I should be leaving. I should be packing my bags and getting out of the apartment, but instead I'm sitting here, paralyzed and replaying the whole thing in my mind. I should have known better than to think I could outsmart him. It's impossible. I can't think the way he does. He has his own logic.

And he knows me so well. He has all of my passageways memorized, places I don't even know myself, dark corners where he can hide and wait for me. You were wrong about him—

Alex can't believe what she is looking at. She blinks, holding the paper out away from her as if keeping her distance from it will make it less real. She feels like she might throw up. The words aren't just familiar. They are her own.

The room spins as she puts down the letter she hasn't seen in eight long years. She tries to absorb the words she's been running from for most of her adult life. A new terror takes hold of her as she realizes that the letter in her hand is the only one she had never sent.

Who could possibly have gotten hold of a letter abandoned years ago in an apartment halfway across the country? There is only one other person who knows what Alex went through back in Wickfield. Only one other person who was right there through all of it. The one she's been hiding from all this time. Her body begins to tremble. The letter can only mean one thing. She's been found.

FORTY-THREE

The scrape of footsteps in the hallway sends the hairs on the back of Alex's neck on end. If someone is out there trying to scare her, she wants to know who it is. She launches herself to the door, flinging it open. She catches only the tail end of a shadow moving across the end of the hall, and the stairwell door opening and quickly slamming shut.

She bolts down the hall and pushes the door open into the stairwell. Breathing heavily, she stands still and listens. Nothing. And then just as she is about to turn back, she hears the echo of shoes somewhere below her. She leans over and looks down into the stairwell. She gasps as she sees the flash of a hand, on a railing several floors down. Alex tucks herself back against the wall. There is a voice finally, clear and deep.

"Sorry, I thought I heard someone. Go on," Howard Demetri says. She listens for another person's voice, but nothing. He must be on the phone. She stands as still as she can and listens.

"It's there. It has to be." His voice is heavy with worry. "Everyone is so damn incompetent. I'm going to go to the beach house to find it myself." *Francis's house?* Alex's chest tightens. She tiptoes back to the banister, leaning forward, over the edge, trying to hear better. What could he be trying to find at the beach house? His voice becomes lower; she strains to hear him.

"No one has been there in months. It'll be easy to get in. I don't think the police ever had the key. Under a garden gnome. It should still be there. I'll go tonight," he says decisively. There is a long pause before he speaks again, his voice a low moan. "Goddamn it, how did it come to this?"

Alex makes the mistake of looking straight down into the endless loop of the banister. The blood rushes out of her arms as she closes her eyes, trying to regain her balance. Then she hears him say, "We both know the knife is still there."

Before she can react to that last horrifying sentence, a click of dress shoes echoes up the marble stairs. Alex moves as quickly as she can, tiptoeing one floor up to the very top landing. There she presses herself against the wall, shuddering at the sound of the hinges scraping open and shut below her.

When the door closes, Alex is left with an image of Francis collapsed in a puddle of blood and Howard Demetri hovering above her.

Her mind buzzes with the potential of catching him there, the knife that he used on Francis in his hand. Or even better, she could find it first—prove what he did to Francis Keen, trap him with all the evidence she needs. When she bursts back into the hallway, Lucy is passing through clutching an iced coffee.

"What's wrong, Alex?" she says, her face dropping. "Are you okay?"

"No, I—" Alex glances behind her. She pulls Lucy down the hall and into her office, shutting the door behind them. Alex sinks against the door, still feeling shaky.

"What happened?"

Alex looks at her assistant. "I think Howard killed Francis."

"What?" Lucy's face goes pale. "No, that doesn't make any sense. Why would he—"

Alex is trembling. She knows she shouldn't tell her assistant, but she can't help it. The words come out anyway. "I think he was trying to shut her up. About an affair he had with one of the girls from the mailroom."

"Oh God, Alex." Lucy's eyes are dark and fearful.

"I just heard him talking about a knife. He is planning on going to get it tonight and hiding the evidence."

"He can't do that. We can't let him."

"Lucy, did you say you had a car?" Alex asks, an idea forming in her mind.

Lucy nods. "I do, yeah. It's not nice or anything, but it works."

"How would you feel about taking a little work trip?"

"Sure. Where?" Lucy asks.

"To Francis Keen's summer house," Alex says.

"The place where she died?" Lucy says in nearly a whisper.

Alex nods. She knows she must look absolutely unhinged but she doesn't care at the moment. All she wants to do is catch Francis Keen's killer. Lucy returns her gaze, hesitating for only a moment before she gives a little fearful nod back.

"Of course. What do we need to do? When do you want to go?"

"Soon. I just need to do something quickly first," Alex says. "Can you meet me at my apartment in an hour?"

"Yes, sure, I'll be there. Just text me the address."

"Thank you so much. And Lucy, please don't tell anyone," Alex says. "It's important."

"I promise," Lucy agrees, her eyes sparkling. "It's our secret."

FORTY-FOUR

When she gets to her apartment, Alex locks the door and rushes to her bedroom. She goes into the closet and reaches up to the top shelf. Her fingers close around the small metal lockbox where she keeps the important pieces of her life from before New York. These were the only things she took with her. She'd kept it at Sam's Hardware, in the back where there was a small storage area that served as the employee break room. "You can hold on to this for me, right?" she had asked him once, not long before the end.

She remembers the way Sam looked at her. He'd hesitated, clearly wanting to say something else. "Of course. It'll be right here. It won't move. Are you sure you don't need anything else?" But she'd been too scared to tell him. She hadn't even wanted to risk coming downtown to bring him the box. What if someone saw her walking down the shoulder of the road toward town and told Brian? She'd shaken her head and given Sam a grateful squeeze on the shoulder. "I'll come back for it. I'm just not sure when yet."

Now Alex places her fingers on the dials and lines up the numbers until the lever pops open. She hasn't opened the box in years. There was no need. Every time she happened to glance at it in her closet, it gave her such a pang of anxiety that she would quickly look away. She was trying to move on, she'd told herself. If she was going to start over, she didn't need to look at all of the evidence that she was once the scared young woman in an abusive relationship. But now she wants proof. She pushes back the top of the box.

It is mostly empty. She'd saved only a few mementos from her other life. A small plasticky phone from a convenience store; the stubs of several used bus tickets that had brought her here; a social security card for Bess Christopherson, the name she bore until she turned twenty-two years old. There is a thin stack of photographs, the shiny paper curly with age. In one, her six-year-old self squints into the camera. It is summer and she is wearing her typical mishmash of secondhand shorts and a top; her two front teeth are missing. Her mother's tan arm loops around her shoulders, and she gazes down at her with a maternal smile. This was, of course, before her mom's boyfriend, Sid, entered the picture and stole her attention. Another photo of her on her first day at work, standing behind the counter wearing a trademark red apron with *Sam's* scrawled in cursive across the chest. Alex feels the ache at the back of her throat and puts the photos aside.

She finds what she is looking for at the very bottom of the box. She pulls it out gently: a copy of the *Herald* from August 2014. She holds it by the edges, careful not to bend it. The newspaper has yellowed and is as fragile as a butterfly wing. She unfolds it delicately, like an archivist at a museum, peeling back the pages until she finds Francis's letter.

Dear Lost Girl,

It's a mystery of the human condition that often we seek out situations that are not good for us. Sometimes for a while they even allow us to pretend we are not hurting ourselves. Often staying inside the delusion feels easier than the alternative, which is usually some version of a dark room where you can't see any doors. I need you to listen to me when I tell you it is not easier to stay. That a month or a year of stumbling around searching in the dark will be better than slowly allowing your life force to be stolen. It is no exaggeration to say that that is what he is doing to you.

People like him need you to be scared that something is wrong with you so that you don't look at what is wrong with him. He wants to keep the focus on you, to make you nervous, too scared of your own imagined deficiencies to be able to even see any of his.

But we do not need to analyze him for a moment longer. He has taken far too much of your time already. The goal right now needs to be about getting out of this horrible and already dangerous situation. You need to find a safe place to go. You've written about your family not being able to support you. If they are not an option, I need you to know that there is help out there, there are shelters devoted to women's safety. It isn't ideal, I understand that, but for now, while you transition away from dependence on him, it is invaluable.

The next time he leaves, I want you to make a list of places you have always wanted to go. This should be fun. I have a feeling you are a bit of an adventurous spirit. Now I want you to choose one of them, it doesn't even matter really which one as long as it is far away from him, somewhere he has no connection to whatsoever. I want you to find a women's help center in that place, and then I need you to get on a bus, a plane, whatever you can afford, and get the hell out of there. Do you hear me? Things are going to be hard for right now, but you will be giving yourself the biggest gift of all. Your whole future.

You don't need him in order to be special. Just like Dorothy and her ruby slippers, you will realize that everything you need has been inside you all along.

Go now. Quickly, before it is too late.

Sincerely,
Constance

Alex doesn't realize until she puts the paper down that she is crying, gulping for breath. Her face is wet with tears. All those years ago, she'd followed the advice of a woman she'd never met and moved thousands of miles away to a city she'd never been to in order to save her own life.

A car honks outside. Standing up, Alex wipes her eyes and looks out the window to where a small white car is double-parked with its emergency lights on. She grabs her phone and a charger and shoves them into her purse. As she heads to the door, she still has the words Francis wrote in response to her letters as a young woman begging for help imprinted in her brain. They are a mantra she memorized and still repeats to herself in order to keep going. And now, even more than that, they are a calling to find Francis's killer.

FORTY-FIVE

They've driven for almost four hours with only a single quick stop. Now Alex is jittery, hopped up on gas station coffee and the giant Snickers bar she consumed to keep herself awake as they creep along the expressway in deep summer traffic, Lucy's dilapidated Hyundai dwarfed by giant SUV Mercedes, Volvos, and BMWs. But now they are nearly to the end of the famous peninsula that juts out into the Atlantic and the traffic has finally thinned.

"Look, this is the turn," Alex says, pointing at the exit for East Morehead. Lucy grips the steering wheel as they veer off toward the coastal town where Francis Keen spent her summers, and her last day alive.

Alex glances at her phone. It's nearly 5 p.m. If Howard leaves the *Herald* once the paper goes to press, that will give them at least four hours to hunt down the missing knife.

"So, this is where the rich spend their summers?" Lucy cranes her head as they pass a row of businesses in whitewashed buildings, a few cafés, a Pilates studio, a few shops with caftans and handmade pottery in the windows. People linger at outside tables with gem-colored drinks. They look so worry-free that Alex wants to park the car and join them, to be absorbed into their lives and forget what she is actually doing here.

"Look at this," Lucy scoffs, waving her hand out the window at a bakery for dogs. Alex looks up, surprised at the bitterness in her voice. "These people have so much money they have to invent ways to spend it."

"It doesn't mean they're happy though," Alex says quietly, reminding herself of what she knows deep down is true, that no amount of privilege can buy you contentment.

"No, I'm sure you're right," Lucy agrees begrudgingly. "But they're idiots not to be. What does anyone with a beach house have to worry about?" She waves her hand dismissively.

Getting murdered, for one, Alex thinks.

"I think Francis's place is up here just a little way," she says instead, looking down at the map on her phone. They pass a public beach. A few holdouts are still in the water, their towels empty on the sand. The waves rock them gently on their golden crests as the sun starts its descent. How long has it been since Alex has had a real vacation? For a moment she pictures Tom in the driver's seat. She imagines them coming here for a romantic weekend, checking into a hotel by the beach, lingering over lobster and bottles of white wine at one of the beachside restaurants. *No, no, that's no good.* She shakes her head, dissolving the image of Tom, of beach walks and sun-kissed skin and evening cocktails, from her mind.

Lucy doesn't seem tired at all. If anything, she is more energetic now than at the start of the drive. Her eyes are bright and focused as Alex directs her down one of the side streets, fringed in tall trees, their silhouettes bending in the late summer light. The houses back here look like they are straight from a fairy tale, sprawling cottages shingled with cedar and landscaped with sea grasses and massive hydrangeas. It's the kind of low-key wealth that you only find in New England. Alex glances at the map and sees that past their manicured lawns there is a crescent of beach invisible from the road. She looks at the houses, which are set back from the street and spaced far enough apart to not have to interact with each other. You wouldn't have to worry about your neighbors bothering you in a place like this, Alex thinks. You wouldn't be able to hear anyone scream either.

They round a curve and drive along a stacked-stone fence. "This is it," Alex says, glancing back to make sure they aren't being followed. They turn onto a long drive bumpy with cobblestones. The house comes into view at the end of the drive. It is three floors with graying wood shingling and white trim. A cheerful blue door opens onto a wide front porch. The driveway is still blocked off by a crisscross of police tape, sagging and faded.

"We probably don't want anyone knowing we're here, right?" Alex says, pointing to a hedge down the road.

"Oh, right, smart," Lucy says, rolling the Hyundai very slowly behind a stand of trees. As they step out of the car, the smell of freshly cut grass and the tang of ocean hit Alex's nose. It makes her think of being a child, back in the before times. The nostalgia feels almost painful. They walk silently toward the house, slowing to step over the fence in a spot where the stones have toppled.

A bank of clouds has blown in and the sky has turned a milky green. They look toward the house. The windows are dark and opaque.

Alex glances at Lucy, feeling another stab of guilt for bringing her here. This whole thing could get her into so much trouble. She has tried not to think of the possibility of getting caught, but it is there.

"You don't have to come with," Alex says suddenly. "You should wait in the car and I'll just do this on my own."

But Lucy ignores Alex, her eyes fixed on the house. "Where did you say the key was?"

"Howard said it was under a garden gnome."

"That's ridiculous," Lucy mumbles.

"You want to tackle this side and I'll look around back?" Alex asks. Lucy nods, and they split. Alex moves past the house with its perfectly weathered shutters and stone accents and out into the backyard. She stops to take in the view, which looks like it's out of a postcard, a lush green lawn cradled on two sides by pretty wild foliage and flowering plants framing a view of the Atlantic, which seems to appear there as if by magic, shimmering right above the edge of the yard.

The grass has been mowed, though not recently. The blades tickle her ankles as she walks through it. As she approaches the water, she sees the slender curve of beach, dipping down from a line of sea grasses wavering ever so slightly in the breeze. The honey-colored sand looks warm and inviting. If Alex had a house like this, she would spend all of her time down here just listening and watching. She thinks of Francis following this same path. Would she have stood in this spot and gazed at the ocean on the day she died? She forces herself to turn away and keep searching for the key.

She walks to the far edge of the property and comes up to a row of raised garden beds. Left to their own devices, they have still managed to seed. Clumps of green tomatoes cling to their stalks, while some farther down have ripened and burst open uneaten. Snap peas with nothing to climb droop over the sides of the bed, their pods eaten away by animals. Another gift Francis left behind without even meaning to, Alex thinks.

She spots the gnome finally, tucked away behind the last bed. Lucy comes around the side of the house, and Alex calls her to it. The gnome is bigger than she expected, made of solid concrete worn down by the weather, moss growing up its side. She can still make out its cherubic face, its plump hands on its waist framing a round belly. Lucy tilts it back, grunting with effort, and Alex drops onto her knees in the grass; she sees a glimmer of a silver key pressed into the dark soil and pulls it up from under a layer of dirt, wiping it on her shirt.

"Okay, let's go," Lucy says. They dash back across the lawn, ducking back against the side of the house. Alex's hands shake as she fits the key into the back door's lock and twists the handle.

Alex's skin prickles as the door swings open into Francis's back foyer. The flashlight from her phone bounces around the mudroom. She doesn't know what she expected to find, but she hadn't thought it would feel so lived-in. Francis's shoes are still stacked on a tray next to the door. A set of light jackets, a market tote, and sun hats hang from a row of wooden pegs, just waiting for her return from the city. Beyond the entrance is a wide hallway that opens into a large open living room with a giant fireplace. It is stylish and cozy, a bright quilt thrown over the arm of a plush cream sofa. No one knows why Francis came up here that weekend, but looking around, Alex has the suspicion that this was a place she could come to sort herself out.

"What are we looking for exactly?" Lucy says.

"A knife." She lifts the top off a box shaped like a wooden dove and looks inside at a set of fireplace matches. She replaces the lid. "That's what Howard implied, anyway, that the murder weapon is here somewhere in the house. He just didn't seem to know where."

They come to a spacious kitchen. Everything is still where Francis must have placed it. It's on the small side for such a big house. Wide white cupboards ring a center island topped with a rough wood chopping block. Alex runs her fingertips across the surface; from the amount of nicks in it, she can tell that Francis must have liked to cook.

Alex stops and looks out the kitchen window. It is getting dark outside, the edges of the yard blurring into shadows. It would be strange to be here all alone, she thinks.

"How would we know which knife?" Lucy asks, pulling a large chef's knife from a butcher block and extending it in front of her.

Alex shakes her head. "I don't think it is a kitchen knife. I think it might be decorative," she says, thinking of the elaborate embossing on the case. "Look for some sort of design on the hilt."

Lucy returns the knife to its slot. "I'm confused. Wouldn't the police have found it already if it was here?"

"Apparently the detective in charge of Francis's case was pretty incompetent. He might not have even tried that hard to find it," Alex says. "Even Howard thinks that it is still here, so I think it must be true."

"He didn't say where?"

"No. I wish." Alex wonders if Howard had been drinking when he drove up that night. She can imagine him parking out on the street and stumbling up the cobblestone drive, a flask tucked up his sleeve.

"How much time do you think we have?" Lucy asks nervously.

"If he left right after work? I don't know, with traffic maybe three hours now?" Alex guesses. "But he could have ducked out earlier."

Lucy looks anxiously at her phone. Alex can see the bubbles of text on the screen. She types something quickly on it and then presses the side, making the screen go dark. Alex has another pang of sympathy for her assistant. Here she is in the middle of nowhere with her boss instead of out somewhere with her friends. It's hardly the thing a twentysomething wants to be doing on a summer evening.

"Thank you for driving, Lucy. I really appreciate you helping me with everything. I don't think I could have gotten here without you."

"It's nothing, I wanted to. For Francis," she says quickly, slipping the phone into her pocket. "Should we divide up again to cover more ground?"

"Yeah, that makes sense. Want to look and see if you find anything else in here and in the living room? I'm going to go look for her office."

"Perfect." Lucy seems more excited now about their mission. "We should keep the lights off or the neighbors might see us and call the cops."

It's true, Alex realizes. With the fading daylight they will have to be cautious and rely on their phones for light. As she steps back into the hall, she has another thought. "Oh, and Lucy, if you find the knife, definitely don't touch it. You don't want to get fingerprints on it." Alex has only a vague idea of what happens when you turn something in to the police, but she has Raymond's stern voice in her mind as she walks to the back of the house: *Don't mess with the evidence, Alexis*.

Alex holds up her phone. The thin beam shines out onto a worn woven runner leading into the back of the house. She wonders where Francis was standing when she realized she was in danger. Was it here in the hall? Did she run? Or was someone waiting to surprise her? Perhaps she never saw it coming at all. An involuntary shudder jerks her shoulders. She swallows and forces herself farther into the house. It will be hard to find anything in an old house like this. Now that the light is almost gone it could be nearly impossible. Maybe this was a bad idea.

The hall opens into a modest-sized office room. It contains a wall of bookshelves and a desk that faces out toward a bank of windows overlooking the dark lawn. Under the deep blue of the sky, the ocean churns darkly. She sits down at Francis's desk. It's less grand than the one in her New York office, but what a view. It's a small wooden desk with a row of drawers to one side. The wood is nicked and stained with rings from coffee mugs left to sit as she wrote.

Alex opens the drawers one by one. She finds the usual desk things inside, a jumble of pens and paper clips, some old bills. She finds a stack of letters with a rubber band around them. She flips through them, looking for her own, but none are familiar. The computer surprises her by humming to life when she bumps the mouse. There are no blinds or curtains covering the windows and Alex has a terrible feeling that someone is watching as she sits in front of it, the screen sending a haze of bright white light into the room. Surely the police have already looked through her computer.

The log-in to Francis's email. Alex types in the log-in to her own email, an homage to her former self: LostGirl93. The screen refreshes. And she sees that it has been reset to her own and she watches with disappointment as her own inbox fills the screen. She logs back out and explores the desktop. It is a mess. But Francis has also saved things on this computer.

She drags the mouse over to the deleted files. The email at the very top is dated the seventh of October from Howard Demetri. That was easy.

"Oh my God. We've got him," Alex mutters, clicking open the email. She leans in to read.

My Dearest Francis,

I know you didn't want to talk to me today, but I need you to read this. Forgive me, but I know you have to, it is your sworn pledge, isn't it? So, I can cross my fingers now and hope that you will continue to honor it. All I want is for you to hear me out for the length of this letter. I have always been better at writing than talking. You know that more than anyone. What I started to tell you at the bar before you ran away from me is this: I am going to leave Regina. This is not some grand gesture I'm making for you alone. It is the last sane choice in an untenable situation. I have made mistakes. I know that what happened, what I have caused, willed to happen, was unfair to her, to you, to myself. But you know that my marriage was nearly arranged. It was one of complete convenience. I have never let myself love anyone until you came into my office. The moment you sat down in front of me for the interview all those years ago, it was the strangest feeling. Familiar, as though I was looking into a mirror. But I wasn't seeing myself, I was seeing the potential of what life could be. It flashed before my eyes, and even then, I knew that I'd made a mistake. What you said about it being unfair to her is right. I live with the regret of what I've done to Regina, but I can't live my life for her any longer.

It has been the honor of my life to spend twenty years with the woman I love just down the hall. I told myself it could be enough. But it isn't. I ache for the moments we could have together. I used to think that this job alone could sustain me, could give me meaning that would make up for all the lies I told myself. But you've taught me better. I know that this can be us; I am done living a lie for a career. What does it mean in the end? What does any of it matter beyond being with your beloved one? I no longer care about anything else. I've already told her, Francis. It is done. I will meet you at the beach house. Please stay and wait for me there.

I love you.
Howard

Alex reads and rereads the words, staring and trying to make sense of them until the screen blurs in front of her. Howard was not trying to threaten Francis; he was professing his love to her. Why would he kill the woman he loves?

Alex's image of Francis also crumbles. Despite what Jonathan told her, she has only ever believed that her idol could be perfect. Alex thinks of the indentation on Howard's ring finger and of the anger radiating off Regina while they waited in his office.

All this time Alex has only imagined Francis in a supporting role in all the drama, an impartial bystander dragged into things against her will. But Francis wasn't some unsuspecting innocent who stumbled upon an affair—she was the one having the affair herself. Francis wasn't perfect. Not even close. The thought makes Alex sit back, a startled sort of relief in her limbs. She should have known that life is more complex, reality more bendable, than you can ever come to expect. If Francis wasn't some saintly figure, maybe Alex doesn't have to be either, she thinks, realizing that she doesn't know Francis the way she thought she did. She doesn't know her at all.

FORTY-SIX

Alex's phone buzzes in her hand. *Jonathan Amin.* She rushes to answer it. "Jonathan, I've found something. Howard Demetri—"

Jonathan cuts her off. "Alex, listen to me for a minute. I have to tell you something."

"What is it?" Alex asks, excitement still bubbling up in her chest as she scans the letter once more.

There's a long, heavy breath into the receiver. "They're here, in the office. They've come for him."

"Who's there?" She stops and looks up into the still darkness of the house.

"The police. He's being arrested in front of everyone. He did it. Apparently they found something that ties him to the murder."

"The sheath," Alex whispers.

"How did you know?" he demands, suspicious.

"I did some poking around in his office the other night." Alex squirms. "I saw it there and had a hunch it might be connected."

"Wait, are you the one who went to the police?" It's hard to miss the accusatory tone to his voice.

"No! No, I was trying to find something, I don't know—evidence of his affair maybe, or something connecting him to those threatening letters I keep getting sent. And then I saw the sheath with the missing knife, and something in me knew right away that it was the knife that killed Francis."

"How have you managed to find more out in the last two weeks than the cops did in all this time?"

"Jonathan, about that. Please don't be mad at me, but I'm at Francis's summer house."

"What? Oh boy. Alex, I—"

"Listen to me. I'm looking at Francis's computer right now. There is a note that was in a deleted folder on her desktop. It's dated the day Francis was killed. It's from Howard telling her he is about to leave his wife."

"That's—wait, what?" His voice echoes, and she can picture him standing against the railing of the stairwell, a perplexed look on his face.

"But why would he have written to Francis that he was going to leave his wife and then kill her?" Jonathan asks.

"Because he didn't do it, Jonathan. He was absolutely in love with her." She can see the beam of Lucy's flashlight bouncing off the walls in the hallway.

"I think I'm going to be sick." He moans, "I don't know what to believe anymore, Alex. None of it makes sense. There's something really strange going on." There is a clatter of utensils coming from the kitchen, the sound of metal scraping against wood. "What was that noise?"

"I brought Lucy with me. I don't have a car and she said she was happy to drive, so we left right away." She is rereading the letter, scanning it for any clues she might have missed.

"Who?" Jonathan's voice drops.

"*Lucy*, Jonathan. *Francis's* assistant." Alex hears a drawer open in the kitchen.

"Seriously. Who are you talking about?" Jonathan's voice goes cold. "Francis never had an assistant."

Alex's heart plummets into her stomach. She lifts her fingertips from the keyboard, glancing back into the darkness over her shoulder. She lowers her voice. "What do you mean? She must have. Lucy knows everything about Francis."

"No, Alex. That is impossible. Francis wouldn't have let someone help her if she was hanging from the side of a cliff," Jonathan says, his voice starting to sound worried.

Alex stops moving, stops breathing. Surely he is wrong. The sounds in the kitchen have stopped. She whispers, "But the things she told me about those girls . . ."

"What *girls*?"

"The ones that Howard tried to sleep with. The young ones. From the mailroom." Alex realizes that she hasn't told Jonathan everything she knows about their boss.

"What? You think Howard—" He starts out sounding incredulous, but his tone quickly changes to fear. "Alex, I don't know what is happening, but I think you should get out of there."

"Why would Lucy lie?" Her voice is barely audible. Suddenly the words of Francis's obituary come back to her. *She suffered no fools.* In her memory she sees Lucy's rosebud lips moving and the words of the obit coming out of her mouth verbatim. In the hall, the light from Lucy's flashlight goes off.

"Alex. Please be safe," Jonathan begs. She nods into the dark of Francis's study and hangs up the phone.

As she rises quietly from the desk, Alex thinks that the only reason you would memorize and repeat an obit is if you didn't actually know the person you were talking about.

FORTY-SEVEN

Alex pockets the phone and moves toward the hallway. The house is fully dark now, a maze of bluish shadows that she navigates as quietly as possible. The silence roars in her eardrums. It's been so long since Alex has been away from the city, she has forgotten the pitch black of the nighttime world. In her apartment the light always finds its way in. The streetlights sneak their way around the cracks of her curtains, the headlights move across her wall. But here the darkness is startling. It gives Alex a strange floating feeling as if she is walking into a void. She passes a window, her phone's flashlight bouncing off the glass. She can hear the sound of insects chirping outside. The lights of a neighbor's house far in the distance sparkle through the trees.

Alex could run now. She could leave the house and dash across the lawn and knock on their door. But what would she say? That she has illegally entered a dead woman's home searching for clues to implicate her boss in murder? She'd be lucky if they didn't call the police immediately.

A creak comes from the kitchen, and her heart constricts. There has got to be an explanation. This is Lucy after all. Not some stranger. She should let Lucy be the one to tell her what it is. So, instead of running, she turns toward the dark kitchen. Her ears prick as she reaches the doorway. There is no sound at all now except her own lungs filling and emptying and the scrape of her footsteps as she moves through the house. She shouldn't jump to conclusions about her sweet assistant. She'll just ask her what is going on.

"Lucy?" she calls into the kitchen, trying to sound as casual as possible. She remembers some advice from one of Francis's letters: *People are not inclined to open up if confronted.* She'll start slow. "Hey, Lucy, are you still back here?" She tries to keep her voice light despite the tremor that has taken hold of her body.

"Alex?" Lucy's voice cuts through the dark. It is deeper than normal, raspy. "Were you talking to someone?"

Alex puts a hand on the center island to orient herself as she follows it around the side of the kitchen. She moves the light of her phone toward Lucy's voice. Lucy stands at the edge of the counter.

"Jonathan called. He wanted to tell me that he found something in Howard's agenda that we'd missed," Alex lies, not wanting her to know that no one is coming. "Howard should actually be here sooner than we thought." She can see Lucy's silhouette shuffle uncomfortably at the news. Lucy frowns down into the glow of her phone for a moment and Alex can see the black shine of fear across her eyes.

"Was that it?" She is barely audible.

"They had gone on dates, apparently. Francis and Howard were lovers, not enemies." She watches Lucy carefully.

"Oh, wow, that's a surprise," she chokes out.

"Lucy, it makes me question whether he really was interested in young girls like you said." Lucy takes a big step back.

"Jonathan also told me that Francis Keen never had an assistant." Now Alex doesn't even have to see her expression; she can feel the panic coming from Lucy as she backs away. It vibrates through the room, bounces off the floors, filling Francis Keen's kitchen with anxious terror.

"That's strange." Her laugh is hollow.

"What is going on, Lucy? Why would someone lie about being an assistant?" She comes up against the far end of the counter.

Alex takes another step toward Lucy, closing the space between them. "Lucy, you can tell me what's going on. I am not going to be mad at you. I'm sure you had a reason, I just need to know why."

Lucy's flashlight comes on suddenly. As its blinding beam swings through the dark, Alex has the sick feeling that she has made a terrible and irretractable error in judgment.

"Oh, do you?" Lucy says, her voice hard. She steps toward Alex now, shining the light directly in her eyes. Blinded, Alex steps backward.

She should have known. It all comes crashing in on her. The way Lucy always took the stairs and never the elevator, slipping back behind the newsroom. Skittering through the old part of the building. She'd never even seen her assistant with anyone else in the office, only on her own.

"How did you get in?" Alex asks.

"It's easy to get a job in the mailroom these days." Lucy smiles smugly. "No one wants to do the dirty work anymore. I just applied. Got hired on the spot. They practically begged me to start right away.

"From there it was all about finding the perfect moment. When you were just vulnerable enough. I had to break you down a bit first. It wasn't exactly hard to do. You were so jumpy already. Always thinking someone is out to get you, aren't you, Alex? Maybe you're the one who is actually causing the trouble though, ever think of that?"

"What do you mean?" Alex backs away.

"You gave me quite the gift with Howard."

"Howard? You were always so scared of him. And those young women. You said Howard was a predator, that he tried something." Alex thinks of her boss, stumbling drunk in the hallway, of the young woman he'd taken advantage of. Of Lucy afraid for her job.

"What was I supposed to do? I was trapped. I had to come up with something. You would have found out I was lying. It would have ruined everything."

"Why are you doing this? Did you kill Francis?"

"God, no. Why would I kill Francis?" Her face screws up. "I never even met Francis Keen."

"But why did you pretend to know her?" Alex asks, shielding her eyes.

"I wasn't trying to get closer to Dear Constance, although I hate that column more than just about anything. No, I wanted to get close to *you*." Her voice turns now from derision to pure anger.

Alex stumbles back, trying to understand what is happening. "Why me? We have never even met." Her fingers grab at the air behind her.

"We have, though. Don't you remember?"

Alex's foot slips on the tile. She is falling in slow motion. On the way toward the kitchen floor her head smacks against something sharp. She lands in a pile, her vision swirling with stars. She curls on the floor, a pulsing behind her head.

"Oh dear," she hears Lucy mutter from somewhere behind the light. "That's a real bummer." Alex blinks into the beam of her flashlight. Disoriented, she tries to stand, but her feet slip and she slides back to the floor.

Alex brings her hand to her head and feels the slick of blood between her fingers. She sees it in the beam of Lucy's flashlight, the bright red spattered on the tile and on her hand. The sight of it makes her woozy. The pain comes moments later, a wave of it cascading through her head. It makes Alex's body contract with nausea.

"I did not want you to get hurt, you have to understand that. This was not supposed to happen this way," Lucy whines. "I wanted you to look your best."

"Look my best for what?" Alex chokes out as she tries to stay upright.

"For the apology," she says as if Alex should know what she is talking about.

"What apology, Lucy?" Through the pain in her skull, Alex tries to understand what Lucy is talking about.

"Oh, the one between you and my dear older brother whose life you destroyed so thoroughly."

The shock of it cuts through her pain, rattling through her body as she looks up at Lucy's silhouette.

"*Lulu,*" she whispers. How could she not have recognized the silent little girl with straight-cut bangs and Mary Jane shoes? The one with absolute adoration for her much older brother Brian.

Lucy's posture changes, her hand on her hip, almost bragging. "It's been hard keeping it a secret, I must admit. I knew you wouldn't remember me; I have changed a lot, grown up. But still, it hurts a bit.

The way you stared at me that first time though, I thought for a minute that you'd see right through me. That I'd been caught out."

The horror of it gathers in Alex's chest, beating like wings against the inside of her ribcage. The young man who had ruined her, who had taken the last shred of her innocence, who had made her fearful and paranoid. And now she sees it; she has no idea how she missed it. The same rounded cheeks. The same way of looking at you, lying to you. That should have been the biggest clue of all. Lucy looks down at her. She can dimly make out the smug smile playing on her lips. Alex's head throbs.

Before she can say anything, there's a rush of movement in the dark. Alex's arms are yanked tight behind her before she has the chance to pull away. She feels something hard and unyielding, with sharp plasticky edges, close around her wrists. A zip tie. The horror of what is happening hits Alex. Lucy came prepared.

"Your brother nearly ruined me." If Alex can make her understand what happened back then, Lucy will let her go. She'll have to. Alex is the victim here. She needs her to understand. "He hurt me."

"I don't remember it that way," Lucy says. "Neither does he, of course. He loved you. And you just left in the worst possible way."

Alex realizes, her stomach dropping, that Lucy has no idea what happened. Why would she? There is no way Brian would ever have admitted what he did. He'd probably told his family she ran away. He'd probably told Alex's mother the same thing. She can imagine the hurt he would have conjured in his eyes as he told their families what had happened.

"You always loved him so much," Alex remembers. She tries to comfort Lucy from her position curled back against the cabinet. "It's easy to see things the way we want to when it comes to family—"

But Lucy draws away angrily. "He always said you had trouble with the truth. Don't you pull your helpful bullshit on me," she snaps. "I can see right through it. I know you have no idea what you're doing. God knows how you got this job. Not that I'm complaining. If it wasn't for that announcement in the paper, there is no way I would have found you."

"Is that what he told everyone? That I left him?" Alex asks gently. Despite it all she can see the vulnerable child still inside of Lucy. She remembers the way she'd look up to her big brother, her eyes shining as they followed him around a room. It wasn't too different from how Alex had looked at him at first. Brian had them both under his spell.

"He tried to *kill* me," Alex says in case Lucy didn't know.

Lucy crouches down in front of Alex. The little black hearts stitched into her tights stretch at her knees. She looks down at Alex with concern.

"Did he, Alex? Because it really looked like you tried to kill yourself."

Alex shakes her head. Her wrists throb at the memory of that night. "No."

"He had gone for help. He wanted to rescue you." Even as Lucy says it, Alex can feel reality tilt and shift around her. Her confidence starts to slide away. "And then you just ran away and abandoned him. You didn't even let him know what happened. He was worried sick." She is petulant now, scuffing her toe against the floor.

"That's just not true, Lucy," Alex says, squeezing her eyes shut against the glare of the flashlight. The pain in the back of her skull has intensified, sending a sharp dagger through to her forehead.

Lucy glances down at her palm. In the dark kitchen the screen of her phone gives her face a demonic glow, like a child at a slumber party telling a ghost story.

Alex squirms against the tie but it cuts painfully into her arms. She pleads with Lucy: "Please, Lucy, just let me leave. You don't know what you're doing. Brian is not what you think. He's not a good man, he's—"

Lucy spins back and Alex recognizes the angry clench in her jaw.

"You misunderstood everything," Lucy says, rigid with anger. "And you caused so much suffering for us all. And now I am giving everyone the chance to make things right." Then she closes her mouth tightly, giving a little nod of satisfaction at her pronouncement.

"No, you've got it all wrong," Alex begs.

"Well, soon you'll be able to clear it up," Lucy says, a small smile quivering on her lips.

"What are you talking about?" Alex asks as the room starts to spin.

Lucy gives her a last wolfish smile, the same one as her brother's. How had Alex not seen it sooner?

"When he gets here." She breaks into a full grin as Alex's heart turns to sludge.

Now it is too late. Without another word, Lucy turns on her heel and leaves Alex alone on the cold tile.

FORTY-EIGHT

Alex doesn't know how long she's been slumped on the floor of Francis Keen's kitchen. She can hear the faint ticking of a clock somewhere. The night has turned deep and black, covering the room, removing its contours, and erasing the visible signs of her injuries. She squints up, trying to make out the outline of the window, and winces, the slight motion of her head giving her a dizzy feeling. The bleeding seems to have stopped. She can feel the sticky mess forming on the back of her head, the dried blood tugging uncomfortably at her hair.

Alex can't believe that she has been so naive about Lucy. Looking back, it all makes total sense that her assistant was a fraud. The way she skittered through the halls afraid to be seen, avoiding the elevator; the alarm on her face at every mention of Howard Demetri. There were so many obvious warning signs that Lucy was not to be trusted, and yet, after all this time running from the slightest shadow, Alex had given in to her completely, had trusted her.

A door opens and shuts somewhere far away in the house. Alex's wrists throb at the scars, where they push painfully against the zip tie. There are two voices now. Lucy's, higher-pitched than normal, frantic like it is explaining something. Alex's ears prick nervously as someone replies. The voice is a murmur that she can't make out, but she recognizes the timbre. He is here. She struggles to move, to escape, rolling herself onto her knees and lifting herself partway off the ground, but the ties tear at her wrists and she loses her balance, falling onto her stomach and knocking the wind out of her.

They are coming toward her. She can make out the patter of Lucy's steps, light and eager, and others, his, plodding and deliberate. There is nowhere for Alex to go, no more time to escape. The door opens and a beam of light scurries around the floor, finding her there. She tries to raise her head. To see.

"There she is." Lucy's voice is proud, like Alex is something she's brought to show-and-tell. "I didn't want to have to tie her up. But she would have left."

From her position on the floor, Alex can only see his feet, clad in dark work boots. They come closer to her. She can see a spray of paint on their soles. They are the same kind he wore to jobsites even back then. She remembers how he brought her with him once to his big project, the factory he'd been converting. He'd worn a pair just like these, coated in the red dust from the brick. He was so attractive to her that day, showing her around. Just months later she'd listen, her heart in her throat, to the sound of those boots clunking up the stairs of his condo. She'd watch on high alert as he silently and slowly untied the laces, trying to read his body's cues to see if he was mad at her or not.

"Why is she on her stomach?" His voice sends a vibration of fear through her entire body.

"She must have tipped over," Lucy says. "She wasn't that way when I left her."

"Sloppy, Lulu," he admonishes, kneeling next to Alex. A hand brushes hers and she quivers. His hands are on her shoulders now, lifting her from the floor. She is helpless to stop herself.

"Stop squirming or I'll drop you on your face," he says. Brian, the man who left her for dead. There is a grit to his voice that wasn't there before. He sits her upright, propping her against the cabinets. Alex watches, horrified, as the man she has hidden from for eight years rotates into view before her. He is thicker than before; his once taut and muscular body has filled out into something more solid and terrifying. His muscles contract as he crouches in front of her. His eyes narrow as he examines her, scanning her body, her face. He brings his face close to hers and her throat constricts. A scar. She hadn't expected it. An ugly rope of raised tissue that runs from his forehead to the bridge of his nose and picks up again on his cheek. Despite the years, it is red and angry-looking. Making his once beautiful face something that no one could help but flinch at the way she does now.

She smells something acrid as he comes closer. He's taken up smoking, she realizes, her stomach roiling from the sour smell as he leans in close enough that she can feel the vibrations of his voice next to her ear. "I was always going to find you." Without her even meaning to, her body jerks away from him, her shoulder coming to her ear trying to block him out.

He draws back quickly. "Lulu, what is this?" He must see the blood in her hair.

"I didn't hurt her, she fell," Lucy whines.

"Oh, but you've messed up Bess's head, haven't you? That's no good at all," he says, pulling his hand away from Alex, disgusted. "Or should I say *Alex*?" He smirks. "What a funny choice for a pseudonym. It took me a long minute to understand why you chose it. Then I went and paid a visit to your old friend. Saw the name of the place across the street, all boarded up. Alexander's Market. Alex Marks. Pretty clever."

"Sam?" Alex's heart thumps. "You, you didn't hurt him?"

He cranes his neck, looking down at her. "You really do think I'm some sort of monster."

Alex doesn't say anything. She knows better than to say yes but doesn't have the strength to deny it.

"It didn't help that the old man told the whole town I was the reason you disappeared." He spits out the words. "He couldn't leave anything alone."

Sam had never trusted Brian. He'd always had a good sense for people. Alex should have listened to him, she thinks.

"You tried to ruin my career. Telling Sam all those lies about me.

And then I think maybe you died, but imagine my surprise when I find out you lived. They wouldn't let me see you in the hospital. Wouldn't even confirm you were there, but I knew you had to be. Do you know how hard that was for me? To have you just disappear. To never see my girlfriend again, the love of my life."

"It devastated him," Lucy interjects, shaking her head back and forth, stepping forward from where she's been watching in the shadows. "You were gone, so you didn't see the way he was forced to leave his beautiful apartment. He lost everything. He had to come back to grieve at our parents' house. He cried."

Brian raises a hand, silencing his sister. Alex remembers the tears Brian was so fond of producing, how well they worked to sway people. To manipulate her. "You completely fucked my life up," Brian agrees. He was always good at feeling sorry for himself, and she can see it hasn't changed. His face has gotten puffy, his stubble fuller now, with flecks of gray in it. His lips twitch. "It was terrible. A horrible time. But I got help, I healed myself. I did the work, Alex. More than you can say."

Did the work? Healed himself? She'd spent so much time hiding from Brian that she'd forgotten what he really was, an unbelievable, pathological narcissist. She isn't going to get anywhere by accusing him of anything, Alex thinks, reminding herself of how to stay safe. She has to go along with it.

"That's really great, I am so glad you found something—"

His laugh is sharp. An act to cover up the anger that she can tell by the clenched palms and snarling mouth has already begun to take hold. He hasn't changed at all. "Oh, are you? I couldn't find you to tell you how much I'd changed though. You can imagine how that would make someone crazy."

"What do you want from me?" Alex asks, unable to sit there listening to him lie.

"I would like an apology, to start. I've had to live with some pretty horrible things said about me for the past eight years, you know. The speculation in a small town, it can be quite intense. The way you just disappeared made it hard to set the record straight."

"You want an apology? After what you did?" Alex says quietly.

"Funny. I remember trying to help a young girl out of a very tricky home situation."

"Tell her what you told me, Brian," Lucy steps in, prodding him.

Alex had only met Brian's Lulu once during their time dating. It was on an incredibly awkward weekend with his parents at their huge, austere lake house. She remembers the mother, vacant-staring, and the father with his face like a brick, how he would slap Brian on the back a little too hard for it to be affectionate. Lulu was there, too, a withdrawn eleven-year-old wandering around the house like a neglected pet. The entire weekend she followed Brian, her eyes round and adoring. It's the same way she looks at him right now. And just as he did then, he ignores her. He looks down at Alex from his full height now.

"Tell her, Brian. About how bad you felt," Lucy nudges again. She is standing behind Brian, so only Alex can see his face and the irritation on it, how his neck goes tight, the tendons pulsing.

"Enough," Brian yells. "Fuck, Lu. Why did you put me in this situation?" From the ground, Alex watches his fists clench. She remembers those hands. They are strong and slightly stubby, the thumbs curving inward. They repulse her.

Alex watches Lucy's face when he turns on her, how she flinches, hurt, then rearranges her features back to the way they were before he can even see. Alex remembers doing it herself. "You always said you wanted to have a chance to do it right. Remember you said you wished you had been there to help her deal with whatever happened. You told me once how it ate you up inside. I thought if I found her for you, that you could both have a chance to say you're sorry."

The audacity of Brian to confuse the story like that, to twist it and misrepresent it as if he hadn't been there at all, like he wasn't the one in control of things the entire time.

"God, Lu, you really are a fucking idiot." Brian rakes his hands through his hair in frustration. He spins back angrily toward his sister. "What am I supposed to do now?"

"Well, I thought you two could talk. Alex, she really isn't so bad,

Brian. She is just confused. Tell her what happened that day, how you wanted to save her, to protect her from harm, but she ran away." Lucy is shrinking into herself.

"Yes, tell me, Brian," Alex croaks from the ground. "I hadn't realized."

He looks back and forth, caught between the two of them. "That's not going to happen. And anyway, what do I even care? The thing you don't understand is that I've moved on."

Alex's terror is displaced by her anger now. *He* has moved on? While she has spent the last eight years running from him, looking out her apartment window thinking that every shadowy figure is there to kill her? She bites her lip to keep from saying something that will cause him to hurt her.

Lucy seems to be trying to salvage the situation. "Well, if you don't want to have an apology and talk, then we can just let her go. Pretend it didn't happen. I'm sure she won't tell anyone."

Brian turns and looks Alex over, hunched up on the kitchen floor. Not the way he did then, with love or anger or a combination of the two, but perhaps even more terrifyingly with no emotion whatsoever.

"Oh, Lulu. You really aren't very smart, are you? Of course she'll tell."

"I won't," Alex says, desperate to convince them. "I've gone years and years without telling a single soul." He looks confused for a moment, as though he might actually be considering it. Alex feels hope flutter up in her chest. She pictures herself escaping, running across the lawn to the neighbor's house like she should have done to begin with.

"We'll just deny it," Lucy agrees, her voice full of panic.

"I can deny it, sure. I have nothing to do with it, nothing anyone can trace to me anyway. But not you. You fucked her up, Lu," he says, wrinkling his nose as he surveys Alex. "She's a mess. All covered in blood, look at her." He waves a hand at Alex like she is a shattered jar of mayonnaise at a grocery store.

"That was an accident." Lucy's voice wobbles. "She fell. I didn't do it."

"Doesn't matter. Now she's tied up. You know what that is, Lulu?"

She shakes her head, eyes wide. He's enjoying this, Alex thinks suddenly. He's taking pleasure in tormenting Lucy just like he relished torturing Alex when she was young. Brian whistles, shaking his head as Lucy quivers next to him. "The way you messed her up, held her against her will. I'm no expert, but I'm pretty sure it's a felony. This kind of shit can ruin a person."

"What do I do, oh God." Lucy looks like she might be starting to hyperventilate.

"Let me fucking think," Brian says sharply. They move to the far side of the kitchen to discuss Alex's fate. Their voices blend together in a low murmur. It's incredible to Alex that she once thought of that man as cosmopolitan, that he seemed like any sort of ticket out of her misery. How hard it is to know anything about love when you are young and have no examples to follow, how easy it is to be led astray.

"No! Brian!" Lucy's sharp cry makes Alex's blood speed up in her veins. The voices grow lower, and finally she hears Lucy's mumble of acceptance. Brian's boots scrape toward her. The light from his flashlight trails along the floor and then his face, that raised scar, appears once more in her frame of vision.

"I was not planning on hurting you. Remember that I had nothing to do with this. This time it is on my sister, not me." Lucy goes pale behind him.

Alex screams but his hand clamps down over her mouth.

"Shut up or I will do it right now. I'll be right back. I just have to get some things."

Her chest burns as she squirms and fights with all the strength she has in her, thrashing her legs out but coming up against nothing but air.

Dear Constance,

I made a plan like you told me to. I almost left in time. Mentally I had already packed a bag. In my mind I was walking down the side of the highway, nearly at the bus stop. But physically I was still there in his apartment, my limbs heavy and tired, my brain in a fog. I looked at the clock. I still had six hours until he came home for the day.

I looked around. What do you take with you to start over? I went into our bedroom and looked around at the stark gray duvet cover, the sleek white bedside tables, the artful alarm clock without any numbers made from a cylinder of concrete. Nothing soft or comforting in sight. I don't know now how I was so impressed by it. It should have been a warning. It was so clearly a reflection of who he is, calculated and cold without a single soft place to nestle your way into.

I walked around the apartment and realized that nothing in the whole place represented me. It was only Brian. I had basically disappeared. I found a few of my things, clothes tucked into drawers, a set of pens. I took a bottle of water from the refrigerator. I tucked them all into my tote bag. There was only one more stop to make before the bus and it was a long walk into town from here. I stopped in front of a mirror in the entryway. My arms looked thin through the sleeves of my sweatshirt. You are inside there, I thought. My eyes were dark with fear and lack of sleep. I pulled my hood up. I didn't need people seeing me on the walk. Okay, you have to go now. You have to run.

I picked up the bag and turned to the door just as the handle began to turn. I watched in total shock as the door swung open. Brian smiled when he saw me, taking in my bag, my sweatshirt. He must have known right away but he didn't react, not at first.

"You're heading out?" he asked. I imagined rushing past him, running down the stairs and onto the road, flagging down whoever I could. But the staircase behind him was empty. The

grasses next to the road rippled in the wind. There was no one to help. And even if there was, who would they believe? A young girl in emotional distress or a man wearing a pressed pair of khakis and a work shirt? In Wickfield? I already knew the answer.

"You're home early," I said.

"Yeah, I wanted to make sure I stopped you from doing anything stupid." How had he known? He was moving in on me and I stumbled backward, toward the living room.

"What is this?" he said, holding up a white envelope. The ground dropped out. He knew.

"How did you get that?"

"Buddy of mine in the condo office has access to the mailboxes. I told him to let me know if he saw anything come through that I should be aware of."

He seemed surprisingly calm, and for a moment I thought that I'd misread the whole thing. That it was going to be okay.

But instinctively, my hands jerked up, trying to protect my throat. I stood there quivering, my eyes darting from his eyes—calm and blue—to the door. I allowed myself to imagine turning the lock and slipping outside before he jerked my attention back to him.

"You thought you were going to make a fool of me?" he said through gritted teeth. Not a question, an accusation. "What if people found out that you were writing to her?" I didn't tell him that it wasn't the first time, that I'd written twenty, maybe thirty letters to Dear Constance before the one he'd intercepted. "What if they knew it was me? That would ruin my life, don't you understand?"

"No one would have known." My voice revolted, trembling despite my attempts to keep it steady. "It's an advice column. It's anonymous."

His big blue eyes were confused. The way he couldn't understand made him even angrier. "Well, they sure as hell aren't going to now." He turned his back to me, going into the kitchen and rummaging around in a drawer.

"Brian?" Fear had already gripped my insides. The not knowing what he was going to do made my body hum with fear.

Then he did something unexpected. He came back to me and put a hand gently on my shoulder. "You've been depressed," he said. "So terrible to hear that." He took hold of my hand almost tenderly.

"No, only a little bit," I said. A small smile spread across his face as he turned my palm up. For a blissful moment I thought he was going to let it all go.

"I'll make it look like a suicide," he said in a way that sounded like he'd just come up with the idea, but I could tell he hadn't. I knew that he'd been practicing saying the words to me for a while, and now that they were finally out, he was relishing them.

I let out a weird, strangled laugh. "No one would believe that." I was having trouble comprehending what he was saying. It couldn't be real.

"Oh no?" He turned my wrist over, his eyes traveling to the vulnerable pale flesh swimming with blue veins. "You've withdrawn from all of your friends. Your mom thinks you're 'pretty depressed.'" He made air quotes with his free hand. I remembered then the last conversation I'd had with my mom and my heart shattered. "I think they would."

I tried to twist away, but that only made him grip my arm harder. I lost my balance and fell hard into the wall, gasping loudly as I fought for breath. He looked down at me, slumped over still struggling to stand, and he smiled. He was happy to be in control. You had tried to save me, Constance, but I had waited too long. I should have left when I had the chance. I realized then that my hesitation had cost me everything.

It wasn't as easy as he expected. I fought for my life, squirming and twisting until he held the knife under my chin and told me to stop. Until then I still couldn't believe he wanted to hurt me, to really hurt me. After all, this was a man who had gently gazed into my eyes a hundred times, who had met my mother, who

I'd shared the closest bond I'd ever known with. What was it he said that first night? I thought about the way he pulled me close to him in bed, his voice low and comforting. "Do you know how much I love you? I want to protect you from anything bad that could happen to you."

The words rang in my ears as he looped an arm over my neck and dragged me toward the hall, an X-Acto knife in one hand. He extended and retracted the blade with his thumb as he marched me into the bathroom. Inside, he flung me into the shower, flicking the water on. I held up my hands to protect my eyes from the spray. Not hesitating, he brought the knife across my wrists, one quick slice, superficial at first. I gasped at the bright blood. He turned the spray of the water toward me, drenching my clothes. I pulled away, but he gripped my arm and this time the knife came down at an angle. I screamed, trying to stay up, to fight back, but the glass was slick behind me, and I lost my balance. I screamed again, kicking and flailing, watching my blood turn pink in the shower basin. His jaw was set in that familiar way as he came at me. I pulled myself up and reached an arm to the nozzle of the shower, spraying it on him. "You stupid bitch," he yelled, waving the knife blindly. I shoved past him out of the shower and tried to run, but his hand closed around a fistful of my hair, jerking me violently back. I landed on the floor next to the shower. Out of the water all the pain was sharper. My wrists were a mess of blood now that I was no longer under the shower, and it pumped out onto the white bathmat bright deep red.

I finally went still, too weak to stand. He watched me as I lay there. The love of my life. Isn't that what I called him to you once, Constance? I am never to be trusted again with my own heart.

He had to set the stage to make this look like it was my fault. The ultimate gaslighting finale to this nightmare he'd created. My vision was getting blurry around the edges, but I could see him crouching down, wiping the handle of the X-Acto knife. My pulse was getting weak now. He leaned over me, and for the first time

I saw right through him. By hurting me he had fully released me.
He was weak and stupid and very afraid because inside he knew
he was a husk of a person.

I let my eyes flutter shut. I thought at that moment only of the
words you wrote. The response that was printed in the Herald *for*
the whole world to see but was a secret I'd kept hidden, folded up
and tucked in my little lockbox. I didn't need it anymore. I had it
memorized. I repeated the words you wrote over and over like a
prayer, flashing in front of the red of my eyelids. "I want you to
make a list of places you have always wanted to go . . . somewhere
he has no connection to whatsoever."

I was surprised that I still felt some strength in my hand when
he put the knife in it, curling my fingers around the hilt. I stayed
quiet, my eyes closed. He couldn't be here when I died, he had to
make sure of it. He leaned over me. I could feel his breath on my
face. Could hear it. My eyes flew open, locking with his, and I drove
the knife up at him. He screamed in pain, reeling back from me.

"Fuck. You stupid fucking—" He pressed a towel to his head,
crying in agony, his neck craned backward. My eyes fluttered. He
couldn't let his blood mingle with mine on the floor. He grabbed
the knife from my hand and ran it under the faucet, moaning the
entire time. This time he put it out of my reach beyond the blood-
soaked bathmat.

When I heard the door click shut, I forced my eyes open. I
dragged myself from the shower to the bedroom. My phone was
still in my bag. It took the remainder of my strength to reach it.
The screen was slippery with blood as I dialed. So much blood in
a body, it comes and comes.

"What is your emergency," a voice said. But I couldn't answer.
I hung up before I had to try to explain, and dialed one more
number. This time I could only gasp. "Sam," I croaked weakly.

I could hear his voice coming from very far away. "Where are
you?" But I could no longer speak.

FORTY-NINE

Lucy won't look at Alex as they hoist her up from the ground, each of them taking one of her arms and pulling her roughly to stand.

"Walk," Brian commands. Her feet flop uselessly at the ground, her legs rubbery.

Alex's vision spins as she moves, the floor shifting and tilting wildly in her peripheral vision. There is something wrong with her head, she thinks with growing panic. They inch painfully down the hall toward the front of the house.

"In here," Brian says, guiding them into the living room. They drop Alex onto a low sofa.

"Close the blinds," Brian instructs Lucy. She scampers to all the windows, doing what he says and pulling the curtains across for good measure. Brian switches on a small table lamp. It lets off a yellowy glow. Alex blinks, taking in the built-in bookshelves heaving with hardcovers, the soot-stained mantel, and above it a large oil painting of a choppy ocean with seagulls swooping into the waves. She squints, trying to get a clearer view, and her head explodes in pain.

Alex moans slightly.

Brian stands above her looking down. His voice is calm. He is in control. "We have to get her out of here. Less messy. You pull my car around and open the trunk. We can probably drag her over that break in the fence. You can follow me. We'll find a place on the way back. Somewhere in the woods."

"I'm going back with you?" Lucy asks quietly.

"Where the hell else would you go? You're not going to fucking leave me to deal with this on my own." The irritation in his voice makes Lucy flinch.

"I've got an apartment in the city. My roommate will wonder what happened to me . . ." Lucy trails off. "I thought after I did this for you, I might stay there. I could even keep my mailroom job. No one has to know."

Brian's face breaks into a mean grin. The scar stretches grotesquely across his cheek as he laughs at her. "Lulu, you idiot. You think you're going to keep your job? *No.* You are not going to live out some city girl fantasy. You did this and you are going to take care of it now. You're coming with me."

Lucy's chin clenches helplessly. She opens her mouth to speak, but there is the sound of something falling and breaking in the hallway behind them.

At once Brian is on top of Alex. He pulls her up from the sofa, his thick arm circling her neck as though she is somehow responsible. "What's that?" He growls, his mouth close to her ear as Alex gasps for breath. "Lulu, go look."

Lucy pales, looking back into the dark of the hall. "But I don't have anything to defend myself with. I—"

"Find something. I kind of have my hands full with your mess right now," he snaps at her. Lucy pulls a cast iron poker from next to the fireplace. She holds it out with one arm, pointing her phone with the other. Her fragile shoulders shake as she heads into the hallway. For what feels like an eternity there is no sound but Brian's breathing, ragged and arhythmic.

"The back door is wide open," Lucy's faint voice calls back, frantic.

Brian's grip on Alex's neck tightens. "Who did you tell," he hisses into Alex's hair. She struggles, trying to pull away as she gasps for breath.

"Who's there?" Lucy's thin voice echoes from the hall.

For a moment Alex imagines Howard Demetri has shown up, just like he said he would. She'd be happy to see him now, she realizes, imagining his long frame filling the doorway. Howard seems like the kind of person who could put an end to all of this. He'd have the police with him, of course; they'd listen to someone like Howard, wouldn't they? Alex's head is pulsing, woozy. But Howard isn't coming, she reminds herself, replaying the conversation with Jonathan. It feels distant, a memory so vague now that she can't quite decide if it actually happened. Her peripheral vision has a dark halo around it.

"I'm just meeting a friend here," a voice says, too cheerful for the situation. Alex squints at the door, a mix of relief and terror filling her as a woman's body fills the doorframe.

"Janice!" Alex croaks. "No. You can't be here."

"Shut up," Brian shouts down at her as Janice steps into the room. She takes in Alex, covered in dried blood and trapped beneath the crush of Brian's arm, and starts toward her. "Alex, my God, are you okay? What did you assholes do to her?"

"Who the fuck is this?" Brian says, jerking Alex back. She can hear the stress in his voice. He's losing control. There's nothing Brian hates more. And there is never a time when he is more dangerous. She realizes that he really didn't have a plan for when he came here. Lucy must have told him and he just got in his car and drove, eager to stick his face in hers and tell her how much she'd fucked him up, to try to gaslight her again. But this time he doesn't have some master plan to help him get away with her murder. This time it will have to be spur of the moment, which Alex knows is not his specialty.

"I called your office when Howard was arrested, and Jonathan told me you were here. Thought you might need some help, but looks like you brought some friends with you?" Janice glances at Lucy, then Brian. Alex watches her eyes land on the scar. Alex notices the slight shudder as Janice realizes she's gotten herself into something very bad.

"Stay back," Brian shouts at Janice. She hesitates a few feet inside the doorway.

"What do we do now?" Lucy cries from the edge of the room. All this time she has been standing back watching.

"We'll bring them both," Brian says. "Lu, bring me the zip ties."

"Oh, I'm not going anywhere," Janice assures them, planting her feet firmly. "I've seen enough true crime documentaries to know how that works out."

"You're going wherever the fuck I tell you," Brian says. "Lu! Bring me the fucking ties."

But Lucy is looking past him toward the front of the house. She's not moving.

"Let her go," a deep voice commands from the far door.

The beam of a flashlight hits Alex square in the eyes. She blinks, and the light moves past her. Now Alex can see the outline of a figure. He is stooped, thin arms held rigid. He advances on them. As he steps into the room, she can see he's holding a gun.

"Raymond?" Alex gasps, disbelieving.

Brian's arm drops from Alex's neck as he brings it up to shield his face. She uses this moment to twist from his grip, pulling herself away from him into the middle of the room. She is too dizzy on her feet and wobbles, collapsing onto the carpet. Brian starts for her, but Raymond steps closer, nimble on his feet. The gun is steady.

"Step away from her or I will shoot you." The voice booms out of Raymond's slight body.

"Brian," Lucy pleads, "he has a gun."

"Oh, please," Brian says dismissively. "It's just some old guy."

Raymond takes a deliberate step deeper into the living room, the gun locked on Brian.

"Please do what he says, Brian," Lucy shrieks from behind him.

"I'm going to do whatever the fuck I want," Brian snarls, stepping toward Alex.

"I wouldn't," Raymond says.

"Or what, you'll shoot me?" Brian scoffs.

The violent velocity of a bullet pierces the air just to the right of Brian's head, exploding against the mantel. Lucy ducks, and crumples to the ground. She lands near Alex on the carpet, tucking her knees around her head. "Oh my God, Brian." Her scream turns into a low moan.

Raymond looks surprisingly calm. "The next one is going straight through your Neanderthal skull if you don't move away from my friend there."

"Oh? This is your friend?" Brian scoffs. He lets out a bitter laugh as he looks down at Alex, kicking her in the ribs hard enough that Alex gasps for breath. "Please. Do you even know her real name? You can't trust this one. She'll try to tell the whole world a bunch of lies about you. Make you out to be a bad person when all you've ever done is help her."

"Right, you really do seem like a great guy." Janice's voice is thick with sarcasm. Brian turns on her, seething, and she backs into the wall. Alex struggles to pull herself up on her elbows, the throbbing in her skull making her body heavy.

"Do any of you know what a mess this girl was when I found her working at a hardware store in the middle of nowhere?" Brian roars, turning around the room. "Twenty-two years old and still living at home. She couldn't even say her name without her face getting all red. I helped her. I got her out of her mom's house. Out of her dead-end job. And how did she repay me? She disfigured me." He points at his own face, mottled red with fury. The scar glows white.

"No, that doesn't add up," Raymond says, taking a step toward him. Alex watches the gun quiver slightly in Raymond's hand, his finger lightly pressing on the trigger.

"Stop," Lucy sobs, her fingers clenched in front of her. "Just stop it." Raymond glances at her, and in that split second, Brian barrels across the room toward him.

"Ray! He's moving!" Janice yells. But it's too late. With shocking speed Brian lunges at Raymond, yanking his arm to the side and sending a knee straight into his diaphragm. Alex watches, horrified, as Raymond falls to the floor. He wheezes helplessly. Brian's foot leaves the ground ready to strike. *He is going to kill him,* Alex thinks, her heart clenched. His heel comes down hard and she hears something crack below his boot, a shattering of bones. A shaky groan of pain comes from Raymond.

"Ray!" Janice screams.

Alex's eyes travel across the carpet to where the gun has fallen. She rolls away from it and reaches behind her, the zip tie cutting into her as she stretches her hands out toward it, nearly there. Lucy spots it now too. She leaps across the floor toward Alex, her fingers closing around the barrel. Alex watches, her vision tunneling, as Lucy stands, the gun in her hand. She swings it at Janice, who backs away from Raymond's crumpled body.

She points the gun at Alex. The barrel of it blurs in Alex's line of vision. Staring her down.

Brian grins. "Oh, too bad your little rescue committee failed you. Bring the car around, Lu. I'm not letting her get away this time." The air in the room shifts.

"This time?" Lucy says tentatively, her eyes bouncing between them. "What do you mean? I thought you said that she was depressed. That she left a bloody mess in your apartment, and you never saw her again?"

Lucy hasn't been trying to prove Alex's guilt all this time, Alex realizes. She was trying to prove Brian's innocence. All she wants is what Alex wanted all that time ago, for the person she loves to not be a monster.

"The only accident is that she made it out alive. She was going to fuck me over. Just like she'll do to you if you give her half a chance. She'd been writing in to that advice columnist trying to get my reputation smeared."

"No one would have known it was you," Alex says quietly, the room spinning.

"You don't think someone would have figured it out? And if you were telling some stranger, who's to say you weren't out spreading rumors about me to other people? I know you told Sam a bunch of lies about what a victim you were. I could see it the way he looked at me."

"I never did. You had me way too scared of you to ever do that." The room starts to tilt again.

"I would have lost everything, and for what reason? Because I was dating some young nobody who had some deluded fantasy of being better than she was." He is close to Alex now, his face ruddy with anger.

She can see the whites of his eyes crisscrossed with angry red threads. The scar is the least ugly part about him.

Brian turns toward Lucy. "Give me the gun," he commands, holding his palm out. "You don't know what to do with it." Lucy looks down at it in her hands. She's grown pale and quiet.

"No," she says. The word sends a ripple of shock through the room.

"What?" Brian says as though he must have misheard her.

"Why did you lie to me?" She is crying now, her shoulders shaking, but the gun stays rigid in her hand.

"Lulu, what are you talking about? I was trying to protect you."

Alex is losing consciousness now. Stars swoop and spin across her vision as she struggles to stay awake.

"No—no, you weren't," Lucy says. "I can't believe I've been so stupid. You were trying to protect *you*. You only ever cared about yourself."

"Lulu," Brian starts.

"No. Stay away from me." The barrel of the gun swoops up away from Alex.

"What the fuck, Lu?" Brian says. "You stupid bitch. Give me the gun."

"No." She raises it and pulls the trigger.

There is a loud thump of a body hitting the floor. Alex strains to see what is happening, but her vision has gone dark. She hears screaming somewhere that fades into nothing.

FIFTY

The ceiling is the first thing Alex sees when her eyes flutter open. A grid of pockmarked gypsum panels interspersed with track lighting. Her head lolls to the side. She is in a bed. A stiff white sheet covers her up to her chest. There is a clock on the wall, old-fashioned, round like the clocks in her grade school. She squints at the glowing face of it: 10:47. She can't see a window, so she doesn't know if it is morning or night.

"Alex," someone says. She tries to move her head in the other direction but she's getting tired again. She can only make out the dark shape of someone sitting in a chair before her eyelids tug down again, her eyes closing involuntarily.

She goes like this in and out of consciousness for an untold amount of time. Machines beep periodically around her. Their little red lights flash reassuringly. She thinks Janice and Raymond are there with her once, but when she opens her eyes again, they are gone and there are no chairs there at all. Once she wakes up and there is a man in the doorway, his mantis-like limbs coming toward her. Her chest seizes. The image fades, disappearing behind her lids, and when she wakes again, she isn't sure if he was ever there.

She doesn't know if it has been days or only hours when she finally emerges from the fog of what happened. Finally, her eyes blink open and stay that way. She is in a hospital room. A woman in a doctor's coat comes into the room and makes her look at a bright light.

"You had a significant head trauma, but you got here just in time to stop the bleeding. You're going to be fine soon enough." Alex glances down to where a tube sends a steady drip of something nice into her arm. Her wrist lies exposed to the air. She catches the nurse looking at it as she switches out the IV bag. She gives Alex a sympathetic squeeze on the shoulder. Alex's eyes close again.

They open to the sound of a chair being dragged across the room. There is someone sitting next to her when she wakes again. A pair of pointy black shoes with *Prada* stamped on the toes flash in her peripheral vision as two long legs crisscross impatiently next to her.

Her eyes finally focus on the woman the shoes belong to. The high cheekbones, the perfect outline of her nose, the precise rose-colored lipstick.

"Regina?" Alex's voice cracks.

"Oh, good. You're awake," she says, in a voice colder than you'd expect from someone who has come to offer their sympathies.

"Am I?" Alex mumbles, trying to understand why Regina is here.

"Quite the drama up at the beach house, I hear. Something about a girl from the mailroom murdering her own brother?" she says distastefully. Alex's head throbs as she tries to remember what happened. Francis's house. Brian. Her stomach turns. What happened to Raymond? She looks around for a sign of him. Did he visit her? She can't remember.

"Raymond?" she croaks out. "Do you know where he is?"

"I'm sorry. I don't know who you're talking about." Regina looks momentarily flustered, annoyed by the off-script questioning.

She continues: "As you know, we can't have our staff going around behaving badly. I spoke to Daddy, and he wasn't so sure, but you'll be happy that I've convinced him to keep you on." She smooths her platinum-blond hair, swept into a chignon the size of a giant cinnamon roll on the top of her head. "I told him you were trying to prove that Howard killed Francis. You did us a service at the *Herald*. I came to thank you, actually."

"Thank me?"

"Without all your nosing around, there is no way Howard would have gotten caught. I never would have known."

Alex's vision blurs as she tries to focus on what Regina is saying. Did she prove Howard's guilt? In her half-loopy medicated state, Alex is having trouble remembering. There was a letter, something on the computer at Francis Keen's house. Did Howard say that he loved her?

"What are you mumbling?" Regina snaps.

"Nothing." Alex coughs.

"Anyway, I should be going. I just came to pay my respects and to let you know that you still have a job. I thought it might inspire you to get back at it more quickly. Nothing like a goal, am I right?"

Her job. Alex remembers the rush of adrenaline she felt putting the words together, unfolding the puzzle of someone's deepest dilemmas and arranging them on the page. There are the letters of people she thought of even here from her hospital bed. Images of their lives that play out against the backs of her heavy-lidded eyes during half-waking moments. Sometimes she has even thought of something she wants to say to them, to write down, but found herself asleep again before she could try to reach for a pen.

"Thank you," Alex says. Her throat feels dry and scratchy.

"Oh, I brought you a card," Regina says as she stands, leaning forward to place an envelope on the flesh-colored hospital tray next to Alex's bed.

Regina gathers herself, straightening the cream-colored sweater. So pressed and perfect. Alex wonders how she must appear to Regina. Terrible, she assumes. She can see only her own scarred wrists on the bed and the wild curls of hair in her peripheral vision. She must look like a nightmare to someone like Regina, whose entire existence is so perfectly curated it may as well be put in a gallery to admire like some sort of incredible performance art. Alex watches her lift her Chanel bag off the top of a contraption with a digitized screen. Despite being dressed down, Regina looks every bit as perfect and glamorous as in the first photo Alex saw of her and Howard at the Met Gala, in that miraculous shimmering fish scale dress. Incredible, really, for a woman whose husband just went to jail and is awaiting trial for murder.

As Regina goes to the door, Alex picks up the card and slides it open. *Get well soon*, written on thick cardstock in perfect tilted script. But that isn't what makes Alex cry out. The notecard accidentally falls from her fingers, fluttering to the floor. It lands face up, a green background with a thin gold line embossed around the edge.

"I know," Alex whispers. "I know about Howard and Francis," she says gently to Regina's back as her hand freezes on the door.

Regina rotates slowly on her heels, turning back toward her. Coming back to the end of the bed, she looks down at Alex and her eyes narrow. "What did you say?"

"You knew about the two of them, didn't you? You told her you did."

"No, I had no idea about her and Howard, only that Howard was having an affair," Regina says in her clipped way.

Alex's voice remains calm. "I found the note, Regina. *I know.* Wasn't that what it said? I'm a little bit addled at the moment, but something like that is hard to forget. So short and to the point." She registers a flutter of anxiety in Regina's eyes and continues. "It would be tempting to want to punish someone your husband cheated with so brazenly and for so long."

"I didn't." Her mouth opens and closes.

"It was your handwriting though. You have incredible penmanship. I'm quite envious of it, really."

"You can't prove anything with a note, darling," Regina says, though her knees seem to have gone weak and she's sunk back into the blue plastic hospital chair beside Alex's bed. "Any woman would be angry at the woman who ruined her marriage."

"It's true. She did ruin it, didn't she?" Alex says with pity in her voice.

"For years and years, I had to deal with it. The way he always gave her the benefit of the doubt, raved about her talent, while with me, well." She snorts, a surprisingly unrefined noise. "You know, the emotional part is always so much harder than the physical anyway. I wasn't ever in love with my husband in a passionate way. But I did love him. I respected him. I expected some level of devotion at least. A token of appreciation for what I did for him. What I sacrificed."

"What was that?" Alex winces as she shifts in her bed. She is suddenly dying of thirst. There is a cup just to the side on the table. She reaches her fingers out to it.

"I could have run the whole place. Been editor in chief. Do you think I wanted to be a fucking socialite? To spend my life holding charity functions?" she demands, standing and crossing the room. "My father would never have allowed it though. He always wanted someone like him to take over. But Howard was nothing like him. He was always full of principles"—she makes air quotes with her fingers—"and ideas." She leans in, confiding in Alex. "Marrying Howard was a perfect way to punish my father while also keeping my hands in the business. I always thought one day I might come back in."

"Until he hired Francis," Alex says, feeling a tiny seed of sympathy. To love someone who would never love you back, to be married to them, is a brutal form of punishment.

"She ruined everything. That's what I thought anyway. My husband was in love with a woman who made everything I've worked for, everything I am, disappear. But it's not true. Of course, I realized it too late. Isn't that the way these things often go? You said it yourself, didn't you, Alex?"

Alex almost has it now. Her finger rests on the edge of the cup. Finally Regina sharpens her eyes on her. She crosses over to the little table.

"I have to say, I didn't expect you to get so involved in all of our drama," she says, picking up the cup.

Alex's whole body feels like a wrung-out sponge. She can practically feel the water on her lips, and stretches out her fingers. Instead of handing the cup to her, Regina takes it with her, setting it on a ledge far across the room. She sits again, straightening her pant legs. "But I'm glad you did. Like I said, I'm grateful you helped put Howard in jail. That's where murderers belong. Now, where were we? Oh, that's right, I believe we were talking about you keeping your job."

Alex marvels at how comfortable the woman is with wielding her power. Regina Whitaker doesn't get caught for crimes. She gets away with them.

Alex hears something at the door and glances past her at the hallway. "And what about the knife?" Alex asks, her voice hoarse.

"What are you talking about?"

"The knife. It was a gift to Howard from you, wasn't it?" Alex says, thinking of the inscription on the leather case.

"Yes, I gave it to him for our twentieth anniversary. What about it?"

"I found it," Alex says as Regina's perfect face falls. "It was under the desk in Francis's office at the beach house. The police have it now."

Regina smiles, and Alex watches her chest fall as she exhales, relieved. "You couldn't have found it. I buried it in the garden."

There is a moment where she realizes what she's done. The two of them stare at one another.

Regina blinks. "Oh, please. I'll just deny it."

"You can't," Alex says, her heart pounding.

"Oh, and why is that?" Regina smirks. A machine next to Alex begins to beep as Regina steps toward her. This is what having no consequences looks like. She is a woman who will do whatever she can to get what she wants, knowing that she will get away with it. She will kill someone. But not right now. Because a slim figure has come to stand in the doorway behind her, quietly slipping into the room through the cracked door.

"Because I heard it, too," Jonathan says. He stands behind Regina, a bouquet of flowers in his hand.

Dear Constance,

I thought it was over for me, I really did. When I heard the door shut, I thought I might only be imagining things. I was hardly able to keep myself from falling asleep by then. I could feel my pulse slow down, like all the blood in my body was coming to a standstill. He'd left, I realized, to avoid getting caught with my body. He'd make sure to come back later so that he could say he found me and put on a little show for everyone, cry some of those fake tears. He'd call 911. Assuming it was all over.

But slowly I got better. And now here I am. I may have choked in the final moments. I may not have left when I needed to, but I had done some smart things to prepare. I contacted one of the women's rescue organizations, which helped me change my name. When he came to find me, there was no one under that name. It allowed me to get better without him, for the wounds to heal. And once I was better, they helped me disappear.

I stepped out into Penn Station. Some people might be afraid of being in a big city, but I felt a stirring in my chest as I emerged into the bright light of Midtown. This was my chance just like you said it was. All this time I'd wanted to escape. And now I had. You were right about that. You were right about everything.

Sincerely,
Lost Girl (now hopefully found)

EPILOGUE

Six Months Later

"Saved your seat," Raymond calls out when Alex walks into the Blue-bird. It's a beautiful Sunday morning and the diner is buzzing with activity. It is that wonderful moment in early winter when the city looks clean and magical. The department store holiday light displays sparkle in a coat of freshly fallen snow. Winter coats spill out into the narrow space as Alex squeezes past to get to the end of the counter.

"How's it going, Alexis, or should I say Constance?" Raymond says, raising his wild eyebrows. "I saw your new column, quite the contentious one this week."

Jonathan had texted her this morning. Apparently there is already a bit of an uproar in the comments section about her latest answer.

The young man from this week's column had written to Constance despondent over the direction his life was headed. He had an unsup-portive family, no real romantic prospects, and a relentless problem with a bully at work. He'd wondered if he could run away from his problems, start fresh in a new location. Of course, Alex knew the typical response would be to tell him to stay put. But she has more nuanced views about these things. Alex may have even been going against what Francis would have said when she wrote her response.

Dear Escape Fantasies,

*You've probably been told that you can't run away from yourself.
Wherever you go, there you are, isn't that the old adage? Though
I appreciate the sentiment, I respectfully disagree. Because there
are certain times you need to go someplace new to put your
life back on course. I'm not saying it will automatically make
you a different person. But it can be hard to change under the
microscope of people we know, hard to stretch ourselves through
the claustrophobia of the familiar.*

*Sometimes the only way to be able to see yourself clearly is
through a fresh lens. So go forward toward your new beginning.
It's not often in life we get to start completely fresh. Savor it.*

Alex smiles, thinking about her answer. It might be her favorite
column to date.

"How are things with you, Ray?" she asks him. It had been touch and
go there for a while. They had been admitted to the same hospital, so
when Alex was allowed to walk around she'd gone and visited his room.
Janice stopped by often as well, and they'd sit and talk over Styrofoam
cups of watery hospital coffee.

"Oh, you know," Raymond says, glancing at the crutches leaning
on the counter. "Getting better. How's the job going? Are you all still
steering the ship without a rudder?"

"Oh, didn't I tell you? We have a new boss, a woman this time,
actually. She seems quite good." Alex had a meeting with the new
editor yesterday. Belinda Robinson, a journalist who came from
magazine reporting and had a Pulitzer Prize under her belt. She'd
been engaging and no-nonsense, and Alex had immediately felt at
ease with her. Most important, they share a vision for Dear Constance.
She was committed to it staying the way it was and to keeping Alex
on in the role.

"Ohhh boy! You think Regina's found out yet?" Raymond asks.
"That's gotta sting."

"I don't know if you get the news in prison." Janice laughs.

"I don't think they lock people that rich up in regular prison. She probably has the internet and fluffy pillows," Alex says, trying to imagine Regina without her cashmere sweaters and designer shoes.

"They probably let her keep all her designer bags," Janice says, "let her get some floofy white emotional support dog." They all chortle.

"Shame about Howard though, always hard to see the higher-ups fall from grace. Even if they deserve it," Raymond says, possibly thinking of himself.

Alex has seen Howard only once since he was released. He was no longer on trial for Francis's murder since Regina's accidental confession, but he didn't have his job back and he never would. Regina's father had made sure of it.

They met briefly at the coffee shop across from the office where she'd first run into Tom. Howard was pale and hunched when he came in, appraising the corporate signage at the counter with a kind of forlorn emptiness that made Alex worry he might suddenly tip over. They found a small table. Howard looked like a little kid when he sat at it and his knees scraped the top. He'd hunched his shoulders apologetically.

"I'm so sorry for the way things happened, Alex," Howard said. "I was so preoccupied when I hired you. I thought I could find out what had happened to Francis myself if the police weren't going to. Stupid, really." He shook his head.

"Not as crazy as you might think," Alex said. "None of this was your fault."

He gave her a dry chuckle. "Oh no? It was, though. I wasn't able to show up for you. I could have made sure you were safe in the office I helmed, for God's sake. All of this is my fault, really." Alex could tell he felt deep regret. "I told myself that if I worked hard enough, it could all be mine. The job I desired, the person I loved. I thought I could keep everything in balance," he said miserably, his knee bouncing under the table. Alex noticed that he hadn't touched his coffee.

"But I couldn't." He removed his glasses, pressing his palms into the corners of his eyes before continuing. "Looking back on it, I would have chosen a smaller life with Francis any day. I would have given up my career; what good has it done for me in the long run anyway? I would have let her take the lead; she could have kept her job writing the column. Now it all seems fairly simple, of course."

"You tried to fix it, didn't you?"

"It was too late then. I knew Regina was connected to it all in some way. From the day Francis died her confidence seemed to blossom. She became more demanding, emboldened. I was grieving, of course, but I wasn't able to show it. There were things she began to say during that time, little digs she started making at me. I had a feeling then that she knew about the affair. I hired a private investigator to help me prove she was the murderer. Of course, her father would make sure his precious daughter was never touched. Even though Regina killed Francis, I still blame myself. If I had been honest about my feelings to Regina from the start, none of it would have happened. Francis would still be alive. The beauty of hindsight." He gave a dry, humorless chuckle.

"Just so you know, before she died Francis read the message you sent her," Alex told him.

"What?" He looked straight at her, shocked.

"I saw her email, the one you wrote. It was in a folder on her desktop; she'd tried to delete it but it was still there. She may not have been able to answer you, but I can promise you one thing, it had been read."

He nodded. "Thank you, Alex. One thing I can say I actually did right in my tenure at the *Herald* was hiring the right people."

"Yes, you can feel good about that," she said. They finished their meeting and stood to leave.

"Oh, I almost forgot." Alex reached down into her bag and pulled out the book of Yeats poems. He took it from her gently, his eyes already clouding.

"How did you . . ." he started to ask, but became overwhelmed with emotion.

"A gift from you to Francis, at least that's what I've been assuming?" He nodded, paging through it until he found the dedication page. His chin trembled slightly as he read it.

Alex continued, "You changed my life for the better. I want you to know that I really appreciate it. I know you changed Francis's too." Tears pooled under his glasses as they said their goodbyes, Alex heading uptown and Howard down, both on foot.

"That was the only thing I could really give him in the end. Telling him that Francis knew he loved her," Alex says to them now, thinking of the empty whiskey bottles in his desk drawer. "He didn't care if he kept the job. I think he might have even preferred leaving in a way. He needs time. It'll be good for him to have a break." She picks up her coffee.

"God, what a mess," Janice says. "I hope he can have a fresh start. He deserves that at least."

"Don't we all?" Raymond says ruefully.

There's a flash of red at the outside window. Alex smiles as Tom pushes through the door of the diner, his headphones around his neck. His face is flushed when he walks in, snow sticking to his hair. He's wearing a hooded sweatshirt from the Strand bookstore.

"Oh, is it casual day at the old Excelsior Building?" Raymond teases. He has been tolerating the added demands on Alex's attention better than she expected. He even seems to like Tom.

"I quit last week," he says, grinning at Alex.

"Oh boy." Raymond rolls his eyes.

"Don't worry. I've been overpaid for years. I have some money saved up. Plus some stocks and other things. And if that doesn't work, I'm sure some horrible company will take me back in to do their bidding."

Janice raises her pencil-thin eyebrows. "What comes next?"

"Well, thought I'd see about writing a novel," Tom says. "I've always wanted to."

"In my day you'd never quit your day job to write a book," Raymond says, giving Alex a disapproving look.

"In your day there weren't even child labor laws," Janice says, sliding a coffee onto the counter in front of Tom. "I'm excited to read it, Tom."

"Thanks, Janice." He smiles gratefully. She blooms under Tom's attention, her cheeks flushing and her posture growing straighter.

"Usual?" she asks. It's taken Tom much less time to become a regular, Alex notes wryly. He already has a usual after mere months of frequenting the Bluebird.

"Yes, ma'am." He grins.

"What about you, Alex?"

"I'll have the blueberry pancakes."

"Oh really? Branching out?"

She shrugs, hiding her smile behind her coffee mug. "I don't know what you're talking about. I'm a very adventurous woman."

"Mmm-hmmm," Janice says, turning back to put the order up in the cook's window. The truth is that Alex doesn't need to follow as many routines as she used to for comfort. She feels strangely safer now that she is no longer hiding.

Her mom is coming up for the holidays. She'd burst into tears when Alex called her, and they both traded apology after apology. Alex had a massive pang of guilt until she remembered how invisible she felt all those years. It will take a while to repair what they've lost, but Alex has a feeling it will work out in the end. She has that feeling about a lot of things now, she thinks, smiling at Tom. He raises his eyebrows at her and smiles, the dimple forming in his left cheek the way it did when they first met all those months ago.

"Alex was the one who told me I should quit, so if it all goes south you can blame her," he says, giving her a sideways grin.

"Oh well, not to worry. I hear she is some sort of advice expert or something," Raymond says, taking a bite of toast.

Far up in the front of the restaurant someone pushes the door open, and a gust of cold air blows through the diner. People grumble around her, but Alex doesn't even feel it. She is so warm inside she can almost see it from afar. She imagines the way the scene would look from the outside, how the camera would pull back from their perfect morning, out through the window and panning across the giant city, catching the blur of millions of people spinning dizzily toward their futures, doing the best they can with whatever they have been given.

ACKNOWLEDGMENTS

Thank you to my amazing editor Lindsay Sagnette and my agent Alexandra Machinist, for making all of my publishing dreams come true. To Danny Yanez for the title and for being such a good friend.

Beyond grateful to Falon Kirby-Hewitt and Maudee Genao for being the best publicist and marketing guru a girl could ask for and Jade Hui—I appreciate you more than I can express.

Really grateful for author friends new and old who I can go to for advice and commiserate with—Jen Hill, C. L. Miller, Clemence Michallon, Megan Collins, Jennifer Wright, and Lauren Magaziner. And to nonpublishing friends who get it and are up for a last minute read or pep talk—looking at you Aimee Davis.

Thank you to all the bookstores who have supported my work, especially my locals over the years—Charter Books in Newport, Terrace Books in Brooklyn, and Curiosity and Co. in Jamestown.

To my mom who always makes time to read new drafts and talks me off the ledge when I'm writing more times than I'd like to admit. So much gratitude goes to Tim O'Connell, the most amazing husband, editor, and new dad. So grateful for the life we've built that allows us to work in this industry.

ABOUT THE AUTHOR

JESSA MAXWELL is the author of *The Golden Spoon* and *I Need You to Read This*. She is also the author and illustrator of five picture books for children. Her comics and cartoons have been published in the *New Yorker* and the *New York Times* and her writing has been published in *Slate*, *Marie Claire*, and many others. She now lives in Jamestown, Rhode Island, with her husband, two cats, and a three-legged dog.